Padre, A Novel

PADRE

A NOVEL

ROBIN HARDY

NAVPRESS

BRINGING TRUTH TO LIFE

NavPress Publishing Group

P.O. Box 35001, Colorado Springs, Colorado 80935

The Navigators is an international Christian organization. Jesus Christ gave His followers the Great Commission to go and make disciples (Matthew 28:19). The aim of The Navigators is to help fulfill that commission by multiplying laborers for Christ in every nation.

NavPress is the publishing ministry of The Navigators. NavPress publications are tools to help Christians grow. Although publications alone cannot make disciples or change lives, they can help believers learn biblical discipleship, and apply what they learn to their lives and ministries.

Library of Congress Catalog Card Number: 94-6440
ISBN 08910-97996

Cover illustration: Larry Selman

The stories and characters in this book are fictitious. Any resemblance to people living or dead is coincidental. Descriptions of turn-of-the-century mining operations in Big Bend were derived from *The Big Bend: A History of the Last Texas Frontier* by Ronnie C. Tyler (Washington, DC: National Park Service Office of Publications, 1975).

The quotation of George MacDonald is from *Proving the Unseen* (Ballantine Books, New York, 1989), page 7.

Hardy, Robin, 1955-
    Padre : a novel / Robin Hardy.
      p. cm.
    ISBN 0-89109-799-6
    1. Man-woman relationships—Texas—Fiction. 2. Women—New York (N.Y.)—Fiction. 3. Women—Travel—Texas—Fiction. 4. Drug trade—Texas—Fiction. I. Title.
PS3558.A62387P33   1994
813'.54—dc20   94-6440
                                          CIP

Printed in the United States of America

FOR A FREE CATALOG OF
NAVPRESS BOOKS & BIBLE STUDIES,
CALL 1-800-366-7788 (USA)
or 1-416-499-4615 (CANADA)

Also by Robin Hardy:

Chataine's Guardian
Stone of Help
Liberation of Lystra
(also published as *High Lord of Lystra*)
Streiker's Bride
Streiker: The Killdeer

PART ONE

1

❖

Royce Lindel looked over the brochures about Big Bend, Texas. "Don't get me wrong; I think it's wonderful that some of these gosh-awful places are open to visit, but that doesn't mean *I* want to go there," she told Marla, who was seated across the table from her. They were eating lunch in a café across the street from the Upper East Side Manhattan building where they worked. "I mean, this brochure doesn't say anything about the motel having indoor plumbing. Am I going to have to wash my hair under a hand pump?" she shuddered, recalling pictures of the Texas frontier from school history books.

Marla shook her blond head. "What if you do? Where's your sense of adventure, Royce?"

"I have a more highly developed sense of comfort," Royce sniffed. "I don't mind camping for a day or so, as long as there's a bathroom close by. I mean," she leaned forward to whisper, "we're not going to have to share a privy with the men, are we?"

Marla almost had to spit out her mouthful of lunch to laugh. "Royce, you are such a straight arrow! There won't *be* any privies. We'll be sleeping in a tent and improvising our own bath-rooms. But if you get to whining too much, I'm sure Mack and Tom will be happy to drop you off at the nearest motel."

Pouting, Royce pulled out a small compact mirror to check her teeth for poppy seeds. She saw the reflection of a twenty-five-year-old face with hazel eyes and an olive complexion. Finding her teeth seed-free, she raised the mirror to fluff her feathery bangs. The small mirror did not capture her best fea-ture: the long, silky brown hair which draped down her back almost to her waist. How to maintain her hair on this upcoming vacation was a primary concern.

"I don't understand why we couldn't have gone upstate to get away from it all," Royce complained. "The Adirondack Upland is as wild as you can get."

"Tom and Mack have been there too many times. They wanted to go somewhere different," Marla said.

"Why didn't they make the travel arrangements, then? Why did I have to do it all? I've hit the limit on two credit cards just arranging this wonderful trip," Royce griped.

"Stop complaining, Roycee." Marla pronounced the *e* in her name whenever she needed to blunt a harsh statement. "It'll be fun. It will certainly be different. It will expand you as a person." As Marla finished her croissant sandwich, Royce eyed her envi-ously. Tall, stately Marla, 28, had thick blond hair and strong, symmetrical features. This particularly impressed Royce, who did not like her own nose. Marla was daring and self-confident, and actually lived in Manhattan.

Royce sighed. "Well, today's Friday. We're leaving Sunday, and I still don't have everything I need." She pulled out another brochure. "This recommends a hat, a jacket (because the nights are cool), hiking or riding boots, depending on which you do— Marla, I've never been on a horse in my life!"

"Mack will show you what to do," Marla replied.

"He doesn't know how to ride," Royce scoffed. "He pretends to know a lot more than he really does." She continued reading:

"Thick socks, a compass, water supplies of one gallon per person per day, dried food, newspaper . . . why newspaper?"

"I don't know," Marla admitted.

Royce glanced at her watch and began gathering up the brochures. "If I expect Martin to let me off early today, I've got to finish that jacket copy." Royce was an advertising copywriter for The Chocolate Conglomerate, a children's book publisher. Marla was its marketing director.

"And I've got a meeting with Wade, that creep in the art department." Marla stood while Royce placed a tip on the table, then they stepped out of the café.

It was a pleasant May afternoon. The tourists with their cameras and awful clothes were blocking the sidewalks as usual, gawking up at the skyscrapers. Royce and Marla pushed through the throng of pedestrians and Marla started into the street in front of a slow-moving car.

"Don't jaywalk, Marla!" Royce scolded.

"All right, chaplain," Marla grumbled, consenting to walk down to the intersection—something she did only when Royce was around.

Royce asked, "Have you talked to Tom today?"

"No, I haven't talked to him since Wednesday. Why?" Marla asked.

"I haven't been able to reach Mack, to let him know the gate number and departure time," Royce said. The light changed and they crossed.

"He'll probably call to find that out late Saturday night," Marla chuckled.

"Probably," Royce muttered. They entered the expansive marble lobby of The Chocolate Conglomerate's building and parted at the elevators.

"I'll be right up. I'm going to scope out the new guy at *Images* magazine," Marla winked. Royce smiled, privately wondering how Tom would feel about that.

Royce rode up to the twenty-fifth floor and entered a small

office with two desks. Sitting at the left-hand desk, she put a sheet of paper into the typewriter and drummed her fingers. Lowly copywriters at this institution were not entitled to computers.

Slowly she began typing: "Barfy the Dog is the pet of every child's dreams. He is scruffy, and friendly, and loyal to his owner, Timmy. But when Timmy is hurt in a speedboat accident, what can a dog do? Plenty, if he's as wonderful as Barfy. Come read how Barfy shows his love for Timmy in this sweet story, written by a real twelve-year-old girl. After you read it, maybe you will want to write your own story about special friends."

Royce read it over, made a few corrections, then triumphantly pulled the sheet from the carriage. "There! That was easy." She put it into an interoffice envelope addressed to Martin and called, "Joe!" The interoffice mail carrier who had been passing by stopped to take the envelope she held out. "Got a big weekend planned?" she asked.

"Parties from dusk to dawn!" he replied, smoothing his hair with a flourish, and she nodded wryly. She had heard about Joe's parties, and frankly, she was waiting to hear about his arrest some day soon. "Hear you're going out of town next week," he mentioned.

"Yeah, and it may be as wild as your party," she said.

"But not as much fun," he guaranteed, tossing the envelope into his cart.

"Probably not," she admitted, turning to her telephone to dial Mack's number. She got his voice mail again. As she had already left one message today, she hung up without leaving another. Irritated, she wondered, "Why do I have to do all the calling?"

The person belonging to the other desk entered the office: "Oh good, you're back."

Royce looked up at the stout woman in an eighties-style business suit. "Hi, Caryn. What did you need?" Caryn and Royce had on ongoing friendly dress feud: Royce thought Caryn's suits were dowdy and Caryn disapproved of Royce's short skirts and long jackets.

"Martin wants to see that copy right away. They're doing the Barfy book jacket layout now," she said.

"Oh, I just sent it by Joe," Royce said, rising from her desk.

"Never mind. I just passed him in the hall. I'll get it," Caryn said. She glanced at Royce's hemline before disappearing down the hall.

Royce sat back down and used the next half hour for a leisurely cleanup of her desk. She filed completed projects and wrote ticklers in her calendar for upcoming ones. Her telephone rang with one long warble, indicating a call from outside the building. As she answered, "Royce Lindel," Caryn came into the office and handed her the copy she had just written, covered with red-inked corrections and notations. Royce strangled a protest and held it up questioningly to Caryn, who shrugged.

"Hello, beautiful. What's up?" asked a cheery male voice over the telephone.

"Mack, where have you been? I've been trying to reach you for days," Royce said in a tone more exasperated than it would have been before she was handed that copy.

"Business, sweetheart," he said, cooler.

"Well, it took some doing, but I've made all the arrangements for our trip to Big Bend. The four of us will fly out of La Guardia Sunday morning to the Dallas/Fort Worth Airport in Texas, catch a connecting flight to El Paso, then take a commuter to Alpine. We'll rent a Jeep there to get us to Study Butte, where a guide will meet us with horses and camping supplies," said Royce.

There was a long silence on the other end of the line. "*This* Sunday?" he finally asked.

"Yes, this Sunday, what do you think? We've been talking about this for weeks, remember?" Royce said.

"I'm sorry, Royce; I can't make it. My boss scheduled me to attend a four-day conference in Miami next week. I have to fly out Sunday afternoon," Mack told her.

Royce was almost—but not quite—speechless: "Mack, this was *your* idea! I didn't want to go tramping around the desert for a week, but you guys just had to 'get away from it all'!"

"So cancel it, Royce," he said coolly.

"I've already charged tickets and everything," she said, tears springing forth. "I'd lose several hundred dollars to cancel this late." Then in a spate of defiance, she said, "We'll just go without you! Marla, Tom and I will go!"

"Yeah, that's a good idea. You and Marla go ahead and go. But I told Tom about this Miami trip, so he's going rock climbing in Watkins Glen next week," Mack said.

This time Royce was silent for about eight seconds. "You told Tom you had a business trip and didn't tell me?"

He paused. "Sorry. I forgot. Tom is right here in this building, and—"

"That's pretty lame," she observed.

"I said I was sorry. Look, I have to go now—"

"Goodbye," Royce said, hanging up. She cradled her head in one hand, looking at the lacerated copy on her desk. "*What* was Martin's problem with this?" She turned with a vengeance on innocent Caryn.

"He said it made the book sound boring," Caryn answered ruefully.

"It IS boring!" Royce exclaimed, tossing the paper in the air. "It's a stupid, boring book! The only reason we're publishing it is that the author is the daughter of Dr. Jack Goodfellow, whom we've been trying to get under contract for three years! They accept a book written by a child and then expect me to write copy better than the book. Why don't they just let me write the book and put her name on it? That would be easier!"

"You need a vacation," Caryn observed, tapping her chin with a pencil.

"You're right. I'm sorry, Caryn. I'm so mad at Mack I could spit."

"So I hear." Caryn's telephone warbled and she turned to answer it.

Royce swept up the copy to crumple it and drop it into the wastepaper basket. Immediately she thought better of that and retrieved it. Then she looked at the calendar—Friday, May 13. Friday the thirteenth. And they were supposed to fly out Sunday. "I wonder if Marla knows," she murmured, picking up her telephone. She dialed an in-house number but got a busy signal. Shortly after she hung up, however, her telephone sounded the two short rings which signaled an in-house call. "Royce," she answered.

"It's Marla. Tom just called and said he made other plans for next week when he found out Mack couldn't go. Did you know about that?"

"Not until ten minutes ago," Royce grumbled. "And if we don't go, I'm out a bunch of money."

"Well then, let's!" Marla exclaimed. "Let's go! You and I! Let's go just as we planned. What do you say?"

"Marla, you marketing people need to get a grip on reality. Neither you nor I have ever been farther from civilization than a Howard Johnson's. We wouldn't last twenty minutes in the Chisos Basin," Royce said flatly.

"But we'll have a guide, and he's bringing all the supplies, which you've already paid for," Marla argued. "Royce, you need to get out of your rut and try something new. Or are you that dependent on Mack?"

Royce bristled, "No. But—our reservations are for four people. It would still be a waste for just two to go."

"Then let's get someone else to go with us," Marla said.

"This late? Not a chance," Royce said.

"No, listen. I know several people who are going on vacation next week," Marla insisted. "There's Guidry—"

"I will not go camping with The Octopus," Royce stated.

"Okay, there's also Renetta Cleary."

"Renetta? In editorial?" Royce asked. She vaguely recalled

a petite, black-haired woman in a dark blue suit.

"Yeah, I know she has next week off and she's not going anywhere," Marla said enthusiastically.

"I don't know . . . Renetta?" Royce mused.

"She's due at a publications committee meeting with me in fifteen minutes. Let's go ask her now. Meet me at her office—you know, by the fax room?" Marla asked.

"Ye-es," Royce said slowly.

"See you there in two minutes." Marla hung up. Royce dubiously put down the receiver and headed for the fax room.

She found Marla near Renetta's open door. "Ready?" Marla asked eagerly. Royce felt as though she were going on a game show totally unprepared, but Marla smelled a sales job, and there was nothing she liked better.

They entered the editor's office together and Renetta glanced up, looking exactly as Royce had remembered her. With her hair pulled tightly back, and wearing tasteful, understated jewelry, she was the quintessential New York editor. Royce pulled down on the hem of her short skirt, feeling like a schoolgirl in Renetta's presence.

Marla opened, "Hi, 'Netta. You know Royce Lindel, don't you?"

"Yes. Copywriter, aren't you?" Renetta nodded at Royce with the slightest air of condescension. Royce comforted herself with the thought that Renetta was several years older—thirty—and had a few gray hairs.

"Yeah, that's right. Listen, aren't you on vacation next week?" Marla asked, sitting on the edge of the large, neatly cluttered desk.

Renetta smiled briefly. "Yes, I have two weeks off."

"Going anywhere?" Marla asked.

"I am going to paint my bedroom and curl up with some good books and Marmion," she replied.

"Her cat," Marla explained in an aside to Royce. "Listen, how would you like to go on the adventure of your life, *free*?

Royce and I were going camping in Big Bend, Texas, with these two guys, but they weaseled out. Royce here has already paid down on the trip, so we just decided we'd go without them. We've got room for two more. How about it?"

"No, thank you," Renetta smiled.

Royce was willing to let the matter drop, but Marla's instinct for sales took control. "Aw, Ren, why not? You were talking about how this pollution is killing your sinuses—five days in the pristine wilderness is just what you need."

"It will be hot as hades," Renetta noted.

"Not in mid-May. And think of the cool, glorious nights," Marla urged.

"With rattlesnakes and scorpions," Renetta added, covering her computer.

Bested on that one, Marla gamely persisted, "Still, think of the vistas you'll be able to capture with your camera. The horses will carry us—"

"Horses?" Renetta looked up with a changed expression.

"Yes, we're hiring horses for the whole trip. We'll be able to explore anywhere we want on horseback. Won't we, Royce?" Marla asked.

"Yes. A guide is meeting us in Study Butte with horses and camping equipment—everything we'll need. A ghost town is there, and an old abandoned cinnabar mine. Then the guide will take us up the Chisos Mountains on horseback," Royce said, growing excited herself.

"The rare Colima Warbler nests in the United States only in the Chisos Mountains," Renetta observed thoughtfully.

"That's right!" Royce exclaimed, although she was hearing that fact for the first time.

"When was the last time *National Geographic* had a layout of that charmer?" asked Marla, in control again.

Renetta's look of concentration was almost scary. "I go free?" she asked.

"All expenses paid, just for the pleasure of your company,"

Marla said triumphantly. On second thought, Royce wished that she had not promised Renetta that. Marla and Renetta both made much more than Royce did.

Renetta's face settled decisively. "When do we leave?"

Royce answered, "Sunday morning. La Guardia, American Airlines flight 204, departing from gate 12 at 6:20 a.m."

Marla added, "Pack light."

"Wait," Royce interjected. "I've got a bundle of brochures that tell all about it and what to pack. Why don't we go shopping after work? We can grab a bite and plan what we need."

"Great idea!" Marla seconded.

Renetta stood, tapping a manuscript into a perfect pile on the corner of her desk. "I'll meet you in the lobby at four o'clock," she said.

As Royce tied up loose ends throughout the day, she reconciled herself to make the most of this trip. The best part about it, she realized, was that she would be risking something new without Mack. He was always ready to help her try new things so he could rescue her, smirking, when she failed. Royce did not like the way he tried to control her, but she could not bring herself to dump him, either. She had always needed a strong male presence in her life. Maybe, she thought vaguely, she could develop enough backbone during this trip to tell him goodbye.

One thing she could not do was produce satisfactory copy for Barfy the Dog. She made several attempts, but they were merely variations of the first. Around 3:45, she gave up. "They're going to have to use that or write their own," she declared, leaving the wrinkled, red-lined sheet out on her desk.

She met Renetta and Marla in the building's cavernous lobby at the designated time, and they strode briskly down the perennially shaded sidewalks to Central Park. They found a roving vendor and bought pizza, which they took to a green, sunny spot in the park. Royce settled on a bench to watch some little girls clamber up on the statue of Alice seated primly on her mushroom, with the Mad Hatter and the White Rabbit scurrying by.

Consulting the brochures, Renetta made a list of necessities in impeccable handwriting. She asked all the right questions about what the guide was providing and what they had to supply themselves, then declared herself ready to shop. As Royce made a move toward the subway station, Renetta said, "No; let's walk."

"To Macy's?" Royce exclaimed. "It's got to be forty blocks!"

"You're about to be doing a lot more walking than that," Renetta said prophetically, turning down the street. Marla grinned back at Royce, who groaned. She already regretted most decisions made today, including that of wearing three-inch heels. *She sure does throw her weight around well for someone so little,* Royce thought, running to catch up.

As they threaded their way single file through the crowded walkways, Royce looked up for a change of scenery. The canyon of skyscrapers loomed protectively, far overhead. She loved the city. She loved the lights, the noise, the traffic. It was home. When Marla wasn't talking it up, the thought of venturing to such a remote area as Texas filled Royce with dread.

"Hey, Ren, want to stop here?" Marla shouted.

They eyed the gaudy pink Trump Tower across the street, but Renetta kept her stride. "I never buy there, on principle," Renetta said, and Royce rolled her eyes. Actually, Royce never shopped there on principle, either—the principle of limited finances.

Before Royce's feet swelled too much they arrived at Macy's, which had giant dolls perched on a bright yellow box above one entrance. Aware of her ballooning credit card debt, Royce practiced remarkable restraint and shopped only for what she needed: a duffel bag, hiking boots, two pairs of jeans and a jacket that matched, and a trendy felt hat. Marla and Renetta spent much more on widely varying purchases: Renetta took practical, wearable gear to the checkout counter, while Marla bought gauzy blouses and imitation-hide cowboy boots.

"You never know who we might meet there," Marla purred,

examining one of her blouses. "Cowboys are so sexy, don't you think?" This time Renetta rolled her eyes. Coming out of the store, Royce looked up at a huge billboard featuring the Marlboro Man.

"Now remember, I have it on good authority that in Texas, it's not 'you all,' it's 'y'all,'" Marla instructed, following her out.

"I'll remember that," Royce promised as she held the door for Renetta, who had her arms full of packages. Glancing at the deepening shadows, Royce said, "I've got to get home. See you Sunday."

"Don't be late, 'cause you've got the tickets!" Marla called.

"Right," Royce sighed.

She folded up her bundles as tightly as possible for the subway ride to Queens. Ignoring the stench, the trash, and the panhandlers, she made the trip in her usual manner of not looking at or speaking to anyone. When the train groaned to her stop, she disembarked and climbed the dingy steps to street level. Gripping her packages securely under her arm, she quickly walked the few blocks to her apartment building. It was familiar territory, but she never relaxed until she was safely locked in her own small apartment.

Once inside, she switched on the kitchen light and gasped as a few cockroaches scurried for cover. "I've told the landlord about those roaches *three times*," she fumed. She checked under the sink where a bucket beneath the pipe held an inch of water. But the pipe appeared to be dry. "Is it fixed, or not?" she muttered.

Rather than hope it was, she went to her telephone and dialed the landlord's number. His answering machine came on. Royce said, "Mr. Hoskins, this is Royce Lindel in 812. Have you fixed my sink? I'm going to be out of town next week, and if it leaks while I'm gone, you're going to be looking at some major repairs. And *please* have someone spray for roaches while I'm gone!" She hung up with a bang.

Checking her own answering machine, she was a little disappointed to find no message from Mack. Part of her had hoped he would consider a trip with her worth rearranging his business schedule.

Dismally, she took her purchases to the bedroom and began packing. Without Marla's buoying presence, all Royce's enthusiasm for this trip had sunk. "Well, if nothing else, it will be fun to see Ms. Cleary get taken down a notch or two," Royce considered. Then she had an uneasy feeling, as though premonition informed her that Ms. Cleary was not the only one about to get mussed on this trip. Dismissing it, Royce sat at her vanity to brush out her hair and plan a last day of self-indulgence before leaving for Texas.

2

❖

Sunday morning Renetta was already at the airline gate when Royce arrived, but Marla did not show up until almost time to board. In anticipation of their arrival in the Lone Star State, they wore their newly purchased jeans and boots. Marla enjoyed drawing stares as they stashed their bags above their first-class seats. Royce, however, fastened her seatbelt and promptly fell asleep. She and Marla slept the entire two-and-a-half-hour flight to Dallas/Fort Worth International Airport; Renetta woke them when they arrived.

Disembarking, Royce immediately noticed several things about this airport: it was much larger than she had expected; it was much newer than La Guardia; and here, the faded Levis worn by the natives made her new blue jeans look gauche. "So I never caught the Western craze," she muttered.

Passing an information center in the airport, Royce paused to look at posters of sites around Texas: the new Morton H. Meyerson Symphony Center in Dallas, the expansive Houston skyline, the opulent Bishop's Palace in Galveston, among others.

Royce frowned, trying to reconcile these pictures with mental images of sagebrush and rusty pumps. Smiling, Renetta watched her. Marla fussed, "Let's go, Royce; we'll miss our connecting flight."

"This is a big place," Royce muttered.

"That's why we need to hurry," Marla said irritably, but they found their gate with thirty minutes to spare.

The flight to El Paso took just over an hour. Marla dozed off again, but Royce and Renetta watched out of the window as the plane lifted off and skimmed over hundreds, then thousands of acres of rolling terrain.

"So much land!" Royce murmured.

"Ever been to Texas before?" Renetta asked.

"No," said Royce. "I've never been south of Virginia, except to Los Angeles. Have you?"

"Actually," said Renetta, "I was born in Port Lavaca. I got my undergraduate degree from the University of Texas at Austin."

Royce gaped. "But you don't have any accent!"

"I do when I want to," Renetta said with an authentic twang. Now Royce had to sit back and revise her mental image of Texans.

They woke Marla upon landing at El Paso International. Passing through the airport, Royce was arrested by a spicy, sultry aroma. Her stomach growled. Just ahead was a genuine Mexican food café, heralded in neon lights. Royce aimed for it and they did not come out again until they had sampled *huevos rancheros* with *picanté* sauce, *carne asada, pollo a la parilla, guacamole,* and *sopaipillas* with honey.

Next door to the café was a gift shop which demanded equal time. Renetta bought a book on the flora of West Texas while Royce and Marla surveyed the jewelry. "Oh, look at these." Marla held up a pair of dangly silver and turquoise earrings. "Ren, come here," she ordered. She held up an earring next to Renetta's face. "These would look great on you. You have to get them."

Renetta gestured impatiently, but glanced at Royce for her opinion. Royce studied the way the silver contrasted with Renetta's black, wavy hair and brought out the gray in her eyes. "They really do look good on you. You should take your hair down," Royce suggested. Renetta left her hair pulled back in a bun but bought the earrings. Royce bought a bracelet and Marla bought an entire ensemble.

Thus fed and adorned, they went off to locate the commuter plane which would take them to Alpine. Alpine was much too small to have regular flights to its little airstrip, but some enterprising soul had begun a one-plane shuttle service back and forth to El Paso during the tourist season. At 11:50 Sunday morning, the three New Yorkers were the only passengers on this leg of their trip. The light plane they found was beat up and its pilot grizzled. Royce had never been on such a small plane before—she kept her seatbelt on and her hands clenched throughout the bumpy ride to Alpine.

After an hour's flight, they arrived in the Texas Royce had been more or less expecting to see: primitive and sparse. As soon as the plane jolted to a stop on a narrow landing strip, the pilot disappeared into an establishment called "The Cockpit." The women were left to haul out their bags themselves. Climbing out, Royce enjoyed a smug sense of Eastern superiority at the sight of the squatty, run-down buildings. Then she looked up at the magnificence of the Del Norte Mountains and her smugness vanished.

They entered the terminal and signed for the rental Jeep with the help of a very short, broad lady in a faded print dress who talked to them as if they were her own children. "Is it just you three? All by yourselves? Oh my, my," she clucked.

"Don't worry; we're perfectly able to take care of ourselves," Marla said briskly.

"You meet your guide where?" asked the woman.

"Study Butte," answered Marla.

"St—oh, ha, ha, ha!" laughed the woman. "Oh, sugar pie,

it's not *study*, it's *stoody*. Stoody Butte, bless your heart." Royce saw Marla blush for the first time ever. The mother hen pressed, "But why there? Why not Terlingua?"

"It's all been prearranged. No problem," Marla insisted as Royce signed the forms and received the keys to their vehicle.

But Mother was not satisfied. "What's his name? Your guide's name? What outfit is he with? Honey, now there's people around that tries to take the tourists, and—"

"We know all about that. We're from New York City," Marla smirked, slinging her bag over her shoulder. The woman would have followed them out to the rental car arguing, but her circa 1950 telephone rang.

While the nag was distracted by the telephone, the three vacationers hurried out and found their vehicle: a dusty, stripped down, open-topped Jeep. They deposited their bags in the back, and Royce delicately wiped off a seat. Before starting out, they prepared themselves: Renetta donned an authentic Stetson, sunscreen, and a down vest over her long-sleeved shirt, and hung her camera around her neck. Marla put on sunglasses, eschewing a hat. She fluffed her loose, shoulder-length hair and arranged her jewelry over her blouse. Royce tied her long hair back into a ponytail and seated her hat above it, studying the effect in a rearview mirror. She also wore a long-sleeved cotton shirt and her new denim jacket. Once ready, they climbed into the Jeep. Royce and Marla sat in front; Renetta was in back with the bags.

At this point they encountered their first difficulty. Royce stared down at the gearshifts—*two* of them. "What am I doing? This is a standard. I can't drive this. Can either of you?" she asked, turning.

Renetta cocked an eyebrow, but Marla snorted, "Greenhorn. Get up and let me drive." Royce moved over and Marla sat in the driver's seat. She started the ignition, shifted gears, and the Jeep lurched backward and died.

"Can you drive this?" Royce demanded.

"Okay, so it's been a few years. I just have to figure out the gear pattern," Marla insisted.

"That was reverse," Renetta offered from the back seat, a hand on the camera dangling from her neck.

"Thank you," Marla acknowledged with a nod. She restarted the engine and moved the stick shift experimentally. They lurched and bucked, but made it to the highway.

"No sweat!" Marla shouted. "We just take 118 south straight to Study Butte, don't we?" she asked, careful to pronounce it *stoody*. Royce nodded, looking for a seatbelt. "Then we're fine as long as we don't have to start and stop much," Marla said.

But Royce spotted a Stop 'N' Go and requested, "Stop, Marla; I need a restroom."

In spite of various essential delays, they were soon speeding out of Alpine. It was a clear day with a crystalline blue sky. As Marla drove singing, "Born to Be Wild," Royce adjusted her hat down low on her forehead, just above her reflective neon sun-shades. Renetta drank from an old-fashioned soft drink bottle in one hand while holding on to the back of Marla's seat with the other.

They entered a part of the highway where mountains reared up steeply on either side. It was a breathtaking sight and a familiar feeling, and suddenly Royce was glad that she had come. Marla was right—it was a stretch she had needed to make.

The hour's drive went quickly. Marla stopped singing as the eerie Chisos Mountains came into view—rugged purple sentinels along the horizon. As they drew closer, Royce took off her shades. The mountains grew to immense proportions and they were still miles away. Royce found herself holding her breath.

Finally, they spotted a small cluster of faded, broken-down buildings off the highway, and a sign informed them that this was indeed Study Butte, population 120. Marla turned off the highway and stopped. She switched off the ignition.

For a moment the three sat in silence, taking in the vastness of the mountains and the desert, the breathing of the wind, and the pathetic remains of human forays into hostile territory.

For the time being, the wilderness had won.

"There's no one here," Renetta said at length.

Marla restarted the Jeep and they lurched forward among some adobe ruins. Then they spotted a man running toward them, waving: "'Lo, ladies, hullo!"

Marla put on the brakes so suddenly that the engine died. The fellow came up to the driver's side and waved her over. "That's okay, sweetheart, these babies are temperamental critters. I got it fer you now." Shifting bags, she reluctantly sat in the back beside Renetta.

"Are you our guide?" Royce asked in dismay. He was very dirty and very smelly. His teeth were black and tobacco drool dribbled down his chin.

"Certainly. The name's Ol' Pete." He started the engine with a roar.

"Where are our horses—our gear?" Royce cried.

"I want to see some identification," Renetta said, but no one paid any attention to her.

"Now honey," he answered Royce, "I couldn't bring all that here by myself. I have to take you to Terlingua—that's where all your gear be." He whipped the Jeep up to the highway then across the highway, striking across the desert in a vaguely southern direction.

"Where are you going?" Royce asked in some alarm.

"Before we hit Terlingua, I thought to show you the ruins of Mariscal Mine. It's a wonder to behold—the old buildings standin' like tombs over the open mineshafts where a hunnerd men died mining the quicksilver ore. That's what they called mercury, ya know." The guide seemed to think that having no road was no reason to slow down. The Jeep careened over rocks and clumps of brush, causing his passengers to grip anything that was solid.

But he also saw no reason not to talk. As they flew through the desert, he shouted over his shoulder: "Around the turn of the century, they worked all by hand, ya know—just picks and shovels and human hands. They carried the cinnabar in bags on their backs up out of the mines—sometimes as much as eighty pounds at a time. They dumped it in tram cars and pushed it by hand to the crusher, which ground the ore fine. Then they burned it in the extractin' furnace to vaporize the quicksilver. It gathered in the baffles of the condensers and ran off into buckets. See, they had to burn fires in the furnace for two, three weeks solid, day and night, to get it hot enough to vaporize the mercury." His remarkable knowledge and chatty manner held their attention in spite of the rough ride.

"The mines were lit by candles—jus' enough light to work, and to delude a man into thinkin' there was solid ground under his feet afore he stepped into an open shaft. And then many men died of 'miner's consumption' from breathin' the dusty air ten hours a day, seven days a week. The miners were paid a dollar a day to work in mines that gave up eleven and a half million pounds of the quicksilver. When the ore ran out, the mines closed and all the people left—all but the souls of the dead miners still workin' the mines, still diggin' the ore, still runnin' it up on the tram cars to the crusher. At eventide, when the light is right, you can still see the blue flames of their candles bobbin' between the shafts." So Ol' Pete talked in a slightly nasal voice as he drove, and Royce gradually forgot the jolts and tobacco drool in listening to him.

Then he became quiet, slowing the Jeep to a gradual stop. He pointed ahead: "Shhh. Look ahead yonder—under the mesquite tree. A mama mule deer has hidden her fawn there. See the spots? I daren't drive nearer. Get your camera and go close. Quiet, now!"

Royce and Marla were instantly out of their seats, tiptoeing forward as they eyed the brush. Renetta sat back, crossing her arms. "I'm not getting out of this Jeep," she said.

About the time Marla said, "I don't see any deer," they heard a scream behind them. They whirled to see Renetta rolling on the ground and the Jeep roaring away.

"Stop!" "Wait! What are you doing?" Royce and Marla screamed as they ran after their guide. But in a moment the Jeep was enveloped in dust on the horizon.

Shaking, they helped Renetta up and brushed her off. "Are you hurt?" Royce asked.

"No. He pushed me out," Renetta said, trembling in anger. She checked the camera that was still dangling from her neck. It was the only possession they retained from the Jeep.

"My money—my credit cards," Marla moaned, gazing after the dust cloud. "I can't believe this. He suckered us!"

Royce shook her head, scanning around them. The wilderness stretched mightily on every side. "Which way is the road?"

The three squinted in the direction the Jeep had gone; it was no longer visible. Renetta looked over at the sun in its afternoon descent. "We should go north," she said, pointing. "Eventually, we'll intersect a highway."

Silently, they began walking. The temptation to voice blame or self-recriminations tugged strongly at Royce, but she knew it would just waste needed energy. So on they trudged, getting an up-close, personal view of Big Bend.

It was really ugly: dry and rocky. What plants grew here were prickly and thorny. Royce stumbled over a depression in the ground, which was uneven and hard to walk on. And there were *bugs*—when Royce accidentally dislodged a rock, something that had been underneath it scuttled away, startling her. From then on, she watched more carefully where she stepped.

They had walked about an hour when Marla said, "I'm getting thirsty."

"Aren't we all," Renetta remarked.

"Shouldn't we be seeing the highway by now? We weren't thirty minutes from where he turned off," Marla persisted.

"We weren't walking," Renetta pointed out. "He was going a good thirty miles an hour."

"We should see it before nightfall," Royce said encouragingly. No one speculated about what would happen if they did not.

On they went. Royce took off her jacket. When her stomach growled she instinctively looked at her watch: 5:15 Texas time. She remembered last having a snack from the Stop 'N' Go in Alpine. Wiping sweat from under her sunglasses, she said nothing, but Marla glanced over when her stomach growled again.

To distract herself, Royce watched Renetta walk. Carrying her down vest over one arm, she strode as quickly and purposefully as if she were on her way to Macy's. Marla walked with much extraneous swinging, and Royce stumbled a lot in her new, unfamiliar boots, but Renetta moved with the economy and precision of a miniature tank. "Renetta!" called Royce. "Did you ever take dance?"

Renetta stopped in surprise. "For about ten years. How did you know?"

"It shows," Royce said.

They kept walking. Royce knew they were going in the right direction because the Chisos Mountains were mostly to their backs. But there was a low ring of hills to the west, on their left. And when the sun touched those hills, the darkness sprang out like a panther. In five minutes Royce went from sweating to shivering, and got back into her jacket. Renetta put on her vest. "What happened to the light?" exclaimed Marla. Renetta shrugged and they began walking faster.

The world around them changed rapidly. Strange shadows grew up on the landscape. A coyote howled somewhere not far off, and living things began moving in the rocks at their feet. Then it was night.

Renetta stopped, and the others did, too. "We can't walk in the dark," she said. "We can't gauge our direction, and we'll just start to wander. We have to stop for the night."

"No!" cried Marla. "We can't! We don't have anything to sleep on! We don't have anything to eat!" She broke into hysterical tears.

"Stop that! Get a grip on yourself!" Renetta ordered. Royce

watched them in amazement. Were these the bookish editor and the self-confident marketing director she had known a few days ago?

Then something caught Royce's eye, and she stared intently. Touching Renetta's arm, she said, "I see a light over there."

3

❖

Marla and Renetta spun to look where Royce pointed. "I see it!" Marla cried. "Come on!"

"Wait!" Renetta restrained her. "We will approach quietly and see who or what it is." She made too much sense for argument, so the other two obediently followed her stealthy lead.

As they came closer, they saw that the light was a flickering campfire. Another twenty-five paces showed them horses, and Royce's heart beat faster. When they drew to within sight of the forms around the campfire, one of the horses whinnied. A man stood to pat it and the women hid behind a bush.

Another man crouched by the fire as he listened to a radio receiver. It looked like he was drawing on a map. A third man lay sprawled on a sleeping bag nearby. They all had the appearance of experienced outdoorsmen, with several days' growth of beard. They were also deliberately flouting the park's rule against ground fires. The man with the map was eating from a pan on the fire—Royce stifled a moan. Renetta put a finger firmly to her lips, and they listened.

"The cocaine's coming tomorrow, in the early a.m.," the man with the map said, turning off the radio. "Here's the drop-off point." He handed the map across to his companion on the sleeping bag.

"By helicopter or light plane?" this man asked, languidly studying the map.

"Helicopter, probably," answered the other, spooning another bite from the hot pan. He blew it cool before tentatively placing it in his mouth.

"We'll be there!" the man on the sleeping bag cracked. He picked up a semiautomatic pistol and squeezed off a couple of rounds into the air.

The other two immediately jumped on him: "Stop that!" "You want the whole world to know we're here?"

Renetta tugged gently on Marla and Royce to draw them back. They moved away a safe distance, then conferenced in whispers: "Well, we've seen enough to tell us who they are," Renetta said. "We must not let them see us. I suggest we wait until they go to sleep, then slip in and take what supplies and horses we can get."

"Ren, they have guns!" Marla squeaked in a whisper.

"What do you suggest, then?" Renetta asked coolly. Marla helplessly shook her head.

Royce said, "I vote with Renetta."

Nodding, Renetta said, "Not a *sound* from here on." They moved like ghosts to the bush on the edge of the campsite and sat noiselessly to wait. They were out of the light of the fire, but unfortunately out of its heat as well. As promised, the night was cool. Royce steeled herself against the shivers.

From the vantage point of anonymity, she observed the three men closely. The one on the sleeping bag, who had fired the shots, was a tall, lean man of Hollywood features and apparently an ego to match. He was in his mid-thirties, with expensively styled, bleached blond hair. He lit a cigarette from the campfire and leaned back to drag on it with a lazy half-smile.

Across the campfire crouched the man with the radio. He was a wiry man, not quite as tall or handsome as the other, but probably five years younger. He had a firm jawline and cute curly hair, and gazed into the fire with a look of determination that reminded Royce of Renetta.

The third man, farther from the campfire, was less distinct, but his age was somewhere between the other two. He was stroking the horses as he watered them from a metal pan. Royce began to puzzle over the incongruity of a drug dealer showing such consideration for the beasts. *I guess it's just people's lives they have no concern for*, she thought. She watched as he lifted a hoof to check the shoe.

Suddenly they were jolted by screams. Marla jumped up, screaming, "Snake! Snake!" and dancing in terror.

The men sprang up. "Who's there? Come out real slow! Keep your hands in sight!" ordered "Hollywood," training his pistol on the bush. With Marla crying, the women did as they were told. They got up and stepped into the light of the fire. Royce stumbled over her boots.

The men gazed at them tensely, and Hollywood demanded, "Who else is there?"

"No one," Renetta answered. "We're alone."

"You expect me to believe that? What the—" Hollywood began a tirade.

Royce desperately interrupted. "It's true. Our guide drove us out here and then dumped us. He stole our rented Jeep and everything in it!" She began a disjointed explanation of how this trip was planned and almost canceled, and how the three of them decided to come anyway. The men listened. As she talked, she unconsciously began looking at the third man for reassurance—the one who had been tending the horses. He had dark brown hair that hung in his eyes and a medium, unremarkable build. But something about his gaze emboldened Royce to spill out the unvarnished, almost complete truth.

"And then we saw your campfire, and we hoped to—to get something to eat and drink, and help in getting our things back," she finished.

The men looked at each other, then the third man murmured, "I'll check it out." He took a high-powered flashlight and strode past Royce. Hollywood, meanwhile, took the camera from around Renetta's neck. First he opened it and ripped out the film, then he swung the camera by the strap and smashed it on a rock.

"Hey!" Renetta cried.

"Sorry. It slipped," he smirked, tossing the remains back to her. While he kept his gun trained on the women, they watched the other man's light shift this way and that until it disappeared. A while later it reappeared and went all around the camp. Then it came swinging back.

"Well, it's only their footprints for at least a mile back—though they didn't just wander up. They came up to the campsite, then backed off, then came up again. Did you really intend just to ask us for help?" he wryly asked Royce. She felt her face redden.

"Great," muttered the man with the gun. "Now what?"

"Kill them," said the short, curly-haired man.

Royce startled. *Surely he's joking.*

"Oh, dry up," said the third, confirming it. He went to a pack and brought out another can of stew, which he emptied into the pan on the fire. "Come eat," he said to the guests.

They rushed the pan, not caring that the stew was lukewarm or that the metal dishes were dirty. While they ate, he passed them cups of water which had to be refilled numerous times. The men watched without comment.

When the newcomers had devoured the last molecules of stew, they handed back plates cleaner than the ones they had been given. "Thank you," Royce whispered to the considerate man. He brushed his hair back from his eyes to look at her, then deliberately looked away.

No one said anything for a while. Finally, the man with the gun pointed it at Marla and said, "What's your name?"

"Marla," she said softly. With her blond hair mussed and her cheeks flushed by the firelight, she looked appealingly vulnerable. "This is Renetta and this is Royce. Are you going to tell us who you are?" As Marla raised her eyes to Hollywood, Royce realized with a sick feeling that she had turned on her flirtation lights.

"Sure," he grinned ironically. "I'm John."

The brown-haired man glanced at him and shifted. "My name is Paul," he told Royce.

Renetta turned to the curly-headed man to ask sarcastically, "And I suppose your name is George?"

"No," he returned with equal sarcasm: "It's Ringo."

"Now that we have introductions out of the way, we can discuss what to do with you," John said pompously. The way he was looking at Marla, Royce figured he already had ideas. She wanted to reach over and slap them both.

"We're going to have to take them to Terlingua," Paul said quietly. "That's the only way we can be sure they'll get help."

"And when do you propose to do that?" demanded Ringo. "If we started off right now, we'd make it there by morning. And if we're at Terlingua in the morning, we won't be where we're *supposed* to be. Let's just give 'em a canteen and point 'em in the right direction."

"I know you're not serious, so don't frighten them," Paul remonstrated. "They'd never make it alone."

"Then we'll just leave 'em here while we go take care of business. We'll come back and take 'em to Terlingua," Ringo suggested.

"We'd have to leave food and water with them," said Paul.

"Leave our supplies? No way!" Ringo declared.

"What are they going to do, steal them?" Paul asked sarcastically.

"I'm not leaving anything with these women unless someone's standing over them," Ringo insisted.

A breath later, Paul said, "Okay."

"What, are you going to stay with them?" Ringo asked.

"We'll draw cards," Paul said, leaning over to a saddlebag. He took out a deck of cards and cut them. "Low card stays. Aces high."

"I'll hold the deck," John said, reaching out.

"Not hardly. Royce'll hold it," Paul said, handing the deck to her.

"Cut it again," John ordered. Royce nervously cut the deck and fanned the cards. She wanted to assure John that if she could have cheated to make sure Paul got the low card, she would.

John drew first, a jack of spades. Ringo drew a nine of clubs. Royce shifted to hold the cards toward Paul, who by then was sitting beside her. He drew the ace of hearts.

"You stay," John grinned at Ringo. He answered with an unintelligible muttering.

As Royce handed the cards back to Paul, he winked at her. She read it as a comforting gesture and smiled faintly.

Before bedding down, the men allowed their visitors to go together on a bathroom trip. They were even given a flashlight and packaged towelettes. "Do you have any dental floss?" Renetta asked.

John howled, but Paul said, "Believe it or not, we ran out."

The women went out a discreet distance to take care of business. "What do you think? Wh-what should we d-do?" Royce asked Renetta. Her teeth chattered, either from the chill or from apprehension.

While Renetta was thinking, Marla said, "I like them. I think they're okay."

Royce spun on her fiercely. "Mary Elizabeth Petrelli, you stop leading that guy on! You don't even know his real name! All we know about them is that they're doing something dangerous and illegal."

Marla made a face at her. "Lighten up, chaplain."

Renetta said, "Our choices are pretty limited. We'll have to cooperate as far as is safe—but Marla, if you get friendly with this man, you can make it rough for Royce and me. They may expect the same cooperation from us."

"I don't have to go on this guilt trip," Marla said stubbornly. They finished what they had come out to do, then returned to the camp.

The men had unrolled all three sleeping bags. "You ladies may sleep wherever you like," John announced, holding his sleeping bag open in an invitation to Marla. She looked inclined to join him until she caught her friends' disapproving glares.

"I don't think there's room," Marla said regretfully as the three women sat together by the fire.

"She'd as soon climb in that bag with a slimy, poisonous tree frog," Ringo snorted.

"Well, let me put your mind at rest," John said gallantly, climbing out of the bag. "You sleep here. I'll sleep on the ground."

"Why—how sweet of you," Marla purred. She immediately got up and tucked herself in John's sleeping bag. He lay down on the ground beside her, an arm under his head for support.

Watching, Paul groaned. With ulterior motives in mind, John had set a precedent which Paul didn't particularly care to follow. After a few moments' struggle with himself, he grumpily extracted himself from his bedroll and yanked on his boots. "Here you go," he reluctantly offered Royce.

Stung by his reluctance, she replied, "No, thank you. I'm fine right here."

"You're going to get cold when the fire dies down," Paul observed, softening. He held his bag open.

"No, really, I'm fine," she insisted, laying her head on her knees.

"Suit yourself," Paul shrugged, removing his boots and climbing back in his bag. Ringo determinedly hunkered down in his bedroll and said not a word.

Muffled talk and giggles came from the area of John's bag across the campfire while Renetta and Royce huddled together. Before long Royce lay down on the dirt with her arm for a pillow and shut her eyes.

Before too much longer she discovered that denim is not a good insulator. While the fire burned down to a glow, the wind whipped through her jacket as if it were a window screen. She awoke, cold from her ears to her toes in their department-store hiking boots. Renetta, asleep, was shivering violently beside her. Royce got up and put what few sticks she could find on the dying embers of the fire. They burned up with a crackle and a warm flash, then she was left colder than before.

As she slumped down, Paul raised up on his elbow. She looked over. Sighing, he shrugged out of the bag and put his boots back on. "Come here," he whispered.

Her pride gone, Royce scrambled over to his bag, then looked guiltily toward Renetta. She was little enough to share the bag. So Royce went back and shook her awake. "Renetta," she whispered.

"What?" Renetta said irritably, sitting up.

"Paul's letting us have his bag. Come on," Royce urged in a whisper. Renetta got right up and went over to where he stood.

"Take off your shoes. Just be sure to shake them out before you put them on in the morning," he muttered. Renetta tossed her boots aside and buried herself in the bag. Royce put down her hat, yanked off her boots, and gratefully crawled into the warm bag beside her. Royce zipped up the bag, then lay on her back and closed her eyes. Muttering under his breath, Paul rolled up his jacket for a pillow and lay down on the dirt a few feet away.

Renetta was the only one who went right to sleep. Royce was too uncomfortable, finding her arm stiff and sore from laying her head on it earlier. She considered rolling her jacket up under her head like Paul did, but was still too cold to take it off. So she shifted around in the narrow bag, trying to get comfortable.

"Be still, Royce," Renetta's voice rang out. Apparently she was one of those people who needed their sleep and didn't much tolerate interruptions. Paul looked over, then rolled on his side away from them. Royce lay still right where she was.

But then her hair became a problem. She preferred sleeping with it draped up over her pillow, out of her face and off her neck. Since she had no pillow, to drape it up here would get it in the dirt. She pulled her ponytail over her shoulder. When it started bothering her, she flipped it away.

"Royce!" Renetta exclaimed, removing it from her face. Paul startled, then lay on his back.

"Pipe down over there, will ya?" Ringo demanded.

Chagrined, Royce tried to tuck the hair behind her but then Renetta shifted and caught some strands. "Ouch!" Royce gasped quietly. She disengaged the strands from Renetta's clothes and placed the ponytail over her shoulder again. She settled down, glancing self-consciously at Paul a few feet away. He needed his sleep, too—for what, she'd rather not know.

Royce closed her eyes. As she began to drift off, she semi-consciously flipped the hair away from her neck. "Royce!" Renetta barked like a little mechanical dog.

Paul sat up. "Okay, 'Ringo,' if you don't give one of these women your bag tonight, I'm gonna use it for target practice while you're still in it!"

Bitterly griping, Ringo climbed out of his bag. Royce, feeling that she had first claim to Paul's bag, unzipped it and gently nudged Renetta out, whispering, "You go to Ringo's."

"Don't push me," Renetta said irritably. But she got up and went to Ringo's bag, where she flopped down. After a few moments, he leaned over her to zip it up.

Everybody settled back down to sleep. Feeling warmer now, Royce took off her jacket and rolled it up for a pillow. She lay on her back and rested her arms on her midsection outside the bag. She pushed up her sleeves. The cool night breeze felt good on her bare arms.

Then she smiled. This was almost comical: Their first night in Big Bend they were camping, all right—in the sleeping bags of three pseudonymous strangers. What would Mack do if he knew?

She felt something light on her forearm and barely opened her eyes. A large, unidentified insect was making its way up her arm—Royce bolted up and shook it off with a scream.

Everyone but Renetta awoke. "What?" "What is it?" It was quite dark.

"It was a bug!" Royce cried.

Paul sat up. "I *promise* that if you wake me *one more time*, I'll make it worth my while!"

John snickered loudly as Paul lay back down heavily. Royce meekly put her head on her jacket, moved her hair out of the way, and tucked all appendages safely inside the sleeping bag. She even went to sleep.

Royce woke once more that night. Everything seemed very quiet at first. Then gradually she distinguished the tiny rustles, flutterings, and scuttles that signaled the busyness of desert night life. A weird hooting sounded nearby, which startled her into scooting closer to Paul, bag and all. He shifted, moaning something, and turned his face in restless sleep toward her.

Curious, she looked down at his face. She could not distinguish much in the dim starlight, but her first estimation of his age seemed right. *He doesn't look like a drug dealer*, she thought. *Or act like one.* He had made no move to carry out his earlier threat. A troubled expression came over his face and he shifted again. Idly wondering what he was dreaming, she settled back down in the bag.

✳ ✳ ✳

Royce awoke when Paul almost stumbled over her in getting up. Somehow she had ended up a lot closer to his side this morning than she had been the night before, even getting a grip on his arm. She opened her eyes just enough to see him shaking out his jacket and putting it on. The sky was a pearl gray in the east.

Paul began to saddle a horse. Ringo came to his side, talking too quietly for Royce to hear what he said. John loaded a gun and shoved it into his belt, then handed another one to Paul. He holstered it as he looked back to where Royce lay. She closed her eyes, pretending still to be asleep.

Footsteps approached. Someone bent down and lightly touched her face, brushing back loose hair. From the vicinity of the horses John's voice asked, "Did you make it worth your while?"

The person beside her stood, and Paul's voice murmured, "In my dreams." Standing over her, he paused, then threw something small out into the desert. Ringo came up with breakfast and they moved beyond Royce's hearing.

Then as Paul and John climbed onto their horses, Ringo said, "Not to worry; I'll take care of 'em, P—."

What did he say? Royce opened her eyes. It wasn't *Paul.* What had he called him? She watched as the two rode off, then, still tired, she went back to sleep.

When she awoke a second time, she sat up with a start. John and Paul had not yet returned. Ringo was cooking ham and reconstituted eggs over the fire, with an old-fashioned coffee pot sitting nearby. Marla and Renetta were still asleep in the other two bags.

Royce crawled out of the warm bag and sat by the fire. Ringo handed her a plate of ham and eggs and poured steaming coffee into a tin cup for her. "Thank you," she said in surprise.

He barely shrugged. "So . . . you girls got a little cold last night, huh?"

"Frozen," she mumbled around a mouthful. "This is good."

He nodded. Somehow, he had lost some churlishness from last night. He glanced over at Renetta's form, curled up like a kitten. "What's her name again?"

"Renetta. Renetta Cleary," Royce answered.

"She's . . . pretty sharp, isn't she?" he asked tentatively.

"Yeah, you could say that," Royce answered, smiling into the cup. She took a cautious sip of coffee. It was very hot and bitter, and woke her thoroughly.

"Is she married?" Ringo asked.

"No," Royce answered.

"Well, like, where does she work?" he asked.

"She's senior editor at The Chocolate Conglomerate in New York City—that's a children's book publisher. We all work there. Marla's marketing director, and I'm a copywriter," Royce said. She had no objections to answering these questions in exchange for breakfast.

By this time Renetta was stirring, and joined them by the fire. Loosed from its bun, her slightly wavy black hair swirled about her petite face so that her gray eyes looked twice as large. She tossed back her hair, and the dangly earrings glinted through black strands. This morning she looked as exotic as the Chisos— quite unlike an editor should look. "I must look a mess," she muttered self-consciously as Royce and Ringo stared at her.

"You look just fine," Royce assured her. Ringo handed her a plate of breakfast and carefully poured a cup of hot coffee for her. Renetta brushed the hair out of her face and began eating. Ringo appeared hopelessly smitten.

"I'm sorry I bothered you last night," Royce began apologetically.

Renetta blinked at her. "I don't remember you bothering me at all. I slept fine." She looked back at the rumpled bedding. "Whose sleeping bag is that?"

"That's mine," Ringo said casually.

Renetta turned her large gray eyes on him. "You gave up your sleeping bag for me? Why . . . thank you, Ringo."

"My name's Buddy," he said suddenly. "Buddy Ferring."

"Buddy," Renetta acknowledged, shaking his hand.

"So what are John's and Paul's real names?" Royce asked.

He hardly glanced at her. "Let them tell you."

"Where did they go?" Royce asked, looking across the desert.

"I wouldn't ask so many questions, if I were you," he said testily. Royce smiled. He might be Buddy to Renetta, but he was still Ringo to her.

A few minutes later Marla woke up, and adjusted her clothes in the sleeping bag before getting out. "So, did you find any more bugs last night, Royce?" she asked smugly.

Royce's face was suddenly tinged with red. "No; did you find any more snakes?" she returned. Marla tossed her head and looked around for John. Ringo—Buddy, that is—allowed her to get her own breakfast, as his attention was focused on Renetta.

When everyone had finished eating, they cleaned up the plates and utensils as best they could with no water. Buddy packed everything away with marvelous compactness and rolled up the sleeping bags to twelve-inch cylinders. Part of the gear, like the coffee pot and plates, he wrapped in a tarp and hid in the rocks, apparently to retrieve later. Then he tamped out the fire and scattered the ashes thoroughly. He saddled his horse and sat to wait.

The minutes passed very slowly. Royce began to feel a vague anxiety. Buddy scanned the flat horizon to the east once or twice, so Royce kept a constant vigilance in that direction. *Why should I care what happens to those men?* she thought in a huff. *They're scum.* Then again, if they did not make it back for some reason, that would certainly cloud her immediate prospects for getting help. In spite of herself, she kept watching the horizon.

They waited as the sun rose higher and higher. Buddy fished out the pack of cards and proposed a game of five-card stud, but Renetta pointed out that they had nothing with which to bet. She seemed more interested in Buddy's horse. She went over to pet it, which Buddy encouraged.

Royce sat down by Marla in the shade of some large rocks.

Marla seemed disinclined to talk, so Royce sat quietly for a while before venturing, "Marla, do you think—"

Alerted by her tone, Marla forestalled her: "Don't lecture me, chaplain."

"I won't," Royce promised. "I just don't know what's going to happen, and I—" She was arrested by the faint, echoing sound of automatic gunfire in the distance.

They all heard the gunfire. They all turned to look in the direction from which it had come. For several tense minutes they saw nothing. Then there was a small disturbance on the southeastern horizon. Royce whipped off her sunglasses and peered.

The disturbance drew closer until she could distinguish two horses in a cloud of dust. And two riders. Coming at an all-out gallop, one of them waved. "They pulled it off," Buddy uttered in relief. Royce shared his sentiment, then chided herself for feeling that way. Yet when she discerned Paul in a buff-colored cowboy hat, her stomach knotted.

Galloping up to the group, John whooped, brandishing a large leather satchel. He threw himself from his horse and zipped the satchel open. Everyone crowded around to look as he pulled out several stacks of hundred-dollar bills. "Here, babe!" He shoved a bundle at Marla, who screeched, "John!"

"And this is for your camera!" He tossed a stack to Renetta. She deliberately peeled two bills from the stack and gave the rest back to him, which he stuffed into his shirt pocket.

Meanwhile, Paul had ridden right past the group. Royce turned to watch. He drew up at the edge of a dry gully and dismounted. Royce began walking, then running toward him. He took something from his horse and began doing something which produced white clouds downwind in the gully.

Royce ran until she had reached him. He glanced at her as he lifted a brown package from a canvas bag and slit it wide open with a hunting knife. He shook out all the fine white powder and dropped the paper into the gully. He did this with a practiced hand twenty times or more until the last package had been emptied. As he sheathed his knife and folded the flat bag, Royce exclaimed, "Why did you do that?"

He did not say anything while he strapped the bag onto the saddle. Then he leaned on the saddle, pushed up his hat, and said, "We're privateers, sort of. We rob the drug runners. It's our personal contribution to the war on drugs."

"That's—that's dangerous!" she cried.

"Well, sure it is. There wouldn't be any money in it, otherwise." He mounted and offered her a hand up. She grasped his hand, put her foot in the stirrup, and swung her leg across the horse's haunches. Sitting behind the saddle, she clutched Paul around the waist and looked down. This was a big horse.

"Besides," Paul added as he turned the horse to rejoin the others, "what do you care?" Royce frowned, declining to answer. Paul clucked to the horse and it began bucking—or so it seemed to Royce. She gasped and cinched Paul around the waist.

"Been riding much?" he asked askance as they loped back to the group.

"Dozens of times!" she said through gritted teeth.

As Paul drew up, Buddy turned with a folded-up bundle. "You'll have to carry some of this, Padre, with all our excess baggage."

Paul dismounted but told Royce, "Stay there. You're fine." He gave up his gun to John, who packed all but one of the guns in a watertight wrap and hid them with the other gear. As Paul strapped the bundle from Buddy to his saddle, Royce asked, "Why did he call you 'Padre'?"

"It's a nickname," Paul replied. "Here, hang your leg over this so it doesn't bounce."

Royce allowed him to drape her leg over the bundle and asked, "Are you a priest?"

He glanced up, amused. "No." He nimbly remounted without her having to dismount. Royce looked around. Marla was sitting behind John on his horse; Renetta was in the saddle of Buddy's horse with Buddy behind her. They were ready to go. But—there was some hesitation. At first Royce did not know what was wrong.

Finally Paul said, "You know, we're closer to the Chisos Basin than Terlingua."

"That'll take us right back by the drop-off point!" Buddy protested with sudden passion.

"No, not at all. That's a good fifteen miles south. And there are more people—more tourists in the Basin area, you know," Paul said.

"Yeah," John muttered.

"We're not doing them any favors by keeping them with us any longer than necessary. There's always the chance we'll get caught," Paul said. Buddy puckered his lips like a small child about to throw a tantrum. Marla was looking anxiously at John's profile. Royce listened quietly.

"Vacation's over, ladies," Paul said decisively, heading east. The other riders followed. He started out at a lope, but John shouted, "Why strain the horses?" Paul slowed to a walk. Royce let her breath out gratefully.

After a few minutes, Royce got accustomed to the gentle sway of the horse's gait. It was a sleek, pretty brown horse. She reached down to pat its haunches, and its tail swept over her hand.

Paul looked back. "His name is Buster."

"The horse's name is Buster? Is he yours?" she asked.

"No." He did not elaborate.

"I'm sorry I kept you awake last night. I'm not used to camping out," she said.

"Obviously. Why did you come?" he asked.

"Well, everybody else wanted to, and it was something different," she said.

"Where are you from?" he asked curiously.

"New York City," she replied.

"Noo Yawk?" he laughed, mimicking her. She reddened slightly, having always imagined herself to speak with unaccented clarity. "Oh, I see. You ran out of things to do in New York, so you came here," he added.

"My thoughts exactly," she muttered. Her gaze traveled from the rocky, bristly ground under the horse's hooves to the limitless stretch of blue mountains that melted into the sky. "It is beautiful, as long as you don't have to be down in it."

"After you've been around people enough, it's solace," he said. "Sometimes, when I'm here . . . I never want to go back."

"Go back where?" she asked.

"The city," he answered vaguely. "The dirty, smelly, crowded city. . . ."

That's all he would say, so Royce gave up trying to converse and looked across at Renetta. She was holding the reins, comfortably in control of the horse while Buddy sat behind her, his mouth close to her ear. Riding with John, Marla was playing with his beard and generally acting like a twelve-year-old. Actually, they all seemed to be having a rather good time.

That thought made Royce wonder what time it was, so she looked at her watch. It said 7:10. She shook it and put it to her ear. In so doing, she accidentally knocked Paul's hat over his eyes. "Sorry," she said as he replaced it. "I'm such a bother."

"That you are," he said with conviction.

"What were you dreaming last night?" she asked, remembering the expression on his face. "You seemed restless."

He looked back in alarm. "Oh? What did I say?"

"Nothing, really. You just kind of moaned," she said.

"That would have been when you gouged me with your fingernails," he remarked.

"I did not!" she exclaimed.

"You should see the marks on my arm."

"When did I do that?" she asked.

"Whenever you heard anything unfamiliar," he said.

"I'm sorry," she said pitifully.

"Stop apologizing. I'm just not used to sleeping with—" he cut off abruptly.

Neither said anything more for the next several minutes. Royce rocked easily on the horse, watching their shadow glide over the uneven ground. When she laid her head on Paul's back, the shadow looked like there was only one person riding. It was comfortable to lean on him. The jacket he wore was gray, old and soft, and made a good pillow even while he was wearing it.

She continued to rest her head on his back until it occurred to her that it might be uncomfortable for him. "Am I bothering you?" she asked, lifting her head.

"A lot, but that's no reason to stop," he said, and she got the impression he had just bitten his tongue again.

He must be married, she thought. *He's married, so he's trying not to be too nice.* She wished she could study his face, but that was hard to do while sitting behind him. She looked back down at the ground. He was wearing pointy-toed cowboy boots made of some exotic skin—she did not ask what, because she did not want to know what animal had died to become boots. But they did look good on him.

His chest expanded in a deep breath. Royce laid her head on his back again. He took the reins in his right hand and put his left over her hand on his waist. Royce lifted her hand and he twined his fingers in hers. He did not say anything or look back.

Surprised at what she was feeling, Royce closed her eyes briefly. When she opened them, she saw a beer can on the ground. Royce looked up and saw a group of tourists heading out on horseback, single file. Marla got quiet.

In another few minutes Royce spotted a directional sign pointing to the Chisos Basin Lodge ahead. The sign sat on the shoulder of a paved road. Presently, they rode into the sprawling conglomerate of shops, restaurants, stables and lodging that accommodated tourists to the Chisos Basin of Big Bend.

They pulled up to the lodge's office and all got down off their horses. Finding her legs unsteady after riding, Royce supported herself against Buster. He held very still for her. "The park rangers will help you get your stuff back," Paul said distantly, pretending to be preoccupied with some doohickey on the saddle. "Just—don't mention us, okay? Uh . . . give 'em something to get home on," he told John.

"Marla's got it," John murmured. He placed his hand behind Marla's head and gave her a deep, sloppy kiss. Renetta immediately extended her hand to Buddy and said, "Thank you for the ride." He looked pained.

Royce turned to Paul, who self-consciously wiped sweat and dirt from his face with a bandanna. He had a brown, freshly sunburned complexion under his beard and the softest brown eyes, which gazed at her with a transparent look of reluctance. "At least tell me your real name," she whispered.

"Why?" he said. "I'll never see you again." That should have hurt her, but he kept any pain bottled up inside himself. He looked at her lips and shifted. Before she could put her arms to his neck he had climbed on his horse and kicked it rather hard. Buster whinnied in protest, reared slightly and turned as ordered. Buddy and John followed Paul's quick departure.

Marla, Renetta and Royce stood looking after them. "He took my phone number," Marla said hopefully.

"Well, that was an interesting experience. Let's go get a room," Renetta said, returning to business as usual.

After renting a double room, the women went shopping at the lodge store for new, clean clothes and toiletries. Then they returned to their room for leisurely baths and preening. Royce could not believe the amount of dirt that washed from her body down to the shower drain. Standing under the warm cascade of water felt so good that Royce lost track of the time, and Marla had to pound on the door for her turn in the tub.

As Royce patiently combed out her long hair, she heard Renetta on the telephone inquiring about the lodge's restaurant. When she hung up, she said, "No reservations are necessary, but a line starts forming at six o'clock. Let's go."

From the bathroom, Marla said, "Did either of you buy a hair dryer?"

Renetta shouted from the door, "You look gorgeous, and if you don't come right now, you're eating alone!"

Royce giggled and fingered the fringe of her new suede jacket, bought at the lodge store. It was so Texan. Marla hurried out in a fancy beaded blouse. Renetta had bought a cotton sweatshirt, and they were all conspicuously wearing authentic western Levis—much heavier, Royce discovered, than the New York knockoffs.

As it was still late afternoon, they were seated at once in the restaurant where they ordered large quantities of Tex-Mex fare. They devoured the fajitas, enchiladas and rice which came to their table. As good as it was, Royce fondly recalled the canned stew they'd eaten the night before.

"Buddy likes you," she said suddenly to Renetta, who shrugged. "They're not drug dealers," Royce added softly. "When I found Paul dumping all the cocaine, he told me that they robbed the drug runners."

"I knew they were okay," breathed Marla. "Maybe he'll call me. . . ." Royce did not think so, but she did not say it. "And didn't you just love the way they talk?" added Marla. "That sexy Texas drawl."

"Our vacation sure didn't last long," Royce lamented, forgetting how hard she had fought against coming.

"We're not done. We've got to find that creep who dumped

us," Renetta said in a hard voice.

Royce shook her head. "I'd rather let the police find him. I just wish . . . we had the chance to get to know them better."

"Not me," Renetta said emphatically, but Marla glanced at Royce in quiet agreement.

After dinner they went strolling around the lodge area. There were a lot of brushy trees and cacti. Royce paused to study a giant specimen with radiating green spikes topped by an ornate plume of white blossoms. Lifting her eyes, she saw the mountains rise steeply right behind the lodge—or so it seemed, for their immensity. They made everything else look fragile and temporal.

The women paused by the lodge office. "It's closed," Renetta noted. "I suppose we had better call the police from our room."

Without great enthusiasm, the three returned to the motel room. Renetta sat on one of the beds and picked up the telephone receiver. Royce suddenly asked, "How are we going to explain the money Marla has?"

Renetta eased the receiver back down on its cradle and the three stared at each other. Then they heard a very slight tapping on their door. They continued to stare at each other. The tapping sounded again. "Who is it?" Renetta called forcefully.

"Buddy," a low voice said. "Open the door."

Before the others could stop her, Marla had run to the door and flung it open. There stood a clean, freshly shaven Buddy. "Y'all come with me real quietly now," he said, glancing around. "Bring your clothes and the money. Don't leave anything here." His urgent tone silenced any questions that even Renetta might have had.

The women silently ransacked the room and slipped out with their dirty clothes in shopping bags bundled under their arms. Buddy paused at their room door to scan the area before leading them out, then they walked briskly through the grounds under the brilliant orange canopy of the sunset. Passing stables and historic markers, Buddy picked a sure course to a specific destination. "Have you talked to the rangers yet?" he asked.

"No," said Renetta; Royce shook her head.

"Okay," he noted. As the purple twilight closed in, they left the lights of civilization behind in favor of the desert. Ahead, Royce saw black figures silhouetted against a watercolor sky. A tail flicked; a head rattled its bridle.

John and Paul waited on their horses as Marla and Royce ran forward. Royce gave Buster's neck an affectionate hug; Paul shook his foot from the stirrup and held out his hand. She took it to clamber up behind him. He crammed her possessions into an already stuffed saddlebag.

As they struck out into the desert, Buddy said, "We stopped at the lodge ourselves to rest and get cleaned up. Padre here turned on the radio and was scanning channels, and ran across a call from a cellular phone nearby. Turns out that one of the lodge employees is a front man for the cartel we robbed. He saw you girls paying for things with Ben Franklins and phoned in his suspicions that you had something to do with the heist. They were coming up to ask you a few questions."

Royce felt cold chills run down her spine. "That's what we get for being greedy. We should've let the shipment pass," Paul muttered bitterly. No one replied. He spurred into an angry gallop and Royce gasped, clutching him. The horse's rocky speed terrified her—she felt as though she were on a roller coaster lurching out of control.

Paul would have kept Buster going at this pace, but a few minutes of it was all Royce could stand. She whimpered, "Paul—stop—I'm going to be sick—"

He reined up so suddenly that the wonderful Mexican dinner Royce had just enjoyed came up as well. She fell from the horse, retching. Then she sat on the ground, crying.

She was sobbing so hard that she hardly heard Paul's anguished apologies. He doused his bandanna with water from his canteen and gave it to her. The other riders came up. "Royce!" Marla cried, sliding down from John's horse.

"What happened?" asked Buddy.

"Royce got sick," Paul said miserably.

Marla sat on the ground and held Royce while she wiped her mouth with the dripping bandanna and cried. "I knew I sh-shouldn't have come . . . I w-wish I hadn't. . . ."

Paul crouched in front of her, clutching his knees. "Please don't cry. Don't be afraid. I won't let anyone hurt you—I swear."

Royce looked up from rivers of tears. "I'm not afraid. I'm embarrassed!"

Marla covered her mouth. Paul sat back, enlightened. "Well, gee, Royce, I don't see why. It was the most graceful barf I've ever seen."

John snickered and Renetta smiled sympathetically. "Thank you," Royce sniffled gamely.

Relieved, Paul handed her his canteen and ordered her to drink up. She refused to put her mouth on it, but poured water into her hand a little bit at a time.

Meanwhile, since they had ridden far enough to put a butte between themselves and the lodge, Paul pulled a map and flashlight from his saddlebags. He, Buddy, and John huddled over the map while Renetta and Marla consoled Royce. "What do you think? Terlingua?" muttered John.

"No. It's too close. That's the first place they'll look for them," Paul answered, scrutinizing the map.

"How about Lajitas, then on up to Presidio?" suggested John.

"I don't trust the Presidio county sheriff," Paul muttered. "And I'd rather get away from the border."

"Let's just take them home with us," Buddy said, looking at Renetta.

The women heard. John coughed uneasily and Marla studied him. Royce got up shakily and stood beside Buster. "It's not your fault," she whispered, petting him.

Paul began folding up the map. "We'll follow 118 up to Alpine and leave them with the sheriff there. Can you ride now, Royce?"

"Sure," she said, shaking in her boots.

Paul told her, "You can tell the sheriff the whole story, only you don't know who we are. By the time he gets his people back down here, we'll be long gone."

He handed her the flashlight, and she placidly held it while he packed the map. Under its light, she saw a white stripe on his finger where a wedding band had been until recently. She raised the light just enough to illuminate his face. Clean-shaven, he had the kind of unpretentious good looks that women often overlooked in favor of a more spectacular appearance, like John's. *The good ones are always taken,* she thought.

He slapped the bag closed and briefly returned her gaze. The meaning of his expression was so clear that she could read it instantly: *I can't let you get to me.* He took off his hat, combed his hair back with his fingers, and deliberately set the hat back in place—all to avoid her eyes.

5

❖

It was a rather subdued riding party that struck out in a
northwesterly direction that evening. As soon as Paul had
located the paved road, he urged Buster to an easy, rhyth-
mic lope. "You okay?" He turned back to Royce, testing the sure-
ness of her grip.

"Yes, I'm fine," she insisted. Actually, she was peeved that he
had taken up the reins with both hands.

The cool night was very pleasant, with sweet, soft breezes.
With a full moon, a clear sky, and no artificial light to blur her
eyes, Royce discovered a keen night sight she never knew she
had. The horses, being shod, found it easy going on the pavement. After the first few moments of tensely gripping Paul,
Royce adjusted to Buster's rhythm and relaxed. When she
caught on to how Paul rocked with the horse's stride, it became
even easier. Royce mentally gloated to Mack, *See? I learned to
ride without you.*

The riders passed out through the park entrance and continued loping up the highway. There were few cars out now, but

when headlights did appear, Paul gave them a wide berth and veered far off the road. "Some people think it's funny to spook the horses," he said back to Royce.

She wondered if that were the only reason he avoided the traffic. She noticed that of the three, John was the only one still carrying a gun. "Why didn't you bring a gun?" she asked.

"I don't like them. They're dangerous," Paul replied.

She laughed, "Everything you're doing is dangerous. You don't make any sense." She added inwardly, *One minute you hold my hand and the next you're cool as ice.* He shrugged.

When they passed the remains of Study Butte, ghostly in the moonlight, Royce asked, "How long are we going to ride?"

"As long as you can stand it," he replied.

Something in his tone ruffled her, so that she asked, "How does your wife feel about your line of work?"

"I'm divorced," he said. "My wife—" He started to add what might have been an explanation, then thought better of it.

Royce looked back to Buddy and Renetta riding behind them. John and Marla were bringing up the rear. "What about Buddy?" she asked. Paul seemed to do a double take, so she asked, "Did you know he told us his real name?"

"Well, 'Buddy' is not his real name either—but that's his choice," Paul said indifferently.

"So is he married?" Royce pressed.

Paul deliberated before answering, "No. He's never been married."

"Why not?" she asked.

"For pete's sake, Royce, ask him!" Paul said touchily.

"Sorry," she muttered. She let go of him with one hand to take off the limp felt hat and let the wind blow through her hair. She had not had time to pull it back in a ponytail when Buddy came for them. Now, she twisted around to stuff the hat in one of the saddlebags.

Paul grabbed at her hand. "Don't get fancy. Hold on to me."

"Why?" she muttered rebelliously under her breath.

"Because it's going to slow us down considerably if I have to stop and scrape you up off the highway!" he retorted.

"Cool your jets," she breathed, finding a place to stuff the hat. She wondered why he was so agitated. Paul merely pushed Buster a little harder, so that she was obliged to hold on with both hands.

The mountains fell away on either side as they followed the glittering highway north. Rocking with the horse's stride tired her, so she leaned her head on Paul's back. Then she sat up and said, "If it bothers you for me to lean on you, I won't."

He cleared his throat. "You're all right."

Royce laid her head back down and watched the shadows of the night race by. She saw a large shape bound beyond a tree twenty feet away. "What was that?" she asked, sitting up.

"Deer, probably."

"You didn't see? It was so big!" she exclaimed.

"I'm watching the road. If Buster steps in a chuckhole at this pace, he'll break a leg," Paul said over his shoulder.

Sighing, Royce turned her head in the other direction. Bushes and cacti sped past nearby, but the dark mountains in the distance stood still. "You don't make any sense," she murmured. "I can't figure you out. You're a nice guy doing dangerous, stupid things."

"Part of my charm," he said drily.

"Well," she said, squeezing him a little, "I like you anyway. It was nice of you to come back for us."

Paul did not react outwardly, but a few seconds later he said, "You . . . have a boyfriend in New York?"

"Yeah. Mack. He's a jerk, but he's cute," Royce said with some cunning.

"I've noticed that most women prefer the cute jerks," he remarked, nodding back at Marla and John. "So I guess Mack has nothing to worry about, letting you come without him."

"Wouldn't you? If you had a business trip and couldn't come?" Royce asked teasingly.

"Not on your life," he said hotly.

Surprised at his tone, Royce sat up and tried to look over his shoulder at his face. "Are you one of those possessive, Cro-Magnon men?"

"I don't know; but I wouldn't sleep with a woman and then send her across the country alone," he said tightly.

"I didn't say we slept together," Royce said quietly.

With a stiff jerk of his head, he said, "It's none of my business."

The realization that he was jealous sent a tingle through her. But why did he keep pulling back? Royce experimentally moved one hand up from his waist to curl it back over his shoulder. He bent his head to her hand and she caressed his smooth cheek. Cautiously, he turned his lips to her fingers.

"Paul! Yo, Paul!" John shouted. "Marla's about to drop off this animal. What say we stop for the night?"

Paul grunted and turned off the highway toward a mountain range which loomed up on their right. They climbed a short way into its slopes, where Paul found a protected, somewhat level spot. He hopped down from Buster and reached up for Royce. She allowed him to lift her down, but wobbled on the suddenly solid ground. He gripped her.

"Get your hands off that woman and get us some grub!" John shouted as he dismounted.

"Oh, dry up," Paul muttered, turning to the saddlebags. He had some difficulty unfastening the bags under Royce's gaze, but finally produced two sacks of trail mix, one of which he handed to John. "No fire tonight," Paul growled, giving the second sack to Royce.

Buddy brought out some canned chicken, which he opened with a Swiss army knife. He ate some out of the can with his fingers before passing it to Renetta. With aplomb, Renetta stuck her fingers in the can as well. Royce shook her head, appalled.

As Royce ate, she watched Renetta wipe her hands and begin helping the men unsaddle the horses and currycomb them.

Is there anything that woman doesn't know something about? Royce wondered.

When all had been sufficiently fed, the men got out their bedrolls and Marla, Royce, and Renetta excused themselves to a short distance away. They took their toiletries, a flashlight, and a canteen. While Renetta brushed her teeth, Marla whispered to Royce, "Did you see the way Paul was looking at you? John said he's fallen like a rock."

"He's . . . nice. I like him," Royce said tentatively.

Renetta spat out her mouthful. "Et tu, Royce? I wish you'd be careful. We still don't know anything about them."

"Buddy told us his name," Royce argued.

"He *told* us. So what? How do I know that 'Buddy Ferring' is his real name?" Renetta demanded.

"She's got a point," Royce told Marla.

"You two are such killjoys," Marla sighed.

In a few moments they returned to the fireless camp. As Renetta took possession of Buddy's sleeping bag, Marla slithered into John's bag and he lay down close by, talking to her in very low tones. Glancing at them, Royce pulled out her new hairbrush and began working tangles out of her hair. Paul rolled up his jacket into a pillow and stretched out on the ground as before. He watched as Royce gathered her hair over her shoulder and ran the brush through it to the ends. She smiled down at him and leaned over to search her shopping bag for a rubber band.

Renetta turned off the flashlight and Royce gingerly tucked herself into Paul's bag. He scooted maybe an inch toward her, but that was all. When her eyes readjusted to the night lights, she looked at Paul and he turned his head toward her.

Only a glint from his eyes was visible, but his breathing seemed uneven. Royce extracted her arm from the sleeping bag and ventured a hand toward him; he intercepted it on the ground between them and squeezed it lightly before letting go. Then he turned his face back up to the sky and closed his eyes.

Royce was momentarily disappointed, as she was expecting at least a good night kiss. But, under the circumstances, she had to appreciate his restraint. It was a refreshing change from Mack.

Royce settled on her back and looked up at the night sky. She thought about Mack as she rubbed her sore legs, trying to ease the cramping enough to go to sleep. She missed Mack like a bad charley horse. Knowing him had made her so cynical that every time she met a new man, she wondered what his agenda was, what were his hidden faults.

She looked over at Paul. His eyes were open, staring up at the stars. Again she saw that disturbed, haunted look. The intensity of it moved her—and scared her, a little. *Renetta is right. We really don't know much about them,* she thought uneasily. Yet— he was so careful about how he touched her, even in such intimate circumstances. What kind of a man guarded himself so closely?

Not realizing that she was watching him, he closed his eyes and drew a deep, tired breath. Then his eyes sprang open again, as if sleeping would leave him vulnerable to a stalking enemy. *What is chasing you?* she wondered, then drifted off to dream of shadows chasing her on Buster.

In the morning, she was roused by Paul leaning over her: "Royce . . . Royce. . . ." She reached up to him sleepily. "Wake up, Royce; we need to get an early start." He eased her out of the sleeping bag.

"It's still dark!" she protested in a mumble. There was no hint of sunrise yet, nor of the moon that had illuminated the night. The men were packing by the light of several flashlights.

"Yeah, but we still have forty miles to Alpine, and half of that with no cover at all," he said.

As Paul began rolling up the sleeping bag, Royce found that she could hardly stand for the stiffness in her legs and posterior. The thought of getting on that horse made her groan. "Do we have to start off right now?"

"Well, look at it this way," Paul offered, tying down the

bedroll, "would you rather ride now, in the cool, with no traffic, or during the day in the heat, visible for miles around?"

"All right, already," Royce grumbled, stretching her stiff muscles. "What have you got to eat? I'm sick of trail mix."

Paul began rummaging through a pack. "Umm . . . here are some cookies." He tossed her a package.

"Fig Newtons," she said. "I haven't had these since I was a kid." She ripped them open and bit into one. They were not too stale or crumbled. "Hey, these are good!" She began stuffing them in her mouth.

"You want to share those?" Marla laughed casually, coming over. Royce peered at her in the flashlight's sidelight, and grudgingly gave her a handful. "I told you this was going to be a great trip," Marla said in a low voice, toying with a cookie as she watched John pack.

"Yeah. Great," muttered Royce, then looked up at Marla's suggestive tone. "How is it great?"

"Cowboys are *so* sexy," Marla sighed.

Royce stared at her watching John, then realized with a sharp pain in her stomach that Marla had found room in that bag for both of them after all. "Oh, Marla, how could you? Have you lost your mind?" Royce hissed.

"Don't preach too much," Marla taunted her, glancing pointedly toward Paul. Royce's face burned at the suggestion that she was a hypocrite—or soon would be.

Renetta came over to ask, "Could I have a few of those?" Royce gave her a generous handful of cookies. Renetta ate them quickly in order to help get the horses ready to ride.

But when John came up with his flashlight looking for a handout, Royce tossed her head and said, "Eat your own stuff. Paul gave these to *me*." She was as mad at him as she was at Marla.

"Ooh, aren't we greedy!" John laughed. "Somebody needs to teach you to share."

"Not with you," she said coldly.

"Oh no?" John bathed her in one of his nuclear smiles, having found a new challenge. Marla stopped eating to stare at them. Buddy and Renetta paused in their saddling of the horses to look. At the sudden silence, Paul turned from his pack toward John.

Intent on ignoring him, Royce was completely unaware of the spotlight. She turned her back on John without further reply and reluctantly folded up the package. "I'll save some for you," she said, handing it to Paul to pack. She unscrewed the top of his canteen and took a long drink, then fished out her toothbrush and some towelettes. "Don't leave without me," she told him, moving away.

But her bravado faltered at the sight of the deep darkness past the rocks, and she turned to Marla. "Want to come with me?" she asked weakly. With a glance at John, Marla went.

As soon as the two returned they all climbed on the horses and set off, ambling down to the highway and proceeding north at a brisk lope. Right away, the mountains receded into the distance on the east and west.

The sky over the mountains in the east began to lighten, then a bright aura appeared over their peaks. Watching the sun rise in a burst of red and gold was very gratifying. It set the nearby stretch of rocks and brush on fire, then continued its westward flow. In the new light, Royce gazed at mammoth boulders standing on end as if tossed aside by a giant's child. It was such a glorious, heartless panorama that it made the thought of another long day of riding almost bearable.

Paul nodded toward the sunrise and remarked, "Beautiful, isn't it?" She squeezed him in reply. "I've always loved this country," he went on in such a low voice that she had to strain to hear him over the hoofbeats. "You can't hardly live here—it'll chew you up and spit you out. But it gets to you—the wildness, the openness. After you've been here awhile, you're different. You learn to look over a distance. Your perceptions change."

"Where are you from?" she asked.

"Texas," he replied. Royce took it at face value. If she did not press him, he might eventually tell her more.

Over the next several hours, it gradually dawned on Royce that riding today was easier than it had been yesterday. She seemed to have gotten the rhythm down—she was able to move with the horse without any conscious effort at all. It was difficult to talk while riding, so there was little conversation.

But then Paul said abruptly, "It started by accident," and Royce snapped to attention. "Ripping off the drug dealers. Buddy and I had spent our vacations camping here for several years in a row. One year we were exploring along the mountains when we literally stumbled across a drug transaction in progress. We knew we were dead men if we didn't do something quick, so Buddy just knocked one guy down, grabbed his Uzi and started spraying everything in sight. Thank goodness he didn't kill anyone—they just scattered. They must have been as surprised as we were. Anyway, Buddy and I were left standing there with all this money and coke. I emptied the stuff over the canyon. We kept the money. The next year when we came back, we brought a radio receiver and a weapons expert."

"John?" she asked.

"Uh, yeah—'John.'"

Royce contemplated this. "What did you do with the money?"

Before Paul chose his answer, John called out, "You hear something?"

Paul drew up on the reins to listen. Suddenly he exclaimed, "Chopper!" There it was, rising from the south. They spurred their horses for the nearest range of mountains to the east. Royce clutched Paul, closing her eyes and clenching her teeth for the rocky ride. But they made it to the slopes without losing her. Darting in the crags amongst the prickly pear, they slid off the horses and pressed against the rock faces as the engine roared overhead.

"Did they see us?" Royce asked, for the helicopter seemed to be hovering. It appeared directly over them, but the mountains kept it from getting too close. Shortly, it continued on its northern course.

When the whirring of its rotor blades had faded, Paul asked John, "Did you see the make?"

"Uh, yeah, it was an OH-58 Kiowa," John replied authoritatively, though he looked shaken.

"An American make? Are you sure?" Buddy quizzed him dubiously.

"What do you know?" John spat, irritated.

"Okay, okay. Let's get out the radio," Paul said to Buddy, who began unpacking it.

"Can he call for help on that thing?" Royce asked anxiously.

"It's just a receiver. There's no transmitter, Royce," Paul said.

While they were stopped to monitor it, Renetta watered the horses. Once Royce had calmed down, her stomach began making threatening noises, so she pulled out the Fig Newtons.

Paul conferred with Buddy, then came over smiling to where Royce stood beside Buster. "I thought you were going to share those with me," he said, trying to sound reproachful.

Royce peered down into the package, came up with the last cookie, and popped it in her mouth. He put both arms around her and backed her up against Buster so he could reach into the pack behind her. Then he brought out a can of Spaghetti-O's. Royce smothered a giggle over the label with the googly eyes. Taking out his knife to open the can, Paul explained, "Buddy likes it." Buddy looked up at the mention of his name. John was already watching.

"And next time, why don't you try eating lunch before dessert?" Paul suggested, handing Royce the can and a fork. She impulsively reached up to give him a friendly kiss on the cheek.

Paul gazed down at her, his smile fading. Seeing the strong attraction between them, John said jokingly, "Hey, Paul, why don't you tell her what you *really* are?"

Paul blanched and turned away. Buddy addressed an

anatomically descriptive vulgarity to John. John replied with a two-word suggestion. Looking at Royce's stricken face, he seemed to realize that he had gone too far. "Hey, it's not that big a deal. It's not like he's an ax-murderer or something," he said defensively.

Paul crouched beside the radio and bowed his head, listening. Buddy knelt beside him. Marla came up to Royce. "Are you going to eat that?" she asked, nodding to the can Royce gripped. Royce handed it to her. Marla ate from the can, directing fiery glances at John. Renetta came over and Marla shared the can with her. The three of them watched the men: Marla angry, Renetta suspicious, Royce frightened.

John turned his back to the glares and sauntered over toward the radio. Glancing at the women, he said something to Paul, who scrambled to his feet and answered in no uncertain terms. John pushed his luck with another snide remark and Paul seized him by the collar. Buddy jumped between them.

Royce turned and ran to the shelter of a rock outcropping twenty feet away. She leaned against the rock, her stomach recoiling with nervous tension as she fought not to throw up. Renetta followed. She came up slowly to Royce and said, "Come away from there—carefully."

Royce looked up. "Huh?"

Renetta pointed. "There's a Gila monster in the crevice right above your head."

Royce leapt away from the rock and looked up. A small, scaly patch of black and orange was visible in a crack. "Are they dangerous?"

"Yes, they're poisonous," Renetta answered. "There's something else. . . ." Renetta went on in a voice that would not be overheard: "There's something about this whole scenario I don't like. The drugs, the money, the fact they came back for us. It's too pat."

"What are you saying?" Royce asked quietly.

"What do we know about them, other than what they've

told us? How do we know there's a cartel looking for us? How do we know these men aren't just what we first suspected?" Renetta posed.

Royce gripped her stomach. "But I saw Paul destroy all that cocaine."

"What you *assumed* was cocaine," Renetta corrected her.

"It doesn't make any sense," Royce argued, anxious to justify Paul.

"It does if they *are* dealers. They would have to either kill us or convince us they *aren't* dealers," Renetta said.

"Then why would they come back for us at the lodge?" Royce asked, perplexed.

"What if we had decided to tell the park officials the whole story?" Renetta demanded. "They would have rounded up these men in a New York minute. So they had to get us away from there—far enough away so that when we finally had a chance to tell someone, it wouldn't matter. Paul said as much himself."

Royce began, "But, the longer we're with them, the more we know—"

"And the more we know, the greater threat we are," Renetta finished. "We have to assume that we are in danger as long as we're with them."

Royce drew an immensely troubled breath. But there was no time to say more; Paul approached and said in a steely voice, "We're ready to go."

Renetta walked carefully around him and he watched her. Then he looked back at Royce with flinty eyes. She lowered her gaze and accompanied him to where the other riders sat waiting. He mounted, then pulled her up behind him. As she settled in place, she looked over at Renetta, who telegraphed, *Be careful.*

6

❖

It was midday now, starting to get hot. All had taken off their coats to ride, and Paul had donned dark glasses. He wore a white, long-sleeved cotton shirt. As they walked the horses down from the shelter of the rocks, Royce watched Paul comb back his hair with his fingers and press his hat in place.

They had barely started off when Buster began hobbling. Paul stopped immediately to check his hooves. While Royce sat behind the saddle, Paul retrieved a small curved instrument from his bag, lifted Buster's left front foot, and gently pried out a rock. He went over the other three hooves and led Buster a few paces to assure himself that the horse was all right. "He's okay," he told Renetta, who was watching intently from behind her dark glasses. Renetta turned to face forward, trying to find a way to hold on without holding Buddy, who sat in the saddle today.

Royce gripped the ridge of the saddle and leaned back as Paul got on, then resumed holding his waist. His cotton shirt was wet with sweat, but she did not mind—she was pretty soggy herself. She felt the hardness of his shoulders under his shirt, and the tension of his stomach muscles. Attempting levity, she patted his stomach. "You can relax now."

"Not till we get to Alpine," he replied instantly.

Royce inhaled and gripped him as they began loping. Without the encumbrance of jackets, she was able to reach her arms farther around him, to feel his breathing and his heart-beat—*Surely she's wrong about them. Oh, please let Renetta be wrong for a change,* she thought miserably.

They continued riding, riding, and the monotony began to tell on Royce. They entered a valley where the mountains on either side crept up almost to the highway, but there was no shade. The sun was big and bright and hot, and malevolently beat down on them at every step. Royce, bouncing on Buster's haunches, tried to distract herself with the spectacular slopes on either hand, but kept finding that she had to close her eyes. They kept closing and would not stay open.

"How much farther to Alpine?" she mumbled.

"About twenty-five miles. We may make it by nightfall," Paul said cheerily. Royce groaned and held on.

Paul kept the group going at a steady lope. The closer they got to Alpine, the harder he pushed—he seemed driven to reach it. After some time, John had to yell at him twice to get him to stop and rest the horses. When they did stop, Royce almost blacked out getting off Buster. But a few minutes under a yucca tree with Paul's canteen made her feel better.

Paul, however, did not notice. He threw himself from the saddle and went right over to talk to John. Soon it was evident they were arguing again. Buddy stood by with tensely folded arms. Marla came over to sit with Royce.

After watering the horses, Renetta joined Royce and Marla in the shade. "They're arguing about what to do with us," Renetta said quietly. "You look pale, Royce."

"I'm all right," she said hastily. "I don't see what the problem is. They're taking us to the sheriff in Alpine."

"That's what Paul said, but it doesn't seem to be a consensus, does it?" Renetta asked.

"I can't believe Paul would let anything happen to me," Royce said stubbornly.

"That's because he hasn't gotten all he wants from you yet. Once he does, he couldn't care less about you," Marla said bitterly. "I think they're a bunch of liars."

Royce stared dismally at Paul and John quarreling. She wasn't wrong to trust him . . . was she?

Paul broke off and strode toward Buster. He leaped up into the saddle and gestured curtly to Royce: "Get on." She climbed up slowly so she could see what the others would do. Buddy took Renetta's arm and dragged her to his horse. After some sullen indecision, John offered a stirrup to Marla.

As they returned to the highway, Royce kept looking behind to make sure everyone followed. She asked Paul, "What were you arguing about?"

"Nothing," he said grimly.

"You're scaring me, Paul," she said quietly.

He expelled a breath. "He didn't see why we should take you to the sheriff. He doesn't see why we should take you any farther at all. But I *know* I've got to get you to Alpine. . . ."

Royce squeezed him. "I trust you. The others think I shouldn't, but I do." He said nothing. When Royce looked over his shoulder, all she could see were his jaw muscles working.

They continued to ride in the relentless sun. Royce began to feel the urge to close her eyes again. She pushed her hat farther down on her sweating brow and concentrated on staying on the horse. She did not even attempt to look at the scenery they passed; it was all so much rock and spiky plants. Rock, and dirt, and that glowering sun. Royce never would have believed how much stamina riding a horse required. She moaned softly from the cramps in her legs, and Paul barely glanced back.

Some time later John shouted, "Yo! The horses are lathering!" Paul ignored him, and they rode on.

"Whoa!" Paul caught at her arm—why, she did not know.

"Are you all right, Royce?" he demanded.

"Yes—yes." She sat up and tightened her grip on him. But a moment later she would have tumbled off the horse had he not grabbed her elbow.

When Royce came to, she was in Paul's arms in the shade of a twisted, deformed tree. Marla was bathing her face with a wet bandanna and Renetta was peering anxiously at her. "What happened?" Royce mumbled, trying to sit up.

"You fainted from heat exhaustion, Roycee," Marla said tenderly, with a scathing look at Paul. "Be still now."

Paul took the canteen Buddy held out and put it to her lips. Royce did not really feel thirsty, but he made her drink. "You just rest a minute," he murmured. "We're only a few miles outside of Alpine."

Renetta glared at him. "Can't you see she's ill? She can't ride any more today!"

"She can make it to Alpine," he said stonily. "Can't you, Royce?"

"Sure. Sure, I can ride," she said, sitting up. But a queer sensation came over her and she slumped back into Paul's arms.

"All right!" Paul said to Renetta, forestalling her gathering storm. "We'll camp here tonight." Buddy began unpacking his horse. John threw Marla's things from his saddle, but stayed on his horse. She looked at him with incredulous, wounded eyes, and one by one the others turned to look at him. Finally he shrugged indifferently and dismounted. Marla's humiliation was painful to watch.

While the others unpacked, relieved themselves, or tended the horses, Royce was content to rest in Paul's arms. He brushed her damp temple with his lips, whispering, "You'll be all right, Royce. I'll get you safely to Alpine or die trying." Royce turned her face up. He bent his head to kiss her but caught Renetta's withering glare and aborted the move.

Buddy produced a meager supper of canned chili and crackers which he offered first to Renetta. She refused it, hanging back to evaluate the situation with a darkening face. So the first serving went to Royce. With food in her stomach and a reprieve from the heat, Royce began to feel much stronger. She smiled encouragingly at Paul as she handed him the can of chili. John sat down with his automatic pistol and began playing with it, unloading and reloading it. Buddy handed a can of chili to Marla, who took it disdainfully.

Paul ate with Royce leaning back against him. She watched him laboriously bring up forkfuls of drippy chili to his mouth. "You're laughing at me," he lightly accused.

"Not at all. I'm admiring your technique. Not just anyone can eat chili with a fork," she returned, her head resting against his chest.

He stuck the fork in the can and set it on the ground, then said, "I don't understand what you see in me . . . but, you make me feel like . . . like maybe I could start over again. . . ." Royce sat up to look in his face and saw his eyes watering. She opened her mouth but he gestured, "Listen—I want to tell you something."

Marla suddenly threw her can of chili against the rocks. "I'm sick of this garbage!" she exclaimed.

"Hey! That wasn't empty! We don't have supplies to waste, woman!" John shouted.

"It's garbage, just like everything else you've been feeding me. And don't you remember my name, *John?*" Marla spat.

"It's not important enough to remember," he sneered.

Marla threw herself toward a large rock in a rage of tears. John laid his gun on the ground and jumped up shouting. Royce sprang up to calm Marla.

"We saved your hide, you ungrateful—"

"You got what you wanted for it!"

"Oh yeah? And you didn't?" John was yelling and Marla was screaming back at him.

Royce was between them, quietly urging, "John, sit down. Marla, listen—now, Marla—"

Renetta seized the gun from the ground and pointed it at

John. "Now, listen!" she shouted, and everyone stared at her. "Marla—Royce—come over here," Renetta said authoritatively. Buddy started to get up but she pointed the gun at him. "Don't move."

"Renetta," Royce said, walking slowly toward her. "Put the gun down. That won't help now."

"We're taking the horses and a pack of supplies," Renetta said.

"Fine with me." Marla defiantly stood beside Renetta.

"Renetta, that is not a good idea," Royce objected firmly.

In nervous excitement, Renetta was swinging the gun from one man to another. They were dangerously spread out: Buddy close to the horses, John near the large rock. Still seated on the ground under the tree, Paul said, "Be careful with that. It's—"

Renetta swung the gun toward him and it went off with a loud crack. Paul fell back into the dirt, writhing. "Paul!" Royce screamed. "Renetta!"

With a wide-eyed look of fear, Renetta shook the gun help-lessly as it continued spraying bullets. Buddy and John hit the dirt with their arms over their heads.

Royce grabbed Renetta by the wrist and wrenched the gun from her frozen fingers. Renetta sat limply as Royce placed the gun gingerly on the ground out of her reach. Buddy and John raised up. Royce threw herself down beside Paul, who was gasp-ing and clutching his abdomen. His white shirt grew sodden with a widening ring of blood.

Royce pried his hands loose to find a fountain of blood pour-ing from his side. Buddy fell down beside her, holding out his bandanna. With shaky fingers, she pressed it over the wound. Paul recoiled in pain.

John retrieved the gun, put on the safety, and bent over Paul. Marla sat apart holding a shivering Renetta. With labored breathing, Paul looked from John to Buddy to Royce, then closed his eyes.

"Look what you did!" Buddy shouted, whirling toward

Renetta. "Look what you did to him, you—you—" It was a stunning reprimand, his being unable to find a vile enough word for the woman he had been infatuated with.

"Oh, dry up," Paul gasped. "It was an accident. She was scared."

"Shhh." Trying not to cry, Royce leaned down to him. She clutched his bloody fingers in one hand and pressed on the wound with the other. He gripped her hand.

Paul squeezed his eyes shut and then opened them. "I always wondered if it would end like this."

"Don't say that," Royce pleaded as the tears came, but he had something else on his mind.

"It was wrong," he told Buddy. "We knew that, and kept doing it."

"The center would have closed years ago without that money, Padre," Buddy reminded him.

"But the end doesn't justify the means. It comes back to haunt you . . . in the end." Paul shut his eyes again.

"This is not 'the end.' We're getting you to the hospital in Alpine!" Buddy declared, jumping up. "Load the horses!" he ordered John, who began throwing things on the animals.

"How are we going to do that?" Royce cried. "He can't ride. He'll bleed to death!"

"Well, he'll die for sure if we just sit here!" Buddy shouted.

"Buddy—" Paul weakly protested.

"Sorry, Padre. Listen, you gotta ride. We gotta get you to the hospital. Can you ride?"

"Sure," Paul gasped.

Buddy cut a length of twine from his pack and tied a fresh bandanna tightly over Paul's wound. Paul moaned and Royce cradled his face, whispering comfort into his lips. Then each taking an arm, Buddy and Royce walked Paul to Buster as John finished repacking the animals.

Buddy mounted, then said, "Help him up behind me. You ride with *her* on my horse." With Royce pushing and Buddy pulling, they managed to get Paul up behind the saddle so he could lean on Buddy.

Royce crawled onto the saddle on Buddy's horse and helped Renetta up behind her. Marla stood beside them, crossing her arms. "I'm not riding with *him*."

"Fine, you can walk!" Royce flared at her. "But we're not waiting for you!" Marla decided she would ride with John after all. So the group started off again as the sun slipped behind the mountains.

Almost as soon as they started out, they had to stop again. Paul, semiconscious, could not keep himself astride the horse. Clutching his shirt sleeves, Buddy yelled at Royce, "Come 'ere! Get the nylon rope out of my right-hand bag!"

Royce flew to the bag and unfastened it, distracted by the sight of blood dripping from Paul's saturated shirt onto his jeans. She held the rope out to Buddy, but he ordered, "Tie his hands together." Royce looked up, shocked. "Tie his hands around me so he doesn't fall off!" Buddy repeated. Royce tied Paul's hands, sticky with drying blood.

Buddy took off again, at a full gallop. John, with Marla, followed. Royce ran back to Buddy's horse, where Renetta waited. Royce was left to get on the animal and make it run herself. Trembling with fear, she kicked it as hard as she could and held on to the saddlehorn for dear life.

The horse knew enough to follow its companions, so all Royce had to do was stay on while it ate up the highway in long strides. *How can he survive this?* she wondered, straining to watch the slumped figure ahead.

Renetta began to cry into Royce's back. "I didn't mean to shoot him."

"I know—and he knows—Renetta. We're—getting him to the hospital," Royce said over her shoulder, her voice punctuated by the sound of hooves hitting pavement.

"If he dies, that makes me—a murderer," Renetta said.

"No, it doesn't. . . ." Royce choked on the thought.

They rode at such a furious pace that Royce wondered if Buddy's feelings had not warped his thinking. Was this really the best thing to do? Should they ride so hard? *Please, Paul, hang on.*

The drumming of the hoofbeats began pounding in Royce's brain. Twilight deepened, and they rounded a bend in the road through the dark valley. *The valley of the shadow of death,* Royce thought with a shudder. She could not bring herself to glance aside at the large, ominous shadows they passed, so she kept her eyes on the figures ahead. One of them was bleeding to death. Then with a start she remembered, *He said he would get me to Alpine or die trying. Is he going to die getting me there?*

They broke out of the mountains and a sign from heaven appeared: "Alpine, 3 mi." Buddy leaned over Buster with fresh demands for speed. Royce gritted her teeth as her horse flattened its ears and poured out power. On the outskirts of town they galloped past an old cemetery—the kind with the large, upright monuments. Royce averted her eyes and thrust away images of an open grave. "No," she gasped.

In minutes they were clattering through the main intersection of the sleepy little town, where the street signal flashed yellow. They hesitated, looking around.

"There!" shouted Royce, pointing to a sign with a blue H and an arrow. They followed it to the Brewster County Hospital, where Buddy roared up to the emergency entrance, yelling at the top of his lungs.

What followed was something of a blur. A nurse and an orderly ran out to untie Paul and carry him in. Falling from her horse, Royce glimpsed his pale, slack face. The others came in behind him and threw themselves breathlessly around the waiting room.

They waited in oppressive silence. Buddy paced like a caged animal. John spread out in a chair, defiantly lighting a cigarette. Renetta sat in shock in the corner with Marla hovering protectively over her. Royce, grievously saddle sore, stood near the door they had taken him through. She looked down in bleak surprise at the dark stains on her new Western shirt and Levis. But it was the grotesque appearance of her hands under the fluorescent lights which shook her. They looked as though they had been washed in blood. Royce sank to her knees under a weight of horror.

Buddy knelt and put an arm around her shoulders. "It's all right. He's still alive," he said softly.

Royce looked up at Buddy's chiseled face and blue eyes. "I don't even know his name," she whispered.

Buddy opened his mouth but at that moment the door swung open. An older man in a white, blood-smeared coat came out, holding an x-ray. Royce and Buddy stood up. All eyes were on the doctor.

"Well, I'd almost say this is one lucky fella." He held up the x-ray to the light for Buddy and Royce. "The slug pierced his external abdominal oblique, then came to rest just a quarter-inch from his aorta here without seriously damaging any vital organs. Let me tell you, if that aorta had been hit, he'd 'a' died in seconds. The bullet's no danger to him where it is, which is good, because we don't have the facilities to operate and remove it. The risk of removal needs ta be evaluated right away at a big-city hospital. But as it is, all that is moot. He won't live to see morning."

"Why not?" Buddy asked, his voice cracking.

"Because he's had a whole lotta blood loss, and he's type O," the doctor explained. "He'll die without a transfusion, but he can't take any but type O. We've got no type O at all. I've sent out an emergency call for some, but by the time we get any, your man will be long gone." Royce leaned helplessly on Buddy.

From the corner of the waiting room Renetta said quietly, "I'm type O." The others stared at her.

"Are you sure?" the doctor demanded.

"Yes, I'm type O," Renetta insisted.

"Oh, Renetta!" breathed Royce.

"Well, get back here and let's see if we can do a cross-match!" the doctor exclaimed. He directed Renetta through a door, shouting orders to a nurse. Then he paused. "By the way, the law requires that I report any gunshot wounds. Don't go anywhere; the sheriff's deputies are coming down to ask you a few questions." The doctor left John and Buddy staring at each other in the waiting room.

"We gotta get out of here," John whispered.

"I'm not leaving the Padre," Buddy said stubbornly, and Royce wanted to hug him in gratitude.

John began to speak on his way out, "If nothing else, I'd better—" He was stopped by the entrance of a large man in khaki, wearing a badge and a cowboy hat.

"This yours?" the officer drawled, holding the semiautomatic pistol and the satchel of money.

"Uhhhh," John stammered.

"Never mind," the officer said. "The sheriff's been called out of town for a spell, so you can save your stories for him. Let's go." Another deputy brought in handcuffs, which they began placing on Buddy and John. Marla submitted to being cuffed, eyeing the sturdy deputy, who eyed her in return.

But when he came to Royce and pulled her hands behind her back, she pleaded, "Please let me stay here—to see what happens. Renetta—"

"We'll tell you everything you need to know," he said curtly.

They were escorted outside to a black and white unit sitting at the emergency entrance. Royce, John and Buddy were put in the back seat; Marla was placed up front between the two deputies.

The suspects were driven to the Brewster County Jail, where a deputy began the process of fingerprinting them. John argued, "Hey, are we under arrest? What are the charges?"

"It could be suspicion of murder, but for now it's smoking in a hospital," the deputy smirked. "Now shut up and turn around," he ordered with a shove.

The deputy escorted Royce to the bathroom to wash her hands before being fingerprinted, so they could get clear prints. Mechanically, she went through the motions of washing at an old, dirty sink. As she reached up for a paper towel, she caught sight of a hollow-eyed face in the mirror that she hardly recognized as herself.

After being processed in, Marla and Royce were taken to one cell, John and Buddy to another, and the barred doors were shut. Royce sank onto a metal bunk bed that had a sliver of mattress. She stared at the cracked concrete floor and the filthy toilet in the corner. Marla leaned against the bars to exchange pleasantries with the deputy on duty.

Before long Renetta was brought in. Royce leapt to the cell bars to watch her being fingerprinted and photographed. As she was placed in the tank with Royce and Marla, Royce demanded, "How is he?"

Renetta shook her head stupidly. "I don't know. They just took blood. They didn't tell me anything. Oh, Royce—I'm so sorry!" Renetta burst into fresh tears and put her arms around Royce's neck.

Royce rocked her like a child, murmuring, "It's okay. He'll be okay." Buddy came to the bars of his cell across the room to watch.

The inmates were given economy TV dinners, plastic forks, and warm water to drink. Royce ate everything, breaking the flimsy fork in the process. Propping his feet up on the desk, the deputy ate a fast-food hamburger. Every now and then he chortled over a show he was watching on a small television set. Hearing snatches of dialogue, Royce recalled that this show was broadcast on Tuesday nights. This must be Tuesday, then. It seemed like a year ago that they had flown in to this town, from another universe. Royce watched the pale blue light from the television flicker across the deputy's face.

Renetta lay down right after supper and went to sleep. Marla eventually tired of eyeball games with the deputy and climbed into the bunk above Renetta. Those were the only two beds in the cell, but it didn't matter. Royce could not have slept on a down-filled mattress that night. She sat on the edge of the lower bunk at Renetta's feet and looked out between the cell bars.

An hour or so later another deputy came in to relieve the first, who stretched and picked up his leather jacket. Before leaving, he said a few words to the new man and nodded toward Marla on the top bunk. The relief man laughed unpleasantly. Then he settled down to watch television and clean his revolver.

Royce heard John snoring, but every once in a while she saw Buddy's form pacing the cell. The guard brewed coffee and was sipping it when his telephone rang. He answered it, listened, said a few words of acknowledgment, and hung up.

Royce stood and gripped the bars. "Was that the hospital?"

The deputy glanced up. "No."

"Could you—find out how he's doing? Just so I'll know if he's alive or not?" she asked.

"You'll find out if we file murder charges in the morning," he said. Royce sank back down on the bunk and saw Buddy's shadow withdraw from the door of his cell.

Royce remained on the bed, leaning her head on the bars as she watched for morning.

7

❖

Royce was jolted to consciousness by the sound of a door slamming. She sat up and instantly held her aching head. It was morning. Two men had entered the jailhouse. One had to be the sheriff—six-foot-four, with a beer belly made prominent by his authoritative stance, and the other was— "Hey!" Royce jumped up, shouting. "Hey, that's him! Ol' Pete! That's the man who robbed us and left us in the desert! And that's my duffel bag!" She pointed through the bars to the bag in the sheriff's hand. The other inmates began sitting up. Ol' Pete looked like a cornered weasel.

The sheriff gestured to a deputy to unlock her cell door, and asked her, "What's your name?"

"Royce Lindel," she said, and gave him her New York City address and phone number.

"Well, that's it," said the sheriff. "We knew he was trying to use stolen credit cards, but we thought 'Royce' was a man."

"And you've reached your limit on every dang card," Ol' Pete said spitefully.

"You thief! And you left us in the middle of that desert to die!" Royce cried angrily.

"Well, ya didn't, didja?" he said in that same nasal, sarcastic tone.

Freed from the cage, Royce was ready to dismember him, but the sheriff intervened. "Okay, okay—book him, boys. Now, Miss Lindel, you come to my office."

He pointed to a room with a textured glass door and Royce stomped in, picking up her duffel bag to look through it. A few things—a very few things—remained.

"Now, Miss Lindel," the sheriff said, shutting the door behind him, "would you like to tell me how you got mixed up with this grifter and the man who was shot?" He settled back into a chair behind a desk and took off his hat, revealing slicked-back salt-and-pepper hair. He had deep lines in his face, and eyed her as he reached into his shirt pocket for a pack of cigarettes.

"How is Paul?" she breathed anxiously.

"You answer my question first," he instructed.

Sighing, Royce began to explain how she and her friends made the trip down, how the grifter posed as their guide and then stranded them in the desert, and how they had stumbled onto the men's campfire. In telling this part of the story, she noticed that the sheriff's expression changed, but he did not say anything. Then, when she was relating the part about the raid and how Paul had dumped all the cocaine, the sheriff interrupted, "Okay, I get the picture: he was accidentally shot hunting rattlesnakes in the desert."

"No; that's not it at all," Royce said in amazement, but the sheriff was hearing no more.

"Now you listen to me," he said sternly, leaning forward and crushing out his cigarette. "We're going to return all your property that was recovered, then we're going to put you on the first plane back to El Paso. Don't worry about Ol' Pete—we'll take good care of him. You're going to fly right back to New York without a word of this to anyone." He opened his door and called a deputy to bring the rest of the things out of the evidence closet.

Royce gaped at him. "What about Paul? The man who was shot? How is he?" The sheriff acted as though he had not even heard her. He gathered the women's bags which the deputy had brought and took Royce by the arm. Briskly, he ordered Renetta and Marla released. They were given their possessions and escorted out in the early morning sunshine to a squad car.

The sheriff drove them straight to the small county airstrip. He sat them in the lobby while he talked to the reservations clerk. Then he went back to tell the women: "You were booked for a return flight Friday, but they've moved you up to today. Your flight out of El Paso's been rescheduled, too—just have 'em check on the computer for gate and departure." He stood over them until the commuter began loading for takeoff.

As he escorted them to the plane, Royce pleaded, "Is he alive? Please, it's very important to us to know. Just tell me that he's alive."

At the door of the plane, the sheriff looked down at her and said, "I'm not going to answer that question, because if you want to come out of this in one piece, you've got to leave now and not look back." The other two passengers watched with interest while he sternly put the three bedraggled women on board.

As the plane taxied down the runway, Royce leaned her head against the window and began to cry. Oblivious of the passengers' stares, she smeared the window with her tears while Renetta leaned against her, crying as well. "Now, y'all," Marla said desperately, "he didn't say he was dead. He didn't arrest Renetta." Royce shook her head against the window.

The plane stopped; Royce put her head down. As minutes passed and they stayed stopped, she looked up. The door opened!

"They're rechecking the hinge—" someone was saying, but Royce was out instantly, hopping down from the wing to the ground past a startled maintenance man. Renetta and Marla followed with their bags. They ran to the rear of "The Cockpit" and watched as the commuter's door was shut and latched, and the plane took off without them.

Shouldering their bags, they skulked the six long blocks back to the hospital. "I don't believe this," Marla muttered.

"Listen, he must be alive, or they wouldn't have released us," Renetta said. "Do you think we can find out for sure?"

"I intend to try," Royce uttered. As they rounded the corner near the hospital, she put out a warning hand and dropped her duffel bag. A deputy's cruiser was parked near the emergency entrance. Crouching, Royce saw that no one was in the car. "Wait here," she whispered.

Royce casually approached the black-and-white unit and glanced down in it. John's gun and satchel were still in the back seat. The door was unlocked. Royce opened it and took the items, then walked briskly back to her friends. "Here." She deposited the things in Marla's hands.

"Are you crazy?" Marla asked without any real wonderment.

"Yes," Royce said. "I'm going to find Paul. You two wait for me."

"Standing out here?" Marla demanded.

"No. Remember that old cemetery we passed on the way here? Wait there. I'll meet you there," Royce said.

"Will do," Renetta said, pushing Marla along.

Royce turned back to scrutinize the beige brick hospital building. Where was he? ICU? Did they even have an intensive care unit here? Circumventing the front entrance, she went around the U-shaped building until she came to the interior of the U, which overlooked a grassy quadrangle. It was a one-story building. Royce began walking along the building, looking in windows. Many of them had closed blinds, but this building was old enough to have windows that actually opened, and screens.

Royce looked in window after window: Empty. Empty. Blinds closed. Elderly man. Custodian cleaning. (Royce ducked.)

Blinds closed. Empty. Buddy.

Royce stopped, staring. Buddy saw her and his eyes got big. He opened the window, pushed out the screen, and Royce climbed in, exclaiming, "They released you, too!"

Lying in bed with tubes in his arm, Paul twisted his head to see her. He was wearing a blue print hospital gown, and had rope burns on his wrists. But his color was good, and his initial expression was that of joyful astonishment. Kneeling by his bedside, Royce leaned close to him and whispered, "How ya doin'?" He gazed at her.

"We thought you'd flown out!" Buddy said as he refastened the screen. John went to the window to look.

"I couldn't," she said, eyes on Paul. "We didn't. I had to know that you were all right."

"I'm all right," he said hoarsely. His face changed; a mask went up. Then he cleared his throat and said, "You've got to leave. Royce, you should have gone on home. You've got to leave right away."

"Why?" asked Royce. "Are you in trouble?"

Paul glanced up at Buddy, who looked at John. "No," Paul said.

"Then why do I have to leave 'right away'?" Royce demanded. Paul did not answer and the mask stayed in place.

Angry, Royce got to her feet. "Fine. I will leave." She opened the window and pushed out the screen again. "By the way, we have something of yours. If you want it, you'll have to come to the old cemetery south of town to get it." She scrambled out of the window, dropping to the ground.

Royce jogged to the highway and headed for the cemetery. It was farther away than she had remembered, and she was wheezing by the time she reached its front gate. When she opened the gate, it screeched on its rusty old hinges. She jumped and looked around, but no one was in sight.

"Marla? Renetta?" Royce called.

A blonde head appeared from behind a crouching stone

angel toward the back of the cemetery. Royce made her way past rows of tombstones and dropped down beside her friends. They had a fast-food feast of burritos, chips, canned soft drinks and apple turnovers spread out, and Royce helped herself. "Did you find Paul?" Renetta asked thickly, without waiting to swallow.

"Yeah, and he was not very happy to see me," Royce said, ripping open a bag of chips with such violence that they flew everywhere. "He was well enough to tell me I should have gone home."

"After all you did for him!" exclaimed Marla.

Royce did not stop to tally up how much she had done for him versus how much he had done for her. "Anyway, I told them we had something of theirs, and if they wanted it back, they had to come here to get it." She bit into a burrito.

"You saw—John?" Marla asked.

Royce nodded. She swallowed and added, "They were all three in Paul's room. Get this: I asked him if they were in trouble, and he said, 'No.' What do you make of that?"

"There are several possibilities—I think," Renetta said humbly. "One: He's lying and they *are* in trouble, and don't want us involved."

Royce squinted, thinking, then shook her head. "There was that black-and-white still at the hospital, but nobody with them and no cuffs on them, or anything. Oh! And when the sheriff took me out of the tank to question me, as I was telling him about the robbery and Paul dumping the coke, he cut me off and said, 'Oh, I see. He got shot accidentally while hunting rattlesnakes.' Then he hustled us to the airport. He must have come right back and released John and Buddy, as well."

Renetta nodded thoughtfully. "Then it could be that they're not in trouble because the sheriff knows what they're doing and wants them to continue. That fact can go one of two ways: either the sheriff is honest and they are honest, or the sheriff is crooked and they are actually drug dealers." The women silently contemplated the unpleasant possibilities.

"Still," Renetta said softly, "I'm glad he's all right."

"What if the sheriff were crooked and they were honest?" Marla asked.

"They'd be dead by now. And probably, so would we," Renetta said, and Royce nodded.

They gathered up their trash. "What, no receptacles?" joked Royce. Marla leaned against the flat back of a stone marker. "I'm so tired."

"You and Renetta go ahead and sleep," Royce said. "I'll keep watch first, in case they come. I'll wake Renetta in a few hours." In spite of her tiredness, Royce was determined to be awake when they came. How long could that take? This sounded like an excellent plan, so Marla and Renetta were soon dead to the world.

Royce scooted out from behind a gravestone just far enough to see the highway. She looked up at the dazzling blue sky through the branches of a large, old mesquite tree. Every now and then a car passed by on the highway, but it seemed worlds away. Here, all was quiet, all was at rest.

Royce blinked heavily. She knew how important it was for her to stay awake, so she got up to look around. The old cemetery was a fascinating place, holding so many hints of spent lives. The marker Marla rested under said, "Jonas Peter Burroughs, born 1815, died March 8, 1901. A loving father and true friend." A double marker nearby indicated the final resting place of a husband and wife who had died within a few weeks of each other, in 1917. Their stone bore a carving of two interlocking hearts carried on wings.

The saddest monument Royce saw was the crouching angel she had noticed from the road. Of gorgeously carved white marble, it was the depiction of a feminine being with wings, bending in grief over the grave below. Her face was hidden between the outstretched arms. Royce looked down at the marker. It was the grave of Sarah Belle Harper, born June 5, 1927; died June 4, 1930. Royce's eyes flooded with tears and she had to turn away.

She wandered up the path, looking idly at the urns and statuettes. One large gray marker caught her eye. It bore the name and dates of the deceased, but the largest space was taken up with this quotation in bold capitals: "I am the resurrection and the life; he who believes in me, though he die, yet shall he live." As she stared at it, her eyes mysteriously began to tear up again, so she stumbled away. Determined not to cry and determined not to sleep, she sat down beside her friends and stonily watched the road. But the limitations of the body could be ignored for only so long, and soon she dropped her head on her arms and joined the others.

✳ ✳ ✳

Royce startled awake and sat up. Not remembering where she was, she gazed in momentary terror at the black tombstones rising up in the twilight. But the sight of Marla and Renetta sleeping peacefully nearby quieted her racing pulse. She put a hand out and found John's gun and satchel up against the marker where Marla had put them. They had not come.

"Good grief," she muttered, shaking the other two. They sat up, yawning.

"What happened?" murmured Renetta, rubbing her eyes.

"They didn't come," Royce said flatly.

"What, don't they want their money?" Marla laughed ironically. The same thought occurred to all three, but Royce reached the satchel first to check for the money. There it was, bundles and bundles of hundred-dollar bills.

"This is perplexing," Renetta admitted.

"No, this is stupid," Royce said, shutting the satchel. "It was stupid to come down here in the first place, stupid not to leave when we could have and stupid to wait hours for questionable characters in a graveyard!"

She put the gun and money in her duffel bag, then got to

92

her feet. "We're going to get a motel room for the night and fly out first thing in the morning. I've had all the fun I can stand."

"What about the money?" Marla asked, nodding to Royce's bag.

"We'll—I don't know. We'll throw it inside the jailhouse and run," Royce said impatiently.

The others readily gathered their things and headed for the rusty iron gate. In the deepening darkness, the cemetery no longer looked an interesting place. It was creepy and forbidding, a depository of bones and ancient fears. The three walked as fast as feasible through the shadows of urns and crosses.

As Royce put her hand on the latch, they heard a familiar *clop-clop, clop-clop.* Three riders approached in the moonlight, loping easily along the highway. Royce's heart thumped and she stiffened.

The riders drew up beside the cemetery entrance and dismounted—Buddy, John, and Paul, with a new blue shirt under his old gray jacket. He came off Buster very slowly.

"You're a little late," Royce said to John.

"Look, the hospital wouldn't release Paul until late this afternoon, and then we had to go get our horses from the Humane Society. Besides, I came hours ago, and no one was here," John said testily. He kept glancing at Marla, who steadfastly looked away.

Renetta went up hesitantly to Paul. "I am so sorry for what I did to you," she said softly, and Buddy looked like warm butter.

"You made it up to me," Paul smiled slightly. "I hear we're the same blood type. I guess you could say" he looked at Royce "that you got under my skin."

Royce lowered her eyes to the bag in her hands. She put it down and zipped it open. "This is yours—" she handed the gun gingerly to John, barrel down, "and this." She pulled out the satchel with the money. "But I suppose the sheriff would have returned them to you, anyway."

The men neither admitted nor denied anything. Royce

hoisted her bag over her shoulder. "It's time we left," she said with hypocritical finality, taking a step.

Paul stepped away from his horse into her path. "Royce." She hardly trusted herself to look up, but when she did, all she could see was the moon behind him, casting his face in deep shadows. He paused, reaching his hand out to her. Then he turned to his saddlebags and pulled out a bundle. He gave her the shopping bag with her dirty clothes and toiletries. "Don't forget your things."

Crimson-faced, she took the bundle and said icily, "Thank you."

That reminded them that Buddy still carried Marla's and Renetta's things. He gave Marla her sack, which she opened and looked through. As Renetta took her shopping bag from Buddy, he held out his hand. "You're okay," he said in forgiving goodwill.

Taking his hand, Renetta seemed caught off guard by his pure, unpretentious goodness. She quietly admitted, "You are, too. You really are." She leaned forward and kissed him on the cheek, then quickly turned away.

Buddy started to say something when John reached out and grabbed Marla's hand. "Aren't you going to tell me goodbye?" he said teasingly, drawing her toward him.

"Yes. Drop dead," Marla said, yanking her hand away.

There was so much more that needed to be said—Royce was loath to part on such a bitter note. She looked at Buddy, wanting to thank him for his loyalty and compassion, but when he looked at her, her eyes began to water dangerously. Royce turned aside only to find herself face to face with Paul, and she was almost undone. Dropping her head, she stepped around him. Without another word the women left the riders standing by their horses.

Royce was glad it was a good brisk walk to the motel, so her tears would have a chance to dry before she had to face the light. "I don't need this. I already have one jerk to cry over at home," she muttered to herself.

Arriving at the motel, they rented a double room which, with economy foremost in mind, was decorated in a cheap Western motif. They flipped a coin to decide who got to bathe first. Since Royce finished dead last, she made the others agree to a twenty-minute time limit.

After a refreshing (albeit lukewarm) shower, Royce used the tub to wash out her spare denims. They turned the water a murky brown. Then she attempted to wash the bloodstains from the shirt she had been wearing, but they merely faded a little. "Nothing's going to remove that," she observed, holding up the shirt. "That blood will be there forever." She raised her dripping hands, remembering how they had been covered in warm blood. "Nothing will remove that," she murmured again.

While Marla watched television and Renetta lay on the bed staring at the ceiling, Royce inventoried her mementoes from this trip: a pretty bracelet, a fringed suede jacket, a ruined shirt and a genuinely stained pair of Levis. She scrutinized the stiff brown spots on the only jeans she had to wear home tomorrow. "I could find a laundromat to dry my denims," she mused, but— who cared?

Is that all you're taking back? came the question. No, there was also a badly bruised rear end and a badly battered heart.

She sat listlessly on the commode lid. How stupid, how futile to meet someone like that and then have to leave with so many questions unanswered. So many what-ifs. What if he loved her? What if he couldn't bear for her to leave? What if . . . they came back knocking on the door tonight?

Royce tried to suppress this wild hope, but it was too late. She summarily dismissed it, and it came creeping back. She slammed the door on it, and it looked in through the window. So she left it in the bathroom with her wet denims and sat on the bed beside Marla to watch television.

Marla was stretched out, coating herself with lotion. "I will be *so glad* to get back to civilization," she avowed.

"Me, too," Royce agreed with a lying vehemence.

"I don't think I'll ever be the same," Renetta murmured from the other bed. Royce looked over to her, crying inwardly, *I know!* and there was that ridiculous Hope beside her again.

"Why, Renetta? Just because you almost killed a man?" Marla tried to laugh off the sober mood.

Royce turned to rebuke Marla, but Renetta said, "Partly. It made me think about things I haven't considered for a long time. It made me think about what I do that is really important. And I decided: not much."

Marla tossed her head, not caring for level-four conversations. "You'll feel better when you get back to the real world."

Renetta looked up. "What makes New York any more real than Texas?"

"You know what I mean," Marla said, exasperated. "I mean, look around. Who would want to live in such a tacky, dreary, *nothing* place?" She waved her arms around the motel room. Royce stared at Marla. *You were the one talking about how this trip would broaden my horizons. Why didn't it broaden yours?* Royce wondered.

Renetta lay back on the bed. "Marla, your mind is so narrow that a new thought couldn't get in sideways."

Marla was attempting a suitably acidic response when there was a knock on the door. Three women bolted up, none of them completely dressed. "Who is it?" Royce called, her heart in her throat.

"Sheriff's deputy," came the answer.

"Uh, just a minute," Royce called back. They quickly pulled on their jeans, then Royce opened the door a crack. "What is it?"

The man in uniform outside said, "The guy that was shot was just readmitted to the hospital with internal bleeding. He needs more blood."

Royce felt a peculiar pain in her chest. "We'll come right with you. Renetta?" Royce asked. She agreed. Royce grabbed her jacket and they accompanied the deputy out into the parking lot. Royce walked beside him; Renetta and Marla followed.

It was a deputy Royce had not seen before. He did not have that distinctive West Texas drawl.

Then Royce remembered the doctor saying that he had sent out a call for type O blood. So why did they need Renetta again? Glancing up, Royce saw they were heading toward a black sedan with its motor running. A man at the wheel turned around—

Royce slammed her body into the deputy, screaming, "Run! Marla! Renetta! Run!" He grabbed her arms and the man behind the wheel bolted out of the car. Royce was able to thrust out a leg and trip him. Renetta and Marla disappeared around the edge of the building.

The second man picked himself up and delivered a stinging slap to Royce's face. He looked after the two who got away and said, "Well, we got one. That'll do." The deputy, whom Royce had belatedly recognized as bogus, shoved her into the back seat of the car and climbed in himself, then they peeled out of the parking lot.

8

With Royce captive in the back seat, the driver turned down the highway. As he drove, he picked up a microphone and said, "Are you listening, boys? I've got the deal of the year for you. You've got something of mine, well now I've got something of yours. You meet me at six a.m. tomorrow at *the place we first met,* and we'll exchange. You give me my property, and I give you yours." He glanced back at Royce, then pulled off to the side of the highway where a new Jeep waited.

Royce was dragged from the sedan and forced into the back seat of the other vehicle, beside an armed man. The first driver exchanged words with her new driver, who then started the engine and roared out on the highway, southbound.

Royce should have been terrified; as it happened, she was quite aware that these men would just as soon kill her as look at her. But a strange exhilaration crowded out the fear. Paul had been telling her the truth all along. He had been afraid of this very thing happening. He did not want her to leave, but he tried to make her, for her sake. Royce tried to think of a time when any man had exhibited such unselfishness on her behalf, and she had to reach clear back to her father to find one.

They were driving through the mountains now, at seventy-five miles an hour. Royce felt as though she were in the middle of a computer simulation. Feeling for her seatbelt, she closed her eyes to block out the mountains rushing past.

So, what had Paul gotten for his trouble in rescuing three stranded women? He'd gotten shot and almost killed, and now stood to lose the income from this trip. What would happen when they could not return the cocaine? Royce had a reliable idea.

Did she regret coming, now? The CJ-7 she was in bounced and pitched wildly over some unnoticed obstruction, and the fear she should have felt earlier surfaced with a vengeance. Did she regret it? Sleeping beside a man who robbed drug runners but was too shy to kiss her in front of Renetta? Who spilled out unsolicited explanations but would not tell her his real name? And what was he about to say before Marla had pitched a fit and Renetta had grabbed the gun?

They broke out of the mountains and the driver turned on his radio in time to hear most of the broadcast message repeated. The vehicle bounced again, all four wheels leaving the pavement. As they landed with a crushing thud, Royce wondered if the driver had a death wish or just considered it all fun.

At eleven p.m. on an empty desert highway, the driver found no reason for restraint and floored the accelerator. "What's the rush?" Royce gasped against the wind, which whipped her hair straight back from her head. The idiot beside her took random potshots at anything that caught his eye as they whizzed by.

In no time at all they were approaching the southern belt of mountains. At Study Butte, the driver actually pulled over to look at a map and a compass. Royce, dizzy, grasped the roll bar beside her. Then, as she feared he would, he left the highway to go careening over rocky ground and low, scraggly bushes.

At length he crossed another paved road and pulled up to the very foot of the misty Chisos Mountains. They angled up a dirt path and a jackrabbit bounded away from the headlights before it could get shot. The driver pulled into a clearing and stopped. Here they had the mountains on their right and a protective ridge of rocks on their left. Beyond the rocks was a clear view of the paved road for miles.

The two men unpacked their supplies of beer, beans, blankets, guns and cigarettes, then spread out to make the best of the wait. As a precaution, they handcuffed Royce to the roll bar beside her seat. She tried the ploy, "Hey, I need to go to the bathroom!" but they just laughed.

The next few hours were some of the most uncomfortable Royce had ever endured. Her suede jacket was warmer than her denim one, but it was insufficient for sitting in the fifty-degree chill. The men ate and drank without offering her any, and chuckled at her pleas for a blanket. Finally one settled down to rest under his blankets while the other kept watch on the road below. At length, Royce dropped off to sleep from fatigue.

$$* * *$$

Sudden movement in the darkness woke her. Both men had moved to look over the rocks at the road. Their backs were to Royce. She could hear the sound of a motor from below.

"'S that them?" one asked the other, who was peering through binoculars. Royce squinted at their shadowy forms.

"Looks like it," he replied, at which the other turned aside to cock a high-powered rifle. He put his eye to the infrared scope and aimed carefully.

Instantly Royce realized that these guys were not interested in a trade at all—they were going to kill whoever had come with the money. And that had to be Paul.

Royce broke into a cold sweat. She had to do something—

anything—to warn him. In desperation, she glanced around the Jeep. She found that by unbuckling her seatbelt and stretching her right leg around the driver's seat, she could just reach the steering wheel with the toe of her boot. A few more inches up. . . .

The man with the rifle suddenly lowered it, saying, "Hey, that's—" Royce's toe hit the horn and sounded a long blast. The men jerked around angrily and Royce instinctively ducked. The Jeep rolled a few inches. Then a barrage of gunfire erupted from the road below. Both men were hit at once.

Horrified, Royce watched them buckle and fall. Was that Paul, who had thanked goodness that Buddy hadn't shot anyone when they had stumbled across the drug runners? What had this guy been about to say before she had hit the horn? He was reacting as if the people below were not the expected party after all. If they weren't, then who were they? The police? Didn't the police shout warnings before they fired? And wouldn't whoever it was be on their way up here now?

Feeling an overwhelming desire to escape, Royce looked around wildly. The Jeep moved again. It was situated just off the dirt road, at the top of a rocky incline of about twenty degrees which was dotted with sparse desert plants as far as she could see, until it faded into the darkness. Royce peered over the seat and guessed that they had neglected to set the parking brake. But they had left the Jeep in gear. Frantically, she kicked the gearshift into neutral and then began rocking back and forth. The Jeep inched forward. She heard the sound of an engine coming up the road to this spot.

She rocked again and the Jeep began to roll a little faster. With the toe of her boot, she nudged the steering wheel until the Jeep turned away from the rocks and toward the slope.

The Jeep rolled down the incline, bouncing and bucking and gaining speed. Royce held on to the roll bar and strained to keep her toe on the steering wheel. The Jeep covered ground quickly, plunging into the shadow of the mountain looming overhead. She could not see a thing.

Branches slashed her face and she stifled a scream. Royce gave up trying to steer and hid her head under her arms. After bouncing along and picking up speed for another thirty seconds, the Jeep crashed into an obstacle and lurched sideways. Royce was thrown from her seat, wrenching the wrist cuffed to the bar. But at least she was stopped.

Holding her breath, she climbed back onto the seat and listened. No car sounds. Then she peered up the slope behind her. Everything was black in the circle of shadow; beyond it, in the moonlight, the rocks glistened like silver.

Royce sat still and listened for probably thirty minutes. Finally, satisfied that she was out of danger, she began working on finding a way out of the handcuffs. She was feeling in the back of the Jeep for a tool when she heard the sudden warning of a rattlesnake nearby. The distinctive, raspy rattle was very close, off to her right somewhere. Royce froze and moved only her eyes to look. But everything was pitch black. She could not see the rattler she heard.

When she stopped moving, the rattle ceased. She held that position in absolute stillness until her muscles began to ache. Ever so slowly, she withdrew to her seat. She stayed there quietly, thinking, *I can't do a thing until morning. Better just sit tight.* Eventually, she closed her eyes and put her head back on the seat.

✳ ✳ ✳

When Royce awoke, morning was well under way. She blinked up at the sky through the tangled branches of the alligator juniper which had halted her ride. Sitting up, she moaned over her aching wrist and aching neck. She rubbed her neck with her free hand and looked over the cracked windshield of the Jeep to find herself stopped on the very edge of an arroyo, the walls of which pitched straight down for twelve feet. There was nothing else within sight of the tree that would have been large enough to prevent the vehicle from plunging down into the dry stream bed.

Royce contemplated her close call a moment, then cautiously stepped out of the Jeep. There was no sign of her visitor from last night. Royce found nothing in the back of the vehicle that she could detach with one hand to free herself. The bar was solid; the cuffs were secure; and Royce began to worry.

At that point she saw something collecting in a puddle under the Jeep. She bent to feel it: oil. "I probably cracked the engine block," she murmured, scrutinizing the wreck. But she reached down again and gathered oil on her fingers, then smeared it around her cuffed wrist. Wincing, she closed her hand in as tight as she could and tried to work the cuff over it. After several minutes of painful crunching, the cuff slipped over her fingers and she was free.

Cradling her hand, she surveyed her success with some satisfaction. Then she began retracing her route back up the slope. The good stiff wind last night had obliterated most of the Jeep's tracks, but she felt fairly sure of the direction. Royce left the vehicle behind without a glance and confidently marched up the incline.

Remembering her first desert trek with Marla and Renetta, she smiled. She was a lot stronger now, and certainly more savvy about the area. All she had to do was get to the road she had seen last night and follow it to the lodge. But first, she intended to pilfer the supplies the men had brought. After walking for a while, however, and not coming to the rocks with the view of the road, she began to realize that her sense of direction must be slightly off.

"Now I know the mountains were over here," she held out her sore left hand, "and the slope was gradual. I must be overcompensating." So she adjusted her course to the right and pressed on. Nothing looked familiar, but she was unsure of much that she had seen last night.

After a long time of walking, she still saw neither the rocks nor the road. Hot and dry, she paused to take off her jacket and wipe her forehead. "Shouldn't I have reached it by now?" she panted. Looking all around, she decided, "It was further into the mountains. I've gotten too far away from the mountains." So she readjusted her course to the left and went on.

Not too much later she realized that she was in trouble. She sat to rest in the shade of a rock, confessing, "I don't know where it is. I can't just wander around." The hunger she began to feel was unpleasant, but the thirst was vicious. It started as a dry mouth, then progressed to such dryness that her tongue stuck to the roof of her mouth.

Scanning the wilderness, Royce wondered if this view would be the last she ever saw. When she thought about dying, she was too weary to be scared. Instead, she was vaguely sad—sad that her life had not amounted to anything more. Sad that she would have no opportunity to change it. What inscription could she leave for a tombstone? "She wrote good copy"?

Royce looked down at a plump, round cactus crowned by a ring of yellow flowers, and it occurred to her that some of these cacti were supposed to contain water. She looked at it more closely. It was covered with many barbed little hooks. She could not open it with her bare hands, and when she remembered that she had not even attempted to strip the Jeep before walking away, she almost cried—without tears.

Casting about on the ground, she found several flat rocks with sharp edges. Using one of these, she was able to hack open the cactus and cut a chunk from its moist inside. When she held it over her mouth and squeezed, it dripped water in a stream.

Royce annihilated the cactus, draining it. That strengthened her so that she looked around for her next move. "If I head north, I will hit the road, eventually." She was sure of that. But when she looked up at the sun, it was straight overhead. She had no clue which way was north.

In lieu of that, she decided to climb the mountain until she could see the road. But wherever she tried to climb, she found her way blocked by thick brambles, massive rocks, or impossible slopes. There was no way up. With bleeding hands and bruised wrist, she soon gave up. Then in another belated insight, she realized that she should have stayed with the Jeep. It had a radio.

By this time, Royce was struggling to keep her composure. It would not do any good to fall apart now. She sat in the shade to think things through. She knew she must not wander around, so she decided to wait until the direction of the sun was clear, and then she would walk north. With that decision out of the way, she dozed off.

Torturous hunger pangs woke her. Royce looked up with blurred vision and ascertained the direction of the sun's descent. Then she began walking slowly away from the mountains at an angle.

A small scorpion in her path lashed its tail at her boot, and she did not even flinch. *Why would anyone want to vacation out here?* she wondered. *Such a desolate, lonely place.* Did a desolate heart find the desert companionable? Paul had started to talk about his divorce, but the wound was still obviously too raw.

Royce looked down at her empty hands. *Wait a minute. I know I was carrying my jacket. My new suede jacket with the fringe.* She looked around halfheartedly for it, then gave up and continued walking.

Why were there deserts on earth? Why did people hurt each other so? She shook her head and glanced at the sun to make sure of her direction. She began to realize that she was not thinking clearly. *Who is he running from out here? His wife? His memories?*

She looked up and suddenly saw Paul not twenty feet away. He was ambling toward her, reaching up to adjust the hat on his head. Uttering a hoarse cry, she rushed to him. He disappeared. After a few bewildered moments, she realized that she had been hallucinating. The thought made her shiver even as the air shimmered with heat.

Blankly, she stumbled on for an indeterminate amount of time, watching the dry, brittle ground pass under her heavy feet. Then she sat in the meager shade of a cactus, too weak to continue.

She raised her eyes in surprise to see Renetta brandishing a gun. It fired, and Paul fell back. Royce looked down at the blood on her hands. She closed her eyes tightly for a moment, and when she opened them, the blood was gone . . . for the moment.

Hunger seized her again. She tried to get up, but her legs folded beneath her. *I can't just sleep here on the ground. My hair will get dirty,* she thought, then lapsed into unconsciousness.

Royce startled awake at a coyote's plaintive howl. The night was cold and dark, and she shivered spasmodically. It was the evening of . . . what was today? How long had she been out here? As she tried to rise, the mountains on the horizon swayed rhythmically in some kind of grotesque rhumba. Royce sank back to the ground. *I'm not ready to die. Dear God, I'm not ready. . . .*

✳ ✳ ✳

Morning broke over the horizon in a splendor of gold. Royce watched it where she lay, without even trying to get up. It was so beautiful. By moving only her eyes, Royce could scan the whole panorama of sunrise, played in glory over the distant mountains.

She closed her eyes in supreme peace. You never saw the sun rise in New York City. She had not seen a sunrise in years, before coming here. Today, she was glad to see it. Opening her eyes once more, she saw another spectacle: a golden rider broke from the ridge of the sun and approached with incredible speed. A horse and rider of fire.

Royce smiled. It was nice that this hallucination had the added realistic touch of dust clouds beneath the horse's hooves. And the sounds of thudding hoofbeats and slapping leather. She dreamily took in the vibrations through the ground as they got stronger and stronger.

But then boots hit the ground near her; she flinched. Her head was lifted and something cold put to her mouth. Royce resisted, but a merciless hand forced the spout to stay at her lips and cooling, soothing water rushed out, bathing her face. She gulped. The stream ran down her throat and she seized the canteen, drinking so quickly that she almost choked. It was withdrawn until she swallowed, then she drank all the wonderful stuff she could hold.

Her mind cleared rapidly, and she looked up at Paul's grimy, sunburned face. His eyes were red and moist. "That's the first time in five years that I've prayed," he whispered.

"Do you have anything to eat?" she asked politely. He breathed out and released her to fetch a new bag of cookies from his saddlebag.

"I thought you might want these," he said, opening the package for her. She took it and sat in the shadow of his horse until she had consumed every last Fig Newton from the carton and drop of water from his canteen.

As he helped her to stand, she looked in disapproval at the black horse. "Where is Buster?" she asked severely.

He smiled wanly. "I didn't have time to bring Buster, Royce. I had to drive down and rent this horse."

Recollections of the immediate past flooded her mind. "Marla, and Renetta—" she began anxiously.

He nodded, taking her hand. "After you were grabbed, they ran to the sheriff's office. He found us, and we heard the message over the radio. Buddy put Marla and Renetta right on the plane, and made sure they stayed on. They're back home by now."

Paul swallowed, gripping her hand. "I took the money to the drop-off point and waited for hours. No one ever showed. The sheriff notified the park rangers and we started searching. I don't know where they had you, Royce, but we're over twenty miles from the rendezvous point."

Royce reached up to his neck and he closed his arms around

her. He bent his face to hers—but then they heard a shrill whistle. Paul looked up and waved to a ranger on horseback. "I've got to get you back. Can you ride now?" he asked. She nodded, and he helped her up to the saddle, where she found herself reasonably steady.

Paul climbed up to sit behind the saddle. "Your wound—" she turned around in concern.

He shrugged it off, "I'm just carrying around a few ounces of extra weight, that's all." He took up the reins around her and they started off at a gentle lope. But his face betrayed his acute discomfort, and he slowed the horse to a walk.

Royce held his arms, overwhelmed by gratitude. She did not know how to begin to thank him; all she knew was that she wasn't letting him out of her sight again. Ever.

They were actually only a thirty-minute ride from the Chisos Basin Lodge area. As it came within view, Paul said hesitantly, "The, uh, the sheriff had to call in the Feds and the DEA. A lot of suits are waiting to talk to you." Royce tensed and nodded. Then she reflected, *Marla and Renetta are gone, so they can't contradict anything I say. . . .*

9

❖

Paul and Royce rode into the compound, where he relinquished her to a ranger standing in front of the park office. As she slid off the horse, she clung to Paul's hand. But he withdrew from her grasp and spurred away. The ranger called after him, "Wait! Hey you—we want to talk to you!"

Paul ignored him. But the Brewster County sheriff stepped out from the office and said, "That's one of the volunteer searchers. I told them that as soon as she was found, they were to notify the other searchers." The sheriff looked at Royce and the ranger nodded.

"Do you need medical attention, miss?" the ranger asked, taking her inside.

"No," Royce said, tearing her eyes from the departing horseman, "but—do you have any lemonade?"

He laughed, "If we don't, we'll send for some. Sit down."

"First, could I just wash my face?" Royce asked. Dark sedans were pulling up outside.

"This way, miss," the sheriff said, taking her arm. As he

walked her back to the restroom, he whispered, "I told them you lied to me about the—" a woman appeared around the corner and he continued without a pause— "restroom is right here." She stared at him, then went on in.

Meticulously, Royce washed her face, neck, and arms as she pondered what she would say. The sheriff had already told them she lied about—what? What had he said? She had to know.

Someone knocked on the door. "Ms. Lindel?"

"Coming," she said.

When Royce emerged, her lemonade was waiting for her, as were a sandwich and six or eight men in suits. While Royce ate the sandwich, they pulled out notepads and tape recorders. The sheriff placed her in a chair in front of them. "Miss Lindel, these men are Federal agents. They want to know what happened." Then he stood against the wall behind their chairs, facing Royce.

She sat still, sipping her drink. "Start at the beginning, please, Ms. Lindel," one man said.

Royce swallowed and began in New York, recounting yet again how the trip was arranged and almost canceled, how she and her friends came anyway; how they were robbed and left in the desert; how they stumbled upon the men's camp.

"There were three of them," she said. "They called themselves John, Paul, and Ringo. They didn't know what to do with us at first, because they had something important to do in the morning. They finally decided that one of them would stay with us while the other two took care of business, then they would take us to Terlingua.

"When the two got back the next morning, they had a lot of money and a lot of bundles of white powder, which I assumed was cocaine. One of them took the bundles and emptied them all over a cliff. He told me they were privateers—they robbed the drug runners.

"After that, they decided to bring us here, because it was closer than Terlingua. They dropped us off at the lodge and left, but then came back and got us a few hours later. They said they heard on their radio a call being made from the lodge—one of the employees was a front man for the drug runners, and had seen us pay for our room and other stuff with hundred-dollar bills. Oh yeah—they had given us some money because everything we had was gone. Anyway, this employee told his drug bosses where he thought we'd gotten the money, and they were coming up to talk to us.

"Our guys decided to take us on up to Alpine, but on the way, they got careless with the gun and one of them got shot—I'm not sure how it happened exactly; I think while he was getting off his horse. His buddies loaded him up on the horse and we rode like crazy to the hospital in Alpine.

"We got him there in time, and one of my friends donated blood for him. Because it was a gunshot wound, the doctor called the sheriff." Here Royce paused, looking down. She did not know what the sheriff had told them. Their stories must be consistent. Royce sipped her lemonade, silently agonizing, while the wall clock ticked away the seconds. The sheriff was quiet.

Finally one of the agents said, "Go on, Ms. Lindel; you're not in trouble."

Light broke on Royce. That's right! She had lied to the sheriff! Royce looked up. "I—I was frightened. I didn't want to be involved any more; I just wanted to go home. So I told the sheriff he had been accidentally shot hunting rattlesnakes. The sheriff let us go."

No one reacted to her statement except the sheriff, who imperceptibly nodded. Emboldened, Royce continued, "The sheriff even gave us a ride to the airport, but when we got on the plane, we found we still had some of the drug money. We were so scared—we were afraid to spend it or even carry it, so we decided to get right off the plane and go back to the sheriff with it.

"But we didn't get there. The two friends of the injured man stopped us and convinced us we'd be getting ourselves in a lot of trouble if we went back to the sheriff and told him the truth.

They assured us we could spend the money freely, that it was unmarked. They said the drug dealers always made sure their cash was clean. Well," Royce put a hand to her face in humiliation, "we were stupid and greedy and listened to them. It was too late to catch another flight to El Paso, so we rented a motel room for the night."

From there, Royce told the rest of the story straightforwardly—how she was kidnapped from the motel and driven to the desert, how her abductors were shot and she escaped. At this point she was burning to know something. "Can I ask you a question? Who shot them? The privateers? You? I want to know what happened," she pleaded.

One of the men answered, "Apparently, there has been a string of these robberies which has created some confusion in the cartel. The boss believed that one of his lieutenants was staging the robberies in order to carve out his own territory. When the lieutenant came to investigate them himself, his sources led him to you. He's the one who arranged your abduction and the exchange. Of course, they were setting up the privateers, intending to kill them when they showed up to make the exchange. But by then the boss had gotten fed up and ordered the lieutenant's execution, as well as that of his underlings. Your kidnappers were almost certainly killed by members of their own cartel. It was quite fortunate that you were able to get away."

This explanation, as well as the sheriff's slight nod, told her that her version of events had been accepted. "Anyway, after that, I tried to get back to the road. But I got lost, and I'm afraid I wandered around until a man on horseback found me this morning," she finished. "I just want to go home. Please, may I go home now?" she asked, working up tears.

"Just a few questions first, Ms. Lindel," said an iron-faced man who had not spoken before. Royce turned to him attentively, but something about his manner unnerved her. He had too much experience under his belt to be fooled by such a novice liar. Royce tried to concentrate on some of the weaker aspects of his appearance—his thinning blond hair, his slender, fortyish build—so that she would not be undone by his hard eyes. "Have you seen any of these men, 'John,' 'Paul,' or 'Ringo,' before Sunday night or after Wednesday evening?" he asked.

"No," she said solemnly.

"And did you know them by any names other than 'John,' 'Paul,' and 'Ringo'?"

"No," she said.

"Have you ever been to this park before?"

"No, and I'm never coming back!" she said tearfully.

"Do you have any of the money that the men gave you?" he asked.

"No. I didn't hold it, and I don't know what happened to it," she answered.

After a silence, he closed his notebook and the others turned off their tape recorders. "You may leave, Ms. Lindel. We will contact you if we have further questions," the iron man said.

"Thanks," she replied dully, mentally chalking up a win.

The sheriff escorted her out to his black-and-white, where her duffel bag sat in the back seat. As he opened the front door for her, she looked up and saw Paul sitting on the black horse, watching from a distance. He slowly nodded. "Wait," Royce pleaded to the sheriff.

He divined her intent and uttered, "You going to expose him *now*? Get in, woman." Tears flooded her eyes. The sheriff glanced at him while gently urging her into the car, then sat at the wheel. As they drove off, he said, "Don't look back."

Royce watched the now-familiar highway to Alpine through a blur of tears. "Did I say the right things to keep everyone out of trouble?"

"Yeah," he said. "You did fine. Don't worry; the DEA ain't interested in prosecuting your friends; they're after the big fish. They just wanted the activity stopped, and that's been done."

"Do you mean . . . he'll never come back to Big Bend?" she asked faintly.

"Not to rob drug dealers," he said. "It's a sure bet they've rerouted their shipments as well. Most of the drugs come up through South Texas, where access is easier. But they get bold and try anything, you know. Flying over the canyons is a piece of cake when you got an isolated area like Big Bend to land in. They thought they were safe enough, till your friends hit. But since the robberies didn't happen all the time, it was no great loss. Still, the fact that they *kept* happening got the boss' dander up, I imagine. And this last heist must have been the straw that broke the camel's back."

"How long have they been robbing the cartel?" she asked.

"Oh, for the past three years, at least. We got so little manpower, and so much in drugs flows over the border—we can't begin to stem the tide. But three years ago we were set for a raid when we saw these guys swoop in on horseback and beat us to the courier and his contact. It was clean and neat—no shots fired, no one hurt. We watched them dump the drugs and ride off. My men were going to intercept them, but then said, 'Wait a minute. Let's see what else they do.'

"Every year since we've had indications of another heist or two, usually during the summer or fall, but once right at Christmas. It's always the same: no one hurt, the drugs destroyed. We made the deliberate decision to leave them be. I think your friends knew it, though I'd never seen them face to face until I got the call from Doc Padgett. They paid the hospital bill in cash, so I gave them a little lecture on gun safety and let them go."

"It must be profitable. I wonder why they didn't go into it full-time," she mused.

The sheriff snorted, "With the army the cartel has? They'd smear your pals over the Bend like butter. But hitting them once or twice a year, they always managed to catch the courier by surprise. He's a clever thief, your Paul. I'll miss him."

"What's his name? Paul's real name?" she asked urgently.

"Honey, I'd be the last person to know," he told her.

They rode the rest of the way to Alpine in silence. As he

pulled up to the county airstrip, she asked, "Did you put my friends Marla and Renetta on the plane?"

"One of Paul's buddies did. He swore he got them off," the sheriff replied.

"What about the money?" she asked quietly.

He turned off the engine and set the brake. As he opened the door and picked up his hat, he leaned over and said, "I ain't seen any money."

When he opened her door, she tentatively noted, "I would think you're entitled to a percentage."

He drew up proudly to his six-foot-four-inch height, and placed his worn, stained hat on the crown of his head. "Nobody owns Sheriff Potts but the people of Brewster County. *Nobody.*"

Royce had never heard that line apart from an old movie. But he said it in all earnestness. As she gazed up at him, she saw the lone lawman from her history books standing between his people and the violence that would eat them alive—the lawman who used any means to assure their peace and safety, even if it meant turning his back on certain gray areas. "Paul trusted you," Royce murmured. "Now I see why."

He picked up her duffel bag and escorted her into the terminal. While she waited for a flight, he brought her a quarter-pound hamburger, extremely greasy french fries, and a double-thick chocolate shake, all of which she greedily consumed. Then dirty, sweaty, and sunburned, she self-consciously boarded the plane with the other commuters, and slept all the way to El Paso. She woke up long enough to make her connecting flight to Dallas/Fort Worth International; however, the plane had been late in arriving and she got disoriented in the large, unfamiliar airport, so she missed her flight to New York City.

Too tired to get angry or scared, Royce hauled her duffel bag to the airport hotel. She had some difficulty getting a room, as her credit cards had been reported stolen. So she sat in the hotel lobby to wait as her story was checked out.

While she waited, she eyed her surroundings. The lobby was

sumptuously decorated in wine and teal, with Oriental carpeting, marble pillars, and huge, arty chandeliers which threw brilliantly colored light throughout the cavernous rooms. Royce blushed fiercely when she recalled quizzing Marla about the availability of indoor plumbing in Texas. Everything was clean to a fault—not even a fingerprint on the brass and wood railings.

That was a notable thing, considering the amount of traffic that flowed through while Royce waited. There were a few in jeans, but they were in a small minority. Most were nattily dressed businesspeople, and Royce was shocked to recognize more than one New York designer outfit. A woman with big blond hair paused near her to check her thickly applied makeup in a tortoise-shell compact, and Royce drew in a breath at the size of the diamond on her finger. It was no cubic zirconia, either.

The woman looked down at Royce's gasp. Observing her ragged state, she murmured, "Yuh poo' deah, cain't you git home?" Royce stared up at her. "Heah, sugah." The woman opened her snakeskin purse and pressed a twenty-dollar bill into Royce's hand. Royce was too shocked to thank her until the woman had moved out of earshot. But she kept the bill.

Soon the reservations clerk informed her that the little misunderstanding was all cleared up. "But, you've reached your limit on this card," the clerk said apologetically as she handed it to Royce.

"You mean I can't get a room for tonight?" Royce fairly wailed.

The clerk hastily answered, "Yes, you can, but the charges for one night's stay have brought you to the limit."

"That's all I need," Royce sighed, signing in. Refusing the bellboy, she dragged her duffel bag up to her room on the eighth floor. Before taking a bath, she opened the window drapes to look out.

She saw the purple and pink remains of a sunset that spread across the horizon. Lights began twinkling from whichever city was beyond the airport—all the beautiful lights that she loved at night. She stood at the window watching the colors deepen and the lights brighten. "There are lights all over the world," she reflected. "There are good people everywhere." Her vision blurred and she quickly shut the drapes.

She took a long bath in the whirlpool tub, using the toiletries the hotel provided, listening to the classical music broadcast out of Dallas. Then she ordered a sandwich from room service. It came on a tray adorned with chips, fresh strawberries, and a bud vase with daisies. She turned out the lights and ate in front of the window, watching the world below. And when she was done, she crawled into bed. A real bed, with clean sheets and foam pillows—! But what she would have given to sleep in Paul's sleeping bag just once more.

After settling up the hotel bill the following morning using her last credit card, Royce was able to get on a flight to La Guardia on standby. Wearing her New York denims that she had fortunately washed in Alpine, she felt a little more civilized and a lot less self-conscious. As she settled into her seat, she looked up and gasped. A man with brown hair was sitting on the aisle seat three rows up. Could it be . . . ? Suddenly that awful Hope which had been born in the motel room was sitting beside her, whispering, "That's Paul, coming to New York to find you."

Mentally strangling Hope, she muttered, "That's ridiculous." But she strained to get a glimpse of his face or what he was wearing. The seatbelt light was on, so she could not get up. Until the plane took off thirty minutes later, she was left to alternately peer ahead and stare around in deliberate unconcern.

As soon as the plane was in the air and the light went off, Royce was devising a reason to go up front. She left her seat and intercepted the flight attendant coming down the aisle: "Excuse me. When you have a moment, may I get some aspirin?" The flight attendant promised some to come right away. Then Royce turned and looked down at the man's face.

Of course, it was not Paul. She knew that. She went back to her seat and gratefully accepted the aspirin when it came. The Hope sitting beside her was dimmer, but still there. "I hope you're not coming all the way back with me to New York City. How will I ever live with you?" she told it.

After arriving at La Guardia, Royce took a cab home to her apartment in Queens. The familiar noise and glare of traffic was comforting. Noticing something in her expression, the cab driver glanced in the rear-view mirror and asked, "Comin' home?"

"Yeah," she said with a breath of relief. "From vacation."

"Yeah?" he said. "Where?"

"Texas. Big Bend!" she laughed.

"Yeah? What was it like?" the cabbie asked.

"Oh, man, it was awful. Hot, and dry, and ugly. Ramshackle buildings and desert and bugs," she shuddered.

"Yeah, well, there's no place worth goin' to outside the Big Apple, if you ask me," he said, then jerked the wheel and cursed at a pedestrian.

"Yeah," Royce murmured, but inside she was experiencing a golden sunrise and blindingly blue sky . . . misty azure mountains and the cool night wind. . . . Paul was right. She had almost died there, but held it no grudges. It was too awesome.

The driver delivered Royce to her building and she surrendered the stranger's twenty. Letting herself into her apartment, she turned on the lights with a sigh and then screamed faintly as the roaches scattered. "I hate bugs!" she shouted. She looked around the apartment for some feeling of welcome, but it seemed cold, cramped, and colorless.

She dropped her travel-worn duffel bag on the floor and headed for the kitchen. First, she checked the bucket under the sink. To her great relief, it was dry. Then sitting down to a microwaved TV dinner, she replayed her answering machine messages. All of them were either wrong numbers or sales calls. Nothing from Mack.

She looked at her calendar. "Today is Saturday. I get to go to work Monday." Unable to face the thought, she crawled into bed and slept the next twelve hours.

10

❖

Sunday morning Royce got up to make herself a cup of instant coffee and sat to drink it at the wobbly breakfast table. She stared at the bare white wall of her apartment, then got up to look out the window. There, she stared at the building across the street.

Restlessly, she flipped through her mail, which was all advertisements or bills. Royce opened a credit card statement and shook her head. "I should have taken pictures, 'cause I won't be going anywhere else for a long time." Then she wondered if Marla still had that money.

Royce washed clothes, ruing the loss of her suede jacket. She fondly fingered the silver and turquoise bracelet on her wrist. The other wrist—not the one with the ugly bruises. "Still, I'm glad I went," she murmured.

All day Royce managed to reflect on her trip without lingering thoughts of *him*. She tiptoed around his memory quietly, fearful of unwittingly summoning that stupid Hope. Remembering all the bold lies she had manufactured for the benefit of the Federal agents made her wince. "Now *that* was stupid. And risky. And . . . unavoidable," she admitted. She recalled him sitting on the black horse, nodding goodbye—impulsively she got up to dial Mack's number. When his answering machine came on, Royce hung up without leaving a message. Actually, the thought of seeing Mack again was revolting. If Paul were really gone forever, she would rather be alone.

✳ ✳ ✳

Monday morning Royce was back at The Chocolate Conglomerate. To fortify herself, she had worn her best white linen suit this morning. It had always been a little tight before, but today it hung almost loosely. And it looked great with a tan.

As she sat at her desk, she slowly picked up the red-lined copy which had been waiting all week for her to return and rewrite it. She stared at it, then put a fresh sheet in her typewriter and began to hammer out this saccharine, sarcastic copy: "UNBELIEVABLE! That's the only word for Barfy the Dog, who saves little Timmy's life in a speedboat accident. You'll either laugh or cry throughout this entire story of a True Friend in Need. Actually written by Serena Goodfellow, twelve-year-old daughter of internationally famous author and lecturer Dr. Jack Goodfellow, this unedited story proves what talent alone can do. Watch for these upcoming titles in the Barfy the Dog series:

Barfy Goes Malling
Barfy Beats Super Mario
Barfy Gets the Flu
Barfy Blasts Off

Demand them at your favorite bookstore!"

Royce yanked the copy from her typewriter and placed it in an interoffice envelope to her supervisor, then left her desk.

She went down the hall toward the fax room and looked in

Renetta's office. It was empty. "Oh, yeah. She had two weeks of vacation," Royce recalled. Then she looked again: the office was *really* empty. The desk was cleaned off and all personal effects removed.

Royce hurried down that hall and up another to Marla's office. She knocked and peeked in. Marla looked up from her desk. "Well, hi; glad you made it back okay," Marla said briskly. She seemed to forget in all but the most general terms about Royce's predicament, last she knew. "Boy, was that some trip or not?"

"Yeah," Royce said softly. "I just looked in Renetta's office, and—"

"Oh, didn't you know? She came in last Friday long enough to quit. On the spot. She cleaned out her desk and left. I heard she's going back to Tex-as," Marla said in a sarcastic singsong. "I guess she decided that any man who wanted her that bad was good enough."

"Buddy?" Royce asked incredulously.

"Who else?" Marla snorted, slamming a drawer. "Certainly not 'John' or 'Paul.' You can bet we'll never hear from them again. Men are all alike—they use you, then dump you. Well, I for one am so glad to be out of that crummy sand pit, with those ignorant hicks. Back to beautiful Manhattan." She strode to the window and took in the view with hardened eyes.

"Yeah . . . well . . ." Royce said hesitantly, "I was wondering— do you have any of that money left? I brought back a lot of bills from the trip, and—"

Marla's face changed ever so slightly, though she still gazed out the window. "No. The sheriff took it from me before he put us on the plane. Jerk."

Royce could hardly believe she was hearing such a bald-faced lie from her friend. *There must have been five thousand dollars in that stack. You make three times what I make, and you're going to stick me with all the expenses for that trip?* Royce gazed at her silently.

Marla glanced at her as she sat behind her nice big desk in her corner office with the window. Reading the disbelief in Royce's face, Marla smirked, "Sorry, Roycee."

Marla's telephone warbled and she answered, "Petrelli. Oh, Wade! Thanks for returning my call. Let me tell you what I needed . . . no, besides that!" she laughed. Royce backed out and shut the door.

She returned to her desk, sat down, and cradled her head in pure despair. *How can I go back to things as they were? Too much inside me has changed. Oh, Paul! I hate you for being too good to be true. Renetta, how could you leave without even saying goodbye? At least you would have understood how I feel.*

Her telephone signaled an outside call. It rang twice, three times. With great effort she answered, "Royce Lindel."

There was a pause, then: "Royce . . . this is Paul."

Her heart almost stopped. "Where are you?"

"Ah, I'm calling from Texas. Fort Worth."

She blurted, "If you're going to call me long distance, why can't you tell me your real name?"

"My name *is* Paul," he said quietly. "Paul Arrendondo."

"Aaronwhat?" she said. He repeated it. "How did you know where to find me?" she asked.

"Buddy told me you and Renetta worked at the same place. She gave me the number," he replied.

"Renetta?" Royce asked. "Where is she?"

"Buddy and I picked her up from the airport yesterday. I don't know where they are now," he said.

"Renetta . . . with Buddy," she said, struggling to comprehend it.

"I don't know what's so strange about that," he said defensively. "Buddy is a great guy, and they have more in common than you realize. You know how horse-crazy Renetta is—well, Buddy's dad owns a ranch outside of San Angelo. The horses we rode are his. And Buddy's mom has a doctorate in classical literature—she was just up in New York City for a symposium in March."

"Oh," she said.

A moment's silence followed. Paul said, "Well . . . all that is beside the point. I wanted to call, because . . . we never got a chance to say goodbye."

"You called me to say goodbye?" she asked weakly.

He exhaled in frustration. "Royce, this isn't very easy for me. And—you don't know anything about me."

"So tell me," she said.

"I'm a Baptist preacher," he said, and Royce dropped the receiver. "Hello? Royce?"

"Yes, I'm here," she said, recovering. "Paul, are you putting me on? You laughed at me when I asked if you were a priest!"

"I was—surprised that you would hit so close to the truth with one clue from Buddy. But, yes . . . I used to be a preacher, anyway. I have a master's degree from the seminary."

"What happened?" she asked.

He sighed, "For a while, I was a real up-and-comer. I had a nice-sized church, I was working on my doctorate, and I was getting recognition from the state Southern Baptist convention. I had my future all mapped out. But my wife was a free-spirited kind of girl—no children—who didn't take to life in a fishbowl. The comments and the criticisms from church members about the way she dressed, the way she wore her hair, her job, her sports car—well, it got to where she couldn't take it anymore and I—I wasn't around much to defend her. She left me for an architect in my congregation, and they moved to Washington state. That was about five years ago.

"My life fell apart after that. The church fired me, and no other church wanted a divorced pastor. Buddy stuck with me, though. He was my youth minister," Paul said.

Royce covered her mouth, then asked, "And John? What was he?"

"Uh, 'John' is not his real name, you know. And, he's married. And he wasn't with my church. He's Episcopalian."

"I see," Royce murmured. "And then—?"

"Then, I took odd jobs until the position of director of a substance abuse center came open. They didn't care that I was divorced; they hired me. They also could hardly pay me because the center was on the verge of bankruptcy all the time. They were trying to take care of not only the addicts but also their families. The children who are shuffled around from place to place because their parents are gone, or homeless. . . .

"Well, anyway—for the first few months after I came on, a philanthropist out of Dallas was subsidizing us. It was a life-saver—we never would've made it through those months without him. But then all of a sudden he jerked the funding out from under us without one word of explanation. Someday I'd like to know why he cut us off like that," he said bitterly.

Then he resumed, "Well, when Buddy and I took our annual trip to Big Bend and ran into the drug runners, it seemed like manna from heaven. Actually, though, I had left God behind with my last church. I figured He wasn't interested in a failure any more than they were. I didn't ask Him what He thought about our little sideline, and sure didn't ask His help doing it. I didn't care if I got killed—the money kept the center going, and I had nothing else to live for.

"But that night, when you stumbled in out of the desert— I can't explain what happened to me. I had still been wearing my wedding band, even since the divorce, to remind myself what a failure I was and what I had lost. The next morning, I took it off and threw it away." He was silent a few seconds, and she silently listened.

Paul went on, "Then, when Renetta shot me, and you leaned over me crying—oh, Lord! I realized how much I wanted to live! I hung on with every last ounce I had, because you wanted me to. But even then I wouldn't pray. I figured that I deserved to die, so why should I plead with God to let me live for the sake of a beautiful girl?

"Then when *you* were taken—Royce, I wished I had died. Then they never showed and you were missing in the desert—

the rangers found the bodies and the wrecked Jeep, but not you. We searched and searched and couldn't find you—I knew then I had to let go of my guilt and pray for your life. He heard me, Royce. After searching that day and most of the night, I prayed at sunup. I knew you wouldn't last another day in the desert, if you were still alive. I prayed, and looked up, and saw you on the ground," he whispered. Royce wiped tears from her face.

"He and I are getting reacquainted," he said. "But—you and I? I can't come to New York, Royce; I can't leave the center. But, it's hardly fair to ask you to come to Fort Worth. But . . . I've got to see you, Royce. I have to see you again."

He stopped talking and Royce cleared her throat. "Let me think about it," she murmured.

"I'll give you my phone number. You call me when you decide what you want to do. If I don't hear from you, I'll know you're not interested." He gave her his number, then said, "Well . . . goodbye, Royce."

"Goodbye, Paul." She laid the receiver down on its cradle and stared at the number she had written down.

Caryn passed by in the hall, saw her, and leaned in. "Royce! There you are! How was your trip?"

Royce looked up with hollow eyes. "Okay," she said.

"Oh . . . well, you got a nice tan. Oh! Have you heard the news?" asked Caryn.

"What news?"

"Our parent company has gone Chapter 11. The Chocolate Conglomerate is going to be sold and 'downsized.' I'm working on my résumé this morning. You'd better, too," Caryn advised.

"Oh!" said Royce, staring.

"Listen, do you have that copy for Martin yet? I'm on my way to his office," said Caryn.

"I already sent it to him," Royce replied in a monotone.

"Oh, good. Well, nice to have you back." Caryn went on down the hall.

Royce stared at her desk, scribbled something, took her purse and left.

About thirty minutes later Caryn came back into the office. "Royce? Oh, rats. Missed her."

The telephone on Royce's desk rang and Caryn reached over to answer it. "Caryn Posner."

"Hi, Caryn. It's Mack. Is Royce around?"

"Hi, Mack. No, she left her desk for a minute. Care to leave a message?" Caryn asked.

"Well, I was just wondering if she made the trip to Big Bend, and how it went," he said vaguely.

"Yes, I think she went, but I'm not sure how much fun it was. It must have done her some good, because she just turned in the best copy she's ever written, according to Martin. It's just what he wanted," Caryn replied.

"Well, good. Why don't you have her call me, then—"

"Oh oh," Caryn said, picking up a paper from the desk.

"What is it?" asked Mack.

"Well, I guess she must have had a good time after all. I just found a note on her desk. All it says is, 'Gone to Texas.'"

PART TWO

11

❖

Royce skipped out of the marble lobby like a kid on the first day of summer vacation. She jaywalked across the street and ran into Central Park. There she kicked off her shoes to pirouette on the grass in her stocking feet. Nobody stared; this was New York. "I do love you, and I'll come back to visit!" she promised her city. "But I've got a date in Fort Worth!"

Winded, she stopped to think. "I've got a million things to do! And the first thing I need to do is call Paul back!" But she was disinclined to call him from her former place of work. She decided to call him from her apartment. But as long as she was in Manhattan, she might as well burn some bridges.

So she took the subway to her bank on Park Avenue and closed out her accounts. After she cashed in her IRAs to settle up her charge accounts, she was left with barely enough for a one-way ticket to Dallas/Fort Worth International. She walked out of the bank lobby rejoicing, "I'm busted! Flat broke! But I'm not bringing a bunch of old debts to a new relationship!"

She took her last ride on the C train to Queens, and cashed

in the rest of her tokens at the bulletproof steel-and-fiberglass booth. Then she ran all the way to her apartment. Unlocking the door, she stepped onto a squishy brown mass. Stupefied, she looked down at the puddles around her feet, welling up from the carpeting. She tiptoed to the kitchen sink and opened the cabinet. Water streamed from the pipe into the overflowing bucket.

"Well! How about that?" she said, wading to the telephone. She picked up the phone and dialed the landlord's apartment. His wife answered, "Yeah?"

"Hello. This is Royce Lindel, in 812. Please tell Mr. Hoskins that my sink is leaking again something awful, and—"

"He'll get to it when he can," she said impatiently.

"Yes, I know," Royce laughed lightly, "but you'd better tell him it's an—" She heard a click. "Hello? Hello?" Royce calmly hung up. She took a precious piece of paper from her purse. Sitting on the table to keep her feet out of the puddles, she dialed a long-distance number.

A female voice answered, "Phoenix Street Center."

Suddenly nervous, Royce said, "Um, Paul Arrendondo, please."

"He's out, honey. Can I take your number?" the woman said.

"Oh, I'm not going to be here," Royce said. "When do you expect him back?"

"I have no idea," the woman answered.

"Well . . . tell him Royce called. I'm coming to Fort Worth. I'll be flying into D/FW this afternoon."

"Okay—what's the name again?" the woman asked, her voice muffled.

"Royce Lindel. I'll call again from the airport."

"Okay, honey. I'll give him the message."

Royce hung up, slightly anxious. She ate a bite from the refrigerator, then went to her bedroom and packed everything of value into two suitcases and the duffel bag. She still wore her best suit, the good white one that she had worn to work that morning. Royce carried her suitcases out gingerly and set them in the hall. Then she tore today's page off the calendar and wrote: "Moving out. Keep the deposit." This she left with her key on the table. She stepped to the door and looked back. She was leaving a lot of junk—but no regrets.

Royce caught a cab to La Guardia, where she purchased a one-way ticket to D/FW. The flight was scheduled to leave in forty minutes. By the time she got her bags checked, she had just enough time for one important phone call.

She got a short stack of quarters and went to the nearest pay phone to dial Paul's number. Her heart seemed to be working unnecessarily hard.

"Phoenix Street Center," said the same woman.

"This is Royce Lindel again. Is Paul in?"

"No; he hasn't gotten back yet, honey."

"Oh dear," Royce muttered. "Well, *please* give him this message: I'm flying into D/FW this afternoon—" She shuffled belongings to look at her ticket. "I'll be arriving on Delta, flight 405, gate 16 at 3:20. I . . . need a ride from the airport."

"Gotcha," said the woman.

"Okay. Thanks," Royce said uneasily, hanging up. There was no time to do anything else but get on the plane.

After boarding, Royce settled back into her seat next to the window and closed her eyes. *This is crazy. What if he doesn't get the message? I should have at least gotten his home phone number.*

Her eyes popped open. Who else would answer his home phone? She began to panic. Here she was, staking her whole future on someone she barely knew. She looked out the window as the plane taxied down the runway. *I can't believe I'm doing this.* There was no other option now but to sit back and ride on the one-way trip she had scheduled.

It seemed endless. At one point Royce put on the head-phones to distractedly watch a lame comedy. The plane was full of passengers, mostly on business. Royce was aware that the man seated next to her kept glancing at her, but she steadfastly stared straight ahead. She did not want to talk to anyone.

Some minutes later a flight attendant came down the aisle with a beverage cart, and Royce removed the headphones to request the tomato juice. As it was handed to her, the man in the aisle seat took the opportunity to smile at her.

Royce smiled demurely in return. He was a nice-looking man, twenty years her senior, with a conservative suit and haircut. "Excuse me for staring," he apologized. "You remind me of my daughter. She's finishing up her junior year at Marymount." He opened his wallet to show her a picture. Royce noted a similarity between his daughter's hair and her own.

"She's lovely," Royce said.

"Her name is Tammy," he smiled. "And I am Forrest Oldham." He offered his hand and Royce shook it.

"Royce Lindel."

"Pleased to meet you—is it Miss Lindel?" he asked.

"Yes—" Royce admitted, reflexively looking away.

He laughed, "There I go, being nosy again. I'm sorry; it's an occupational hazard." Royce raised an eyebrow and he admitted, "I'm a minister of the gospel."

"You are?" she noted. "What denomination?"

"Southern Baptist," he replied.

"You are!" She sat up.

His brow furrowed. "Is that of interest to you?"

"Why, I know someone who was pastor of a Southern Baptist church, and his wife left him, and so the church fired him, and he was just crushed after that. He left the ministry because no other church would hire him," she spilled out.

"I see. How unfortunate," he agreed.

"I don't understand what difference it makes that he got divorced," she went on, unable to stop. "He's a good man, and it just about killed him."

Mr. Oldham looked thoughtful. "Without knowing the specifics, I can't really comment. . . . What is his name?"

Royce sat back. "I . . . think I've said too much already." She sipped her tomato juice.

"I certainly understand," Mr. Oldham said. He took out an appointment calendar from his shirt pocket and began flipping through it.

Royce held her glass and looked down in it for thirty seconds. "His name is Paul Arrendondo."

Mr. Oldham glanced up. "Arrendondo? Oh, yes. Yes, I heard about that. It was several years ago."

"Five years ago. I didn't know him then," she hastened to add.

"I remember that," he mused. "It was sad. He was young, and on fire. I heard him speak once, at a pastor's conference. He had a real gift of insight."

"Then, *why* . . . ?" Royce asked, anxious and afraid to hear more.

"Miss Lindel, you have to understand that it has to do with perceptions, and the way Southern Baptist churches operate. Once his wife left, his church perceived that he had lost control of his domestic situation. And, I understand that he allowed some pastoral duties to slip while he tried to recover. Personally, I feel it would have been best for the church to stand by him at that time, but each congregation is autonomous, and may hire and fire at will. His firing was a very emotional process which split the church, as I recall. That served to further taint him, discouraging other churches from calling him."

"That's not fair!" she said.

"No," he said softly. "It wasn't fair, nor right. But it's not the end. God did not wash His hands of Paul. He'll bring him yet where he needs to be."

Royce looked out the window. Mr. Oldham reached into his breast pocket and pulled out a business card, which he put between her fingers. "If at some point I can help you or Paul, call me."

Blinking rapidly, Royce looked down at the card. He was Dr. Forrest Oldham, pastor of some blurry church in Arlington, Texas. "Thank you," Royce whispered. Dr. Oldham nodded.

By that time they were descending to the runway. Royce wiped her eyes and fastened her seatbelt.

When the plane rolled to a stop and they got up to leave, Dr. Oldham stepped aside to let Royce precede him. She grew nervous as she walked off the plane. Had he gotten her message? Royce stopped to look around the boarding area at all the faces. Dr. Oldham paused inconspicuously nearby.

He wasn't there. He had not come. Royce's breathing grew shallow.

"Royce." She wheeled at her name and saw Paul standing by the telephones. He looked so different! He was clean and freshly shaven, with his hair combed back instead of hanging down in his eyes. He wore a sports coat and slacks—and loafers! she noted in horror. Where was her cowboy? But it was truly Paul, sunburn and all. "I got your message," he said, studying her shocked expression.

Royce dropped her purse and seized him around the neck. She kissed him so forcefully that he fell back against the telephones. "Are you glad to see me?" he gasped and she kissed him again.

There were some winks and nudges in the boarding area, but Royce did not care. She had earned the right to make a spectacle of herself with him. As Paul bent to pick up her purse, she saw Dr. Oldham smile and walk away.

Paul straightened and put his arm around her waist. "You look wonderful," he said with feeling, having never seen her in a skirt. Royce took the purse he held out and slung it triumphantly over her shoulder.

As he walked her to the carousel to pick up her luggage, she confessed, "I was afraid you might not be here."

"Me not come? After calling you and begging you to come?" he said reproachfully.

"No, I mean I wasn't sure you'd get the message," she clarified, touching the buttons on his shirt.

"Nah, Sadie's as reliable as the sunrise. This yours?" he said, reaching for her duffel bag.

"Yes, and those two," she pointed.

Paul lifted those out. "Is this all?" he asked hesitantly.

"Yes." Suddenly she felt a little awkward. "Paul, I . . . quit my job and vacated my apartment. . . . I've got almost no money and no place to stay."

He shouldered the duffel bag harness and picked up the suitcases. Smiling very slightly, he promised, "We'll see what we can work out." Royce took one suitcase from him so she could hold his hand.

He walked her out into the bright sunshine of the parking lot. She turned her face up to the warm sun, inhaling. *This is too good to be happening to me.*

"Here we are." Paul stopped and unlocked the trunk of a late-model, silver-gray Nissan.

"Nice car," she said, running a hand along the top as he loaded her bags.

"It belongs to the center, but I bet you know how it was paid for," he said significantly, leaning beside her to unlock the passenger door. When Royce put her arms around his waist and squeezed, he flinched.

"Have you been to the hospital yet? To get that bullet out?" she demanded.

"No. Get in," he said.

She sat and let him close the door. When he sat behind the wheel, she asked, "Why not?"

"Why should I? The doctor said it's not hurting anything." He started the engine, put on his sunglasses, and fastened his seatbelt. He glanced appreciatively at her legs as he started to drive out of the parking lot, then put on the brakes. "Buckle your seatbelt, Ms. Lindel."

Puckering her lips, she did as requested. It was hard to believe this was her Paul behind the wheel of a car rather than in the saddle. He looked so urban. As she watched him accelerate onto the freeway, her eye landed on one reminder of his alter ego: a cracked, worn leather tag attached to his key ring with the initials PRA burned into the leather. Burned in by a hot tool. That reminded her of what Dr. Oldham had said about Paul's fire, and she wondered if she should tell Paul about him.

They passed a sign that said, "Welcome to Arlington" and Royce sat up. What was the name of Dr. Oldham's church here?

"I can't believe you're really sitting beside me," Paul said softly. "I can't believe how much my life has changed in just a week. I love you, Royce."

"Paul!" she breathed.

"Once I swore I would never trust another woman." He paused to look over his shoulder and change lanes. "But now . . . I'm in your beautiful little hands."

Royce's verbal functions all but collapsed. "I'm so glad I came down," she whispered. It was an inadequate response to his baring of his soul, but he accepted it. He reached out his hand and she pressed it against her cheek. In the thick of traffic, that's about all they could do.

In a few minutes they entered the Fort Worth city limits, and Royce's attention was drawn to the skyline. Paul exited the freeway into a rough-looking area of town. "Where are we going?" Royce asked.

"Aw, I need to check in at the center," Paul said dutifully. Stopping at a red light, he turned toward her: "And then, I'm taking you home with me." Royce caressed his hand with her lips. "Is that all right with you?" he asked rhetorically, smiling.

Beaming, Royce looked out her window. That beautiful Texas sky was beginning to cloud over. It looked like rain. Royce thought of a rainy night with Paul and closed her eyes.

Shortly, he pulled up to a faded red brick building. He parked behind a security fence and got out to open her door. As he helped her out, she reached up to his neck. "Wait just a little while," he promised as he shut and locked her door.

Turning, Royce immediately saw two black sedans parked in the lot, the sight of which disturbed her. Paul did not notice them. He was too busy watching her.

They went to the front of the building and Paul pushed open the glass door. "Sadie?" he called. The front desk was empty.

A man in a dark suit came out of a doorway nearby. "Mr. Arrendondo? Paul Arrendondo?"

"Who are you?" Paul asked curtly.

The man flashed an ID at him. "DEA. We'd like to talk to you about your assistant."

"Let me see that again," Paul said suspiciously. As he studied the ID, he asked, "What about Sadie?"

"Are you aware that Ms. Hurst has been dealing in crack cocaine?" the agent asked.

Royce gasped and Paul's head shot up. "I don't believe it. Not Sadie. That's impossible," Paul declared.

"As a matter of fact, she has recently been using this center as her base of operations," the agent said.

"No. That's impossible," Paul reiterated.

"You've been gone the past two weeks on vacation. Is that correct?" the agent asked.

"Yes," Paul said slowly.

"And you went to—?"

"Big Bend," Paul answered.

"Did you go alone?" the agent asked, looking at Royce.

"I went with some friends of mine. What difference does that make?" Paul asked impatiently.

At this point another man stepped out from the doorway— a man with thinning blond hair and an iron face. "We are interested in certain large infusions of cash which seem to coincide with your Big Bend trips," this man said, and as he looked at Royce, her knees weakened to putty. "Why, hello, Ms. Lindel."

Paul slowly turned to stare incredulously at Royce. "You set me up," he breathed. "You're DEA." Royce opened her mouth in horror, but nothing came out.

Paul exhaled, shaking his head. "What a chump. I fell for it all the way." He turned to Royce with a look of bitter admiration. "You played me like a concert pianist. You were perfect."

The agent at the desk turned Paul around to put handcuffs on him, then shoved him out the front door as Royce watched in mute agony. Then she turned helplessly to the iron-faced man. "Tell him the truth! Tell him I didn't set him up!" she begged.

He sat on the edge of the desk. "Perhaps it's time for you to tell *us* the truth, Ms. Lindel."

12

❖

For the next two hours the drug enforcement agent grilled Royce like a swordfish. He made her tell the story of her trip over and over, starting at the middle, backing up to the beginning, fast-forwarding to the end, then starting all over again. She sat at the receptionist's desk while he paced behind her, peppering her with questions. She had no choice but to tell everything exactly as it had happened.

"But I'm not telling you any names," she said stonily. "You can lock me away for as long as you want, but I'm not naming names."

"Let me see whose names we need," he said, pulling a notepad from his breast pocket. "We have Paul Robert Arrendondo, of course, then there's Walter Grayson Ferring III, Kenneth Perry Cavanaugh, Mary Elizabeth Petrelli, Renetta Meyers Cleary, and Royce Anne Lindel. Is that correct?"

"You know more than I do," she admitted glumly.

"We usually do," he said, putting away his notepad.

"What's going to happen to Paul?" she asked.

"That, I don't know," he said. She looked out the front glass door at the waning light on the building across the street, then put her head down on her arms and began to cry.

"If it's that important to you, I can take you to see him," he said almost kindly.

Royce sprang up, then pulled back suspiciously. "Why would you do that?"

"Why not?" he shrugged. "We're not inhuman." He opened the desk drawer and began rummaging in it, finally pulling out a set of keys. Royce watched him.

He took her outside and locked the front door, then escorted her to the remaining black sedan in the parking lot. After they drove out of the security gate, he left her in the idling car while he shut and locked the gate. Royce's eyes narrowed. *He's being too nice.*

They silently drove a few blocks, and Royce intently memorized every street sign and landmark she could discern in the twilight. Then he turned into the parking lot of an old, apparently abandoned warehouse. A heavy, creaking metal door raised, and he pulled into a large garage at the rear which housed several other cars. As he and Royce got out of the car, another agent closed the door by remote. Then he came up to Royce and removed her purse from her shoulder. "Hey!" she protested.

"We'll return it when you leave," he told her.

The agent with her escorted her up a brightly lit hallway and entered a kind of central room, which contained temporary tables and desks, file cabinets, and computers. Two other agents, a man and a woman, looked up. They were both wearing guns.

The agent with Royce asked, "Are they through with Arrendondo yet?"

"No, I think they're still working him over," the other man said. He presented a file to the first, who appeared to be his superior.

"I promised Ms. Lindel that she could see him when they're done. Wait here," he told Royce, nodding to a folding chair. He left the room with the file. Royce sat heavily next to a table.

The other man departed shortly. That left Royce with the woman agent who, intent on tracking information on her computer screen, ignored Royce.

Sighing, Royce glanced around at the clutter on the table— an empty Kentucky Fried Chicken carton and soft drink cups, printouts, a crossword puzzle book, pencils, a map, and a pile of personal effects sitting on a brown envelope. Underneath a wallet, watch, and loose change was a cracked leather tag with the initials PRA.

Royce froze, then looked up at the agent, seated ten feet away. The woman was totally absorbed in her computer search. Royce eyed the personal effects, experimentally shifting and sighing loudly.

The woman paid no attention. Glancing toward the open door, Royce deftly reached over and dislodged the keys from the pile, then put them in her suit pocket.

Not believing that she had gotten away with it, Royce held her breath, waiting for agents to pounce on her from all sides with drawn guns. But the woman continued her work and nothing happened. If asked, Royce could not have said why she took the keys—only that they represented access to Paul. She did not know yet how she might use them.

After a while Royce said, "I'm thirsty. Can I get something to drink?"

Only then did the woman look up. "When Rick gets back." Royce nodded, using this opportunity to stand and stretch, then sit in another chair farther away from the table.

She waited in that room for a long time. There was no clock, and her solitary working watch had died in Big Bend, so she could only guess that she sat there for an hour. The woman agent finished her computer work and stood intently over the map. Royce leaned back in her chair. "Why would you arrest someone who's helping you?"

The woman looked up impatiently. "Who?"

"Paul Arrendondo, who robbed the drug runners in Big Bend," Royce replied. "I saw him dump out all the cocaine with my own eyes. Then he pumped all the money back into the Phoenix Street Center. Why would you arrest him for that?"

"We can't have a bunch of vigilantes doing our job," the woman said stiffly.

"Yeah, and a great job you're doing, at that," Royce sneered.

"If you want to see him, you'd better shut up," the woman warned. Royce looked away contemptuously, but kept quiet.

Sometime later the agent returned with a noticeably softened attitude. Nodding toward Royce from the doorway, he said, "Okay. You can see him now."

Royce jumped up and followed him down a long hallway. They went around a corner and stopped in front of an unmarked door. The agent unlocked it and pushed it open.

Royce peered into the dark room. She could barely see the figure on a cot in the corner, so she felt for a light switch. "Paul?"

"Don't turn on the light," he said.

"But it's dark in here," she protested softly, coming to sit at his side. "Paul, are you all right?"

"Don't touch me, Royce."

He may as well have hit her. "I didn't set you up, Paul," she said, struggling to control herself. "That agent recognized me from Big Bend. He was one of those who interrogated me at the park office—remember?" He did not answer.

"Paul, you've got to believe me. After all you did for me, I'd never, never double-cross you. I—" She wanted to say, *I love you.* But she realized how hollow that would sound to him now. She had to prove it first. She reached up to his face but he turned away to the wall. "What can I do for you, Paul?" she pleaded.

"You can go back to New York," he said without hesitation.

Royce bowed her head, tears streaming down her face. But there was nothing more to be said. She got up and left the room, covering her eyes from the bright hallway lights. "What now?" she asked the agent.

"You're free to go, Ms. Lindel," he said, shutting and locking the door.

"But what about Paul?" she asked, still shading her eyes.

"I wouldn't worry about him," he said lightly.

Royce removed her hand from her tear-streaked face. "I hate you with all my heart," she said calmly.

He looked at her with a surprised smirk, but somehow could not bring himself to respond in kind.

Another man brought Royce's purse, then the agent walked her to a door which opened into a back alley. "Have a nice flight, Ms. Lindel," he said. Then he shut the door between them.

Royce stood on the outside of the door, slowly turning to scan the dark, smelly, garbage-strewn alley. Fighting down panic, she felt in her pocket for Paul's keys. She still had his keys. Suddenly she knew what she would do. Somehow, she had to find out where Paul lived and get there. Regardless of how he felt about her now, he owed her a place to sleep tonight.

Shouldering her purse strap, Royce strode up the alley to the street. She paused here to make sure of her direction, then turned left and walked down the lonely street with all the menace one hundred and fifteen pounds could carry. A man's figure stepped out of a doorway into her path, and she glared up at him with hateful, dangerous eyes. When he melted back into the doorway, Royce was grateful for having grown up in Queens.

She went down one block and up another; she noted a pawnshop and turned right at the next corner. That brought her to Phoenix Street. From here, it was a quick jaunt to the front door of the faded red brick building.

Royce pulled Paul's keys from her pocket as she glanced up and down the street. There were only four keys on the ring; only two of those were door keys. Royce tried the most likely looking one first. The key turned in the lock.

Right before opening the door, Royce saw the wires outlining the glass of the door. An alarm system. The last thing she needed here was to set off an alarm. Leaning on the door, Royce debated what to do. Had the system been activated? The agent with her had not set the alarm, but someone else could have later.

"One way to find out," she murmured. She opened the door and slipped inside. Apparently nothing happened, but Royce assumed it was a silent alarm. She had to get what she needed and get out quickly.

She turned on the desk light, went straight for the file cabinet and began going through the top drawer. This had held records of the center's operating expenses, and had largely been emptied. Glancing out the front door, she slammed the drawer and went on to the second. This one was locked. Royce paused over it, thinking, then bypassed it and yanked on the bottom drawer. It opened.

Thumbing through the files, Royce muttered, "Aha!" She pulled out a file labeled, "Applicants for Director Position." Royce flipped through the applications until she came to one submitted by Paul R. Arrendondo.

Taking it out, Royce stood over the telephone. This address and phone number were over four years old. She glanced out the door before picking up the receiver and dialing the number on the application. It rang four, five, six times—Royce could not afford to stand there much longer, so she hung up.

She shut the file drawer with one foot as she shoved the application into her purse. Then she paused. When the agent had gotten those keys from the drawer, hadn't she seen—? She opened the drawer and yes, there was a street map of Fort Worth. "Thank you," she said crisply, taking the map and turning off the desk light. Then she slipped outside and relocked the door.

Trotting to the security fence, Royce dug out Paul's keys and selected the Masterlock key. This unlocked the gate. She opened the Nissan's door with the only car key on the ring, and sat behind the wheel.

Here she got nervous. Having rarely driven before, with no

driver's license, in a strange city at night—she started the car, turned on the lights, and felt for the gearshift.

Farsightedly, Paul had bought an automatic. She drove it out of the lot. Then she got out to shut and lock the gate behind her—everything must be left as it had been. She sat behind the wheel again and took off down the street.

Royce drove until she came to a well-lighted grocery store parking lot, where she stopped. She took out the map and job application to find Paul's address—if that were where he still lived.

The map pointed to an apartment complex about ten blocks from where she sat now. Royce started the car and carefully headed toward the indicated street.

At that point the intimations of rain were fulfilled. With a brilliant flash of lightning, it began coming down in sheets. Royce groped for the windshield wiper controls as she squinted up at street signs.

Finally, after crawling along at speeds which infuriated drivers behind her, Royce found the complex. She stared at it in dismay—not that it looked that bad; it was just one of those that sprawled out instead of rising up. There must be six or seven identical buildings. Royce turned into the parking lot and peered through the rain-splattered window, looking for numbers.

She could not see a thing unless she got a closer look. So she parked in one spot, jumped out of the car to check the numbers on the building, then ran back to the car. She drove to the next building to find its numbers. Sighing for her linen suit, she had to get out in the heavy rain four times before she found the building which housed Paul's unit—number 216. Royce pulled into the parking space reserved for the resident of 216, then ran to the building and up the stairwell.

By now she was soaked through. Trembling, she stood in front of 216's door. She was momentarily paralyzed by fear. What if he no longer lived here? How long could she drive around Fort Worth in a stolen car?

Steeling herself, Royce rang the doorbell. She waited, shivering, then rang it again. No answer.

Her hands were shaking so hard that she could barely get out the key ring. She brought up the last key on the ring and put it to the lock.

It did not fit. Royce almost died before realizing that she was trying to insert it upside down. She flipped it over and tried again. The key turned in the deadbolt. Royce opened the door.

It was dark inside. "H-hello?" she called. "Anyone here?" She shut the door behind her and turned on the light.

She was standing in a small, sparsely furnished living room. A television set which had not been dusted in months sat in the corner. This morning's newspaper lay in sections on a coffee table, with the sports section on top. There was a kitchen off this room, and a closed door opposite it.

Royce crossed the room to open that door and turn on the light. This was the bedroom. There was a double bed, hastily made, and a dresser. There were no decorative touches or pictures whatever. "He didn't spend any of that money here, that's for sure. He doesn't spend much time here," she observed. And to her immeasurable relief, there was no indication that anyone else did, either.

Something in the corner of the room, partly hidden by the drapes, caught her eye. She lifted an edge of the drape to find a guitar case. Its thick coating of dust had not been disturbed in a very long time. Royce sensed something too personal for prying eyes and left it alone.

The closet was on the other side of the bed. Royce opened its accordion doors and saw only men's clothes. Then she let out a cry. There, on a high shelf, was Paul's buff-colored cowboy hat. And in a pile on the floor waiting to go to the cleaners was his gray jacket—that sweaty, dusty, precious jacket he had rolled up under his head at night.

She grabbed up the jacket and hugged it. She took it with her like a security blanket to the kitchen, where she opened the refrigerator. As usual, she was starving. It was almost empty except for a few cans of beer. "I thought Baptists didn't drink," she chided, cuddling the jacket. She found some Mexican dinners in the freezer, so she took out a queso dinner and turned on the oven.

The kitchen was not large enough for a table, but there was a bar with two stools pulled up to it. On the bar sat a coffeemaker and a pile of opened mail. Succumbing to curiosity, Royce flipped through the letters. The junk mail had been dropped unopened in the trash can beneath the bar. The rest of it consisted of utility bills, a ticket to a baseball game next Thursday night, a business letter, and a letter addressed to Paul in a feminine handwriting. Part of this letter peeked tantalizingly out of the envelope, but Royce knew better than to read it.

The business letter was lying out, open. Before she could stop herself, Royce had read enough to know that it was from a nonprofit hospital in Dallas offering Paul a place on their staff. Guiltily, she carefully replaced the pile as it had been and returned to the bedroom. Next to the closet was a bathroom just big enough for a toilet, sink, and shower stall.

While her dinner cooked, Royce took a hot shower. She used Paul's shampoo (an off-brand), his loofah sponge, and his oversized bath towel.

She could not find a hair dryer, so Royce wrapped her hair in a smaller towel and investigated his medicine cabinet. He had occasional sinus problems and frequent headaches, she decided. She used his comb on her tangles and unapologetically appropriated his razor to shave her legs.

Royce could not find a bathrobe or pajamas, either. Unwilling to go out in the rain to fetch her suitcases from his car, she rifled his drawers for an undershirt and boxer shorts. Grinning, she tried them on: big, but comfy. As she started to shut the drawer, she spotted something else in it, and dug out a framed picture.

It was a very old photograph of a handsome man in a

cowboy hat, sitting on a horse, with a Bible under his arm. He wore a long black coat and high leather boots, and in his solemn gaze Royce recognized something of Paul. After studying the photo minutely, she respectfully replaced it.

The oven timer buzzed and Royce went to the kitchen to get her TV dinner and a beer. She sat at the bar and ate the hot cheese enchiladas and rice cautiously, blowing frequently. She glanced at the mail pile nearby. *The* letter was in a pink envelope.

Sternly, Royce averted her eyes. To read it was a blatant invasion of privacy. Sure, he had invited her down so they could get to know each other better, but that did not entitle her to read his private, personal mail. Besides, the last thing he had said to her was to order her back to New York.

Royce sipped the beer, wincing at the taste. He did not mean that, and she knew it. Before she went anywhere she was going to make sure he knew that she had not set him up with the DEA. Then, if he still wanted her to leave, she would.

Royce finished the dinner and covered a sudden, unladylike burp. She emptied the rest of the beer down the sink and tossed away the trash. She made a show of looking around the barren little apartment, but the temptation of the forbidden was over-powering. She stood at the bar. With great shame and guilt, she removed the letter from its envelope and opened it up. It said:

May 15

Dear Paul,

You won't believe who I ran into today. Cindi Harveldson. She and Chad are vacationing on the San Juan Islands, and I ran into her at Bellingham. I was shopping, and heard this, "Kris?" and I turned around and it was her! She asked about you, and I told her you were still in Texas.

My divorce from Jason was final last week. On our anniversary. Isn't that ironic? As they say, it was fun while it lasted. But, I don't know, he started getting weird sexually. Into kinky things I just couldn't relate to. I started thinking about you a lot. You were boring but reliable, you know? I didn't have to wonder what or who you were going to bring home.

I'm going to a Women's Empowerment Seminar in Dallas next week, and I'd love to see you. I'll be staying at the Marriott Inn North on LBJ, May 25, 26, & 27th. The number is (214)233-4421. Why don't we get together?

Love always,
Kris

P.S. Bring your guitar. Remember the cabin by Lake O' the Pines? (!!)

Royce replaced the letter in the envelope and returned it to the pile. Contemplatively, she took the towel from her head and hung it up in the bathroom. She picked up her damp clothes from the floor and put them in his hamper. She brushed her teeth with his toothbrush and toothpaste, then turned off the lights and peeked out the bedroom window draperies. The rain was still falling in torrents, with occasional lightning flashes and peals of thunder. Mesmerized, she watched it fall glittering around the streetlamp below.

She slowly pulled the drapes back in place and picked up Paul's jacket. Turning down the bedcovers, she crawled into bed holding his coat. As she laid her head on the pillow and closed her eyes, she murmured, "Kris, you were a fool."

13

❖

In the morning Royce was awakened by a slamming door. Paul said angrily, "Thanks a lot for returning my car. Now do you mind finding my keys?"

She bolted upright. But he was not in the bedroom. He was in the living room beyond, and the door between the two rooms was open a crack.

"Look, when we find out who's responsible, we'll crack some heads." The voice was that of the iron-faced agent who had played nice guy last night.

Paul was not pacified. "I was assured you'd see that she got safely out, and instead you put her on the street with all her things still locked up in my car! I told them she came down without any money or a place to stay!"

"We've checked all the local hotels and shelters, and she hasn't been to any of them. We're checking the airlines now. It's a safe bet that she's flown home," the agent said.

"I don't think she had any home to go back to," Paul said miserably. A muffled plop sounded, as if he'd tossed something down.

"I'm not flying out until you find out what happened to her."

"Look, you have to go today. It's all set up, and we've got no time to spare," the agent argued. "I give you my word we'll track her down."

Paul did not seem to answer, and Royce leaned forward to listen. Finally he said, "Don't . . . harass her, Rick. She won't want anything to do with me, after the things I said to her last r.ight. Just find her so I'll know she's okay. Return her things to her, and be sure she gets that money."

"She'll get all that you've got coming when we wrap it up. She'll never see us or you, if that's what you want," Rick replied.

Paul must have agreed, because the next thing Royce heard was the outside door opening and closing. There was a moment of deathlike silence. She lay back to wait.

Heavy footsteps. Water ran in the kitchen sink, then something was dropped and picked up. Shuffling. Suddenly the bedroom door opened. Paul glanced at the bed and sprang back. "Good morning," she smiled, stretching lazily. He gaped at her as she leaned on her elbow. "I hope you don't mind that I made myself at home. I *was* invited."

"What . . . how . . ." he stammered.

"I took your keys. I found your address in the center's files and I took your car here. Did you put on coffee?" she asked, sniffing.

"Yeees," he said, sinking to the edge of the bed. He eyed his underwear on her.

Royce then remarked, "I assume Rick told you the truth—I didn't set you up."

"Yeah," Paul admitted, glancing away. With a supreme effort, he looked her in the eye. "But I have to leave today."

"Yes, I heard," she said, crawling all the way out from under the covers. He raised an eyebrow at the jacket she held. "We're flying out this morning, is that right? Where are we going?"

"Oh no," he said, trying to maintain a firm expression as she scooted to his side. "You are absolutely not going."

"And where am I not going to?" she murmured, barely brushing her lips against his.

Paul fell off the bed and stood up. "Rick and I worked out a deal. They won't press charges against anyone if I will act as guide on one more trip to Big Bend. They've gotten information to the effect that the big boss is going to personally supervise this next run, and it's going down real soon."

"Great!" Royce exclaimed, bounding up. "Just give me a chance to get dressed and put my hair up. Is that coffee ready? I take mine black, please."

"Royce, you are *not going*," Paul said with finality.

Standing in front of the bathroom mirror, Royce pulled her hair back, murmuring, "I need my brush. Oh, by the way," she said, turning, "did I ever tell you I'm a writer? And I'm thinking about doing an article for *Field & Stream* entitled, 'My Experiences with Drug Privateers in Big Bend.' Don't you think that would make interesting reading?"

"Royce," Paul said threateningly, "I'll just let Rick lock you up until I get back."

"Ooh, that's even better!" she exclaimed. "'How the DEA Detained Me Without Charges While They Escorted Drug Privateers to Big Bend'!"

Paul stood at the bathroom door. "Don't do this to me," he pleaded. "If anything happened to you, I'd die."

"Nothing's going to happen to me. Not when I have you to pray over me," she said cheerfully.

"Don't joke about it, Royce," he said.

"I'm not kidding!" she insisted. She stood directly in front of him and whispered, "I'm perfectly serious."

Paul gripped the door frame and bowed his head. Royce twined her arms around him and kissed him lingeringly. "Get dressed," he muttered. "Our flight leaves in an hour and a half."

Royce had no time for coffee just then. Paul brought her suitcases up from the car, and while she dressed and packed her duffel bag, he called the airline for another first-class ticket.

"Fine," she heard him say from the next room. "Put both tickets on my card. I'll turn this one back in."

As he hung up, Royce appeared in her denims. "I'm ready!"

"Fine," he said. "Now if you're through with my underwear, I'll change and pack."

By the time Royce had poured herself a cup of coffee and taken two sips, Paul was coming out of the bedroom with his bag packed. Royce thrilled at the sight of him in his jeans and boots. But she frowned as he shrugged into a tan jacket. "Wear your gray jacket!" she pleaded.

"Have a heart, Royce; that one smells something awful." He took up her bag along with his and said, "Can I have my keys now?"

"Yes," she laughed. She took them from her purse and handed them over. She held the purse a moment, trying to decide whether she would need it, then tossed it down on the bed. Paul took their bags down to his car, muttering to himself.

On the way to the airport, he got her an egg biscuit and coffee from a fast-food drive-through. "Thank you," she said as he passed the order to her. "Aren't you eating?"

"Rick fed me earlier," he said.

"Ah," she replied, opening the wrapper. As he swung on to the airport freeway, Royce asked, "What about Sadie, Paul? Was she really dealing drugs from the center?"

"Apparently so," he sighed. "Sadie was a former addict, and I guess the pressures of working at the center got to be too much for her, and she relapsed. She didn't start dealing from the center until I left for vacation, of course. While investigating her, the DEA went over our books, which is how they found the cash. I should have done that differently . . ." he mused. "Anyway, part of the deal we made is that she'll receive treatment and no jail time. But the center will have to stay closed until I get back. Then I'll have to hire a new assistant." Royce looked up quickly, but he did not take the hint. She said nothing.

A moment later he glanced at her. "Rick will have a cow

when he finds out I'm bringing you. It's not going to be the cake-walk that our other trips have been. This one could get rough."

He exited to the airport and Royce stared out the window. *What am I doing? Am I crazy?* she screamed at herself. *This is not some dime-store fiction. This is for real.* She gripped the armrest, feeling honest fear.

Paul parked the Nissan in long-term parking and took out their bags. As he walked her to the terminal, he said, "We're flying into Del Rio, where we'll meet some folks from the DEA. They'll take us by helicopter to the Chisos Basin. I'm going to leave you at the lodge, then come back for you when we're done." Royce opened her mouth but Paul insisted, "Don't argue, Royce! I mean it! You stay at the lodge or you don't leave this airport!"

"All right!" she said hastily, secretly relieved. Paul grunted, gratified that his masculine authority remained intact.

He picked up their tickets at the reservations counter in exchange for his first one, then they got their boarding passes. "Where's your hat?" she asked suddenly. "You can't go without your hat!"

He gave her an exasperated look and said, "It's in my bag, Mother. We're boarding." He gestured toward the metal detectors. They found their seats on the plane and Paul stashed their bags overhead. "Window or aisle?" he asked Royce.

"Let me sit on the aisle so I can get out when I need to go to the bathroom," she whispered. He grinned and sat by the window.

As they waited for takeoff, Royce began to feel pangs of guilt. She knew more about him than she had a right to know. He had a right to know that she was a person who read other people's private mail. She shifted uneasily and cleared her throat. Paul, who had been looking out the window, turned around. "Having second thoughts?"

"No," she said slowly.

He leaned toward her. "Royce, you don't have to go. You

don't have to prove anything to me. You can stay at my apartment. I promise we'll pick up where we left off when I get back."

"I want to go," she reiterated. "That's not it. I . . . have
something to confess."

"What?" he asked curiously.

"I . . . I . . . read the letter from your ex-wife," she said lamely.

He sat back, smiling slightly. "Shee, you're nosy."

"I know, and I'm sorry," she said sincerely.

"That's okay," he said, looking out the window again.

But having broached the subject, she could not let it drop.
"She's coming to Dallas this week."

Paul looked over. "I won't be in town, will I?" Royce studied
him and he said, "Oh, I get it. You're worried that I might want
to see her again. Well, let me tell you what I did when I got her
letter: I went to work and called you."

Royce smiled. "You didn't give me your home phone
number."

"No, I gave you the number where I was! I expected you to
call me right back! I sat by that phone for an hour, until I had to
leave. Shee!" He sat back in his seat and Royce laughed. He
held up his hand and she put hers to it, interlocking their fingers.

As soon as they were in the air, Paul relaxed to the point
that he went to sleep. He was leaning slightly toward her, still
holding her hand. A flight attendant came down the aisle and
stopped when she saw Paul. "Would you like a pillow for him?"
she whispered.

"No, he's okay," Royce smiled. He shifted to lay his head on
her shoulder.

"Honeymooners?" the flight attendant asked.

"Does it show?" Royce asked, looking up.

"You can always tell, when the men smile in their sleep,"
she answered, patting Royce's shoulder. "Best wishes." She
moved on.

Royce twisted to look at Paul's face. He certainly did appear
content. Suddenly it struck her: *that* was what seemed different

about him—not what he was wearing, or whether he was in a car or on a horse—but his expression in unguarded moments. That hunted look was gone. Going into the most dangerous situation he would probably ever face, he slept with a look of utter serenity.

Royce thought of what Dr. Oldham had said and a tingle raced up her spine. Kissing Paul lightly on the forehead, she put her head down on his and held his hand.

It was a quick flight. As the airplane put down its landing gear and glided to a stop on the runway, Royce nudged Paul awake. He got up immediately and pulled their bags down from the overhead compartment. As he and Royce disembarked, the flight attendant smiled at him and winked, "Have a wonderful time." He blinked at her.

Paul spotted his two DEA contacts in the boarding area, and they zeroed in on him. They approached, inconspicuously showing their IDs. "Mr. Arrendondo?" They shook his hand and said, "This way, please." As they started off, Royce went with them.

One agent paused to eye her. "Who is this?"

"An informant," Paul said. "Rick found her in Big Bend." They accepted this and went on. Royce flashed a look at Paul, who shrugged guiltily.

The agents took them to a restricted area of the airport, where a pilot waited in a commercial helicopter. They climbed on board; Paul pointed Royce to the seat behind the pilot, and he sat behind her. The two agents sat on the other side. Royce fastened her seatbelt, and as the pilot started the rotor blades, Paul motioned for her to put on the headset at her elbow.

Glancing back at them from behind his sunglasses, the pilot radioed, "Ah, check, Heaven. The Padre is on board. Over."

"Padre, we are still looking. Over," Rick's voice came over the radio.

"Ah, the subject has been located. Over," Paul said. Royce heard it all through the earphones.

"Check. Over and out," Rick replied.

Royce turned around to Paul and mouthed, "He called you 'Padre.'"

"He decided to use that as my code name," Paul replied through the headset.

Royce took off her headset to lean back toward him and ask, "Does he know you were a . . . ?"

Paul lifted off his earphones to hear her, then replied, "Angel, he knows more about me than my own mother does."

The pilot lifted off and Royce sat back, replacing the headset to protect her ears from the loud drone. They headed due west. As soon as Royce's stomach adjusted to the yaw and roll of the helicopter, she pressed her face to the window. They passed over a huge reservoir controlled by a dam, and a winding, muddy brown river. "Is that the Rio Grande?" she asked Paul.

"Yes," he said. She heard a snicker from one of the agents and Paul said, "Hey, she's from New York."

Royce paid no attention, watching the mountains that erupted beneath them. Viewed from above at close range, they staggered the senses. The sight made Royce so dizzy that she closed her eyes and scrunched down in the seat.

Before long she had to look again. They were passing over miles and miles of rolling giants—Royce had not envisioned so many mountains over the whole earth. Then there was the river again—twisting through the mountains, carving a deep path between steep stone canyons. She glanced back at Paul, who was watching out the window behind her.

West of the river she spotted trailers and buildings, and in another few minutes they were setting down in a clear area not far from the lodge. While the blades whirled slowly, the agents, Paul, and Royce climbed out, hauling their bags behind them. Royce covered her face from the swirling dust. When they were clear, the pilot lifted off again.

Before they started for the lodge, one of the agents reached into his pocket and handed Paul a roll of cash. "You're to rent a room under the name of John P. George," he told Paul. (Royce rolled her eyes.) "We'll meet you there shortly."

Paul flipped through the cash, nodding, then stuffed it in his pocket and took hold of Royce with one hand and both bags with the other. They entered the lodge office, where Paul set the bags down and requested a room for two. As she waited, Royce glanced around the familiar rustic environs she had thought she'd never see again.

Dragging on a cigarette, the woman at the reservations desk opened a guest register and Paul laid out some cash. Royce watched surreptitiously as he signed in "Mr. and Mrs. John P. George," tossing off a fictitious address in Houston. Then he took their key and hoisted their bags.

Glancing at the number on the key, he pointed, "This way." Royce accompanied him to a first-floor room which had a large front window looking out to the Basin.

Paul unlocked the door and shoved it open. He dropped the bags on the floor and began looking around the room—in and under lamps and the table, even around the door molding. Royce looked at the two double beds.

Paul smiled briefly at her as he sat on one bed, picked up the telephone receiver and began dismantling it. "What are you doing?" Royce asked.

"Just checking," he said, looking in the mouthpiece and then replacing the disk.

She sat beside him, whispering, "Are we bugged?"

"Probably not," he responded, hanging up the telephone. They looked at each other, then he withdrew all the money from his back pocket and gave it to her. "You hold on to this. I won't need it; you may."

Royce stuffed it into her jeans pocket without looking through it. "I'm scared," she confessed in a whisper.

"Me too," he smiled. He put his arms around her and Royce laid her head against his neck. "You're a good friend," he murmured.

Royce ran a hand over his shirt front. "I want to be more than your friend."

He laughed in a low voice. "Yeah. But you've got to understand, it's easy to be lovers. It's harder to be a good friend. I'd forgo ten lovers for one good friend," he said, looking down at her. At Royce's dubious expression he added, "Maybe you have to be stabbed in the back before you can appreciate that."

As Royce reached up to kiss him, a knock sounded on the door. Grudgingly, she let go of him and Paul got up to open the door. The two DEA agents came in. "Here." One of them handed Paul a leather pouch. "Your horse and supplies are waiting at the stables—you're to ask for the horse 'Prosperity.' Your contacts will meet you at Panther Pass. They'll ask you the name of your horse; you'll tell them, 'Prosperity.' They'll say, 'Oh, so is Prosperity around the corner?' They'll give you the preliminary code words we've intercepted; you'll have to figure out from that where to take them."

"Right," Paul murmured.

"And miss," the agent said, turning to Royce, "you will need to wait here."

"I know," she said.

The two agents stepped out and Paul hesitated. "I'll be right out. Give me just a minute. . . ." He looked back at Royce.

"You've got five minutes," the agent said as he and his partner shut the door.

Royce crossed the room in a few quick strides and landed in Paul's arms. She held his face and kissed him. "I do love you," she said.

A grin flashed across his face. "I know. You can't help yourself." His smile gave way to a vaguely worried expression. "I'll take care of this mess, and get it behind me, then we can talk. Wait here; keep a low profile; and when I come back, we'll talk. . . ." He kissed her deeply, then released her and backed up to the door.

"Wait." Royce leaned down to his duffel bag and unzipped

it, bringing out his buff-colored hat. He took it, combed his hair back with one hand, and fitted the hat on his head, the way he always had before. "Be careful," Royce said weakly.

He nodded and quickly turned out of the room. Royce pulled back the window drapes slightly to watch him stride across the grounds toward the stables.

She sat heavily in a chair and picked up the room key he had left on the table. For a long time she sat staring off into space. She was not actually thinking because she did not know what to think; the situation seemed so unreal.

At length she was moved to action by her growling stomach. She left the room, being careful to lock it, and went to the lodge's restaurant. It was after one o'clock, so the lunch crowd had thinned out. Royce took a plate and began helping herself from the buffet line to barbecued brisket, beans, potato salad, and peach cobbler. She sat at a corner table, glancing occasionally at the other diners. They all looked safely to be tourists.

Royce ate slowly, looking out the large cathedral window at the mountains. *I wish I had thought to ask him how long it would take*, she thought. *But he probably doesn't know.*

A waitress in jeans and cowboy boots refilled her water glass and brought her lunch tab. Little by little the dining room emptied until Royce was all alone. She did not mind at first—there was certainly nothing else she had to rush to—but gradually the silence became threatening. She began to feel exposed and vulnerable. Royce left a ten-dollar bill on the table with her tab and went outside.

It was a clear, radiant afternoon. The tourist season was in full swing, so there were plenty of people about. Royce blended in with them comfortably. She stopped in the lodge store to look around, and saw the rack of fringed suede jackets from which she had bought her first, which she had lost in the desert. Royce promptly found another one that fit.

As she was taking it to the cash register, she slowed beside a display of cowboy hats. Royce found a brown one, similar in shade to her jacket, with a snakeskin band, yet. She tried it on and looked up into the mirror, smiling at the reflection of the hat over her long ponytail. After paying for the items, she happily emerged from the store decked out as a true cowperson. And she did not give a second thought to the snake that had died to adorn her hat.

It seemed natural to wander from there to the stables where a group of tourists were being matched to horses. A hardened cowhand, the Marlboro Man twenty years later, swung around to point at her. "You're what—a hundred ten pounds?"

"Yes," she said lightly.

"Okay, you get Dusty there." A young cowboy brought over a dun-colored horse with a black mane and tail.

"Oh, he's so pretty," Royce breathed, petting the silky nose.

"It's a she," the young cowboy grinned. Royce giggled and covered her mouth. He brought out Western tack and allowed her to help him saddle and bridle Dusty, carefully explaining what everything was for. After helping her into the saddle, he showed her how to hold the reins, how to turn and how to stop.

"You're so nice," Royce smiled down at him. "How much does this ride cost?"

"Ain't you paid?" the teenager looked up in surprise. "It's twenty dollars. A three-hour trail ride."

Royce pulled out a twenty-dollar bill and handed it to him. "I just joined the group," she explained.

"Oh," he said. "You wait here till I get you a canteen, now." He trotted off, and Royce proudly patted Dusty as she looked over the other greenhorns being paired with their horses. Then she reflected that she had better stop spending so freely, as she did not know how long she would be waiting for Paul.

The young cowboy returned with a full canteen and she thanked him. When all were in the saddle—about twenty of them—their guide lined them up single file and began taking them toward the mountains. Royce could hardly help but laugh.

This is what they were supposed to do the first time they had come down.

They passed a sign and her smile vanished. It said, "Panther Pass," with an arrow pointing off to the right—to the place where Paul was to meet his contacts.

14

R oyce twisted in the saddle, straining to see down the path
to Panther Pass. But there was no one within view.

The group of tourists rode on up a dirt trail into the
mountains. It was a very tame ride compared to the wild gallops
Royce had experienced a week ago, but it was still fun. Dusty
reminded her of Buster—she was neither as large nor as spir-
ited, but she was obedient and gentle. Royce patted her con-
tinuously as they rode, and even found a spot between her ears
where she like to be scratched.

The guide pointed out interesting features of the area while
frequently checking back over the line of riders. They ambled
along in the sunshine, admiring the bright scarlet blooms on the
ocotillo and the tiny yellow flowers of the creosote bush. Poised
like a seasoned rider on Dusty's reliable back, Royce appreci-
ated the scenery well enough, but remained vigilant for other
riders on other trips.

At a rest stop Royce removed her jacket and hung it over
the saddle. She petted Dusty's nose and scratched her under the

chin, which caused the horse to stretch out her head for more. Royce hung back from the other tourists enough to discourage conversation, as she did not wish to get engaged in a question-and-answer session about her home or background. The riders soon started off again, continuing on their long, circular route through the hills and rock formations back to the lodge.

Arriving at the stables, Royce helped the young cowboy unsaddle the horses, curry them down and water them. She watched him check for loose shoes and helped him spread fresh hay. When they were done, he took off his straw hat, wiped his brow, and said, "I arter pay you, for the hep you been. What's your name, now?"

"Royce," she said, wiping her hands on her jeans.

"Royce?" he laughed. "That's a funny name. But you're a pretty girl. I'm Billy." They shook grimy hands. He was a lanky, sunburned seventeen-year-old with close-cropped blond hair. "Are you with the group that's from Pasadena?"

"No, I'm from Houston," Royce responded. A confused look passed over Billy's innocent face and Royce said, "Uh, I'd better go get cleaned up for dinner. Thanks for the ride, Billy."

On her way out, the old Marlboro Man leaned in and said, "Now *don't forget* to lock up the stables tonight, Billy. You are always forgettin' to do that!"

"Yessir, I won't forget," Billy replied, blushing. Royce smiled and returned to her room, where she bathed and changed shirts. Proudly, she placed her new hat on the bedside table. Before leaving for dinner, she took the time to hang up Paul's shirts and jeans in the closet.

At the lodge's restaurant she fell right in line with the other vacationers. Unfortunately, a friendly woman promptly turned around and asked, "Now where are you from?"

"Houston," Royce said tentatively.

"Is that right?" the woman exclaimed. "Why, we're from the Park View Drive Baptist Church in Pasadena! My name is Margaret."

You Baptists are everywhere, Royce thought while saying, "Actually, I'm new to Houston. I grew up in New York City."

"Is that right? What brought you to Texas?" Margaret asked. By now several members of her group were listening.

Royce looked down and said, "My husband is from Texas. We're—on our honeymoon." She folded her hands over her unadorned ring finger.

"Well, congratulations! Where is the lucky man?" asked the well-meaning inquisitor.

"You know, I don't know what's keeping him. He told me to go on ahead while he showered. Let me go get him." With a friendly wave, Royce departed the line. Once she was out of their sight, she went around to the coffee shop and bought a sandwich, chips, and soft drink to take back to the motel room.

At the room, she set the items on the table and lashed herself: "Stupid, stupid, stupid! Paul told you to lay low and here you are acting like the Queen of the Tourists." She plopped down at the table, glumly wondering, "Why did I insist on coming? I can't do a thing for him here except get in the way."

Opening the sandwich, she investigated its pimento cheese filling and took a bite. "Well, the only thing to do now is stay in this room until Paul comes back. And if that's days, that will just serve me right."

As she ate, she looked around for the television. She paused in midbite when she finally realized that there *was* no television. This motel did not have television sets! "I don't believe this," she moaned. "It's as bad as no indoor plumbing. I guess I could always buy a book—or three or four—from the gift shop." But not tonight. She was not setting foot outside this room tonight.

So during the longest evening of her entire life, Royce ate her dinner, went through Paul's bag, watched clandestinely out the window, and investigated every inch of the motel room. She washed her hair and used every towel in the bathroom to dry it.

Finally toward ten o'clock she gave up and got into bed. She turned off the bedside lamp and lay down, draping her hair over the pillow. Then she stared up at the ceiling of the darkened room, thinking about Paul. She wondered why in the world he had let her come. He knew better than she how dumb it was. Did he want her with him that much? Royce rolled onto her side, hugging the pillow, and closed her eyes.

Some time later Royce woke with a violent start. She was experiencing a terrible, crushing fear. Her heart was pounding and she was bathed in cold sweat. Was there someone in the room? No, not that she could see or hear. But the terror she felt squeezed her chest until she had to sit up to breathe.

Get out of here. I've got to get out of here. The internal insistence made no sense at all, but Royce, shaking, reached for her jeans and shirt. She dressed as fast as she could for the trembling, hardly able to tie her shoes. Then she put on her suede jacket and opened the door.

It was very late. No one was out; everything was locked up. *What am I doing? Where am I supposed to go?* Royce protested, but the compulsion to leave would hear no arguments. She stepped out, closing the door behind her, and hesitantly walked across the grounds. She saw the stable ahead in the moonlight. Urgently, Royce made for the stable door. It was unlocked— again, Billy had forgotten to lock it. Royce eased the door open, slipped inside, and sank to the dirt.

She sat there a few minutes in bewilderment, peeking out across the grounds. Then she saw a movement in the shadows. She held her breath, watching. A figure stole along the outside of the motel. Then he stopped at one room. He lifted something. Royce heard loud pops and glass shattering. There was a succession of popping noises, like a string of firecrackers going off. As he remained outside the broken window, moving back and forth, Royce realized in horror that he was spraying her room— the room she had just left—with gunfire.

He stopped and ran off. Lights nearby began coming on. Royce leaned against the stable door, hyperventilating.

Now she heard voices and exclamations. Royce watched as

people in nightclothes began coming out. *If they knew where to find me, then Paul is in trouble,* she reasoned. At once, she became supernaturally calm and started thinking: *All I know is that he was supposed to meet his contacts at Panther Pass. I know where that is. Now, how to get there. . . .*

Royce twisted around and looked down the length of the stable. She got up and found Dusty in her stall. "Hi, Dusty. Remember me?" she whispered. Dusty lifted her chin for a scratching. Royce obliged her, reaching for the bridle hanging nearby.

Although it was very dark in the stable, Royce dared not look for a light, not with all the commotion at the motel. Once she had the bridle on Dusty, she led her to a part of the stable that was underneath a gap in the tin roofing. There, enough moonlight shone in so she could see what she was doing.

Following Billy's example from earlier in the day, Royce placed the blanket and saddle on Dusty. Lifting the stirrup, she brought up the cinch and tied it just as Billy had done, even kneeing Dusty gently in the middle to discourage her from puffing her stomach while the cinch was tightened.

That done, Royce led her to the stable door and looked out. The motel lights were on and a crowd was gathered around the door to her room. But no one was paying any attention to the stable.

Still leading Dusty, Royce slipped out of the large double doors and trotted across the dark grounds. Slipping behind the gift shop, she held Dusty still so she could climb into the saddle. Then she took the reins, turned her toward the riding trail, and kicked.

Like magic, Dusty began ambling toward the path. Royce kicked harder and she began trotting. Royce gripped the reins tighter, kicked yet again, and Dusty broke into a reluctant lope.

Scanning the side of the path in the moonlight, Royce found the sign pointing toward Panther Pass and turned down that way. Here she slowed to a walk, being uncertain of what she was looking for or what she would find. Yet she continually kept an eye out for campfires in the distance.

She passed through a narrow juncture in the rocks and continued down the path. It seemed unseasonably cool for how warm it had gotten that day; Royce had trouble controlling her trembling. The mountains loomed ominously overhead and the large rock formations took on unnatural aspects. Royce no longer felt the blood-curdling fear which had impelled her from the motel room, but she was plenty uneasy, considering the circumstances.

Dusty suddenly snorted and balked. Royce kicked her, but she would not budge: something about the size of a hat lay in the middle of the path ahead. Royce dismounted to investigate.

It *was* a hat. Royce picked it up. It was Paul's hat. Even in the dark, she was confident it was his. He had come this way. He had lost his hat and had been unable to go back for it. Royce took it with her as she climbed back into the saddle. She continued her search, trying not to think about the impossibility of what she was trying to do.

She rode for more than an hour, until she came to a curve in the path and a sign marking it as the turn-around point. From here the path led back to the lodge. Royce brought Dusty to a halt. The sensible thing would be to return to the lodge and alert the park rangers. So why did she feel such a reluctance to do that? Dusty swished her tail impatiently.

Suddenly Royce remembered the lodge employee who had phoned his drug bosses about the money she and her friends were spending. Had his identity been uncovered, or was he still at the lodge? How had they known which room was hers and Paul's? How could she know whom to trust?

Royce looked out across the pathless wilderness. Searching for him at random out here was foolish and dangerous, whether she found him or not. She had already been at the mercy of both the desert and the drug dealers, and did not relish the thought of encountering either again.

"If I knew how to pray, I would," she whispered. Then she wondered: Was Paul praying for her? Where had the urgent feeling come from that she must leave that room? Could she go now on the strength of his prayers?

She decided on a plan. Leaving the path, she rode straight toward a prominent peak in the distance, glancing back frequently. Before the path was completely lost to view, she took Paul's hat and placed it atop a tall cactus as a signpost. Then she went on toward the peak, scanning the desert as far as she could see. After she had gone a little farther, she stopped Dusty to pick up a large, rolling bramble. This she jammed down securely on the top of another large cactus. In this way she left frequent signs to guide herself back to the path when she needed it.

After another hour's ride, Royce stopped again to think. This was certainly useless, and she was getting very tired. She decided then and there to cut out this nonsense and go get help.

As she turned Dusty around, something caught her eye. Something flickered in the distance. Royce stared intently. Was that a blue light, or was it her imagination? It flickered again, and Royce remembered what Ol' Pete had said about the blue flames of the miners' lights still being visible. Now Royce was as sensible as they come, and had never in her life given credence to ghost stories, but tonight she was inclined to believe anything.

"Stop that," she said aloud. "You need to find out what that is." She began to ride toward the spot, being careful to mark her path. But minutes passed and she did not see the light again, so she decided that her mind had manufactured what she wanted to see. As she was about to turn back, she saw the light again—definitely a light, and much closer.

Royce climbed down from Dusty and crept forward. There was the light. It was the flame from a small butane stove sitting beside a pickup truck with a shell on it. A horse trailer sat nearby. Three or four figures in sleeping bags were around the stove, and all but one looked to be asleep. This one, a man with an automatic pistol, stood guard as he puffed on a cigarette. Royce watched quietly.

After a moment, one of the figures stirred and sat up. "You might as well let me keep watch now. I can't sleep." As he shucked off his sleeping bag, Royce felt a thrill to her toes. It was Paul.

The other man readily assented and took to his bedroll. Paul picked up the gun and stretched wearily. As he poured himself something to drink from a thermos, Royce felt another twinge: *What's wrong with this picture?*

That was just it. Nothing was wrong, from Paul's demeanor. His situation was just what it was supposed to be. Royce sat back, perplexed. What did this mean? It meant that she had been attacked without his knowledge—someone, somewhere had double-crossed them. Or . . . that she had been attacked with his knowledge. He was not in the room when the shots were fired.

"Royce!" She jerked up at the exclamation. Paul was standing over her, staring in profound amazement. He reached out and pulled her to her feet. "Royce! How in the world—what in heaven's name are you doing here?"

Royce stared at him without answering. He had reason enough to be surprised, but . . . was he surprised because she should have been dead? It made no sense—nothing made any sense—but all those old doubts about the true nature of his activities surfaced. Something in her mind snapped.

"What happened? What's wrong?" he asked, holding her hands. "Royce?"

The man who had just laid down now sat up. "What is it?"

"It's Royce," Paul answered, turning around. "Something's happened. She won't talk to me." He turned back toward her, cupping her hands in his. "You're shivering. Come by the stove," he coaxed. Royce resisted.

"Call Mission and find out what's going on," Paul said to his companion as he gently tugged Royce forward.

This man, who could have played professional football ten years ago, opened the shell of the truck and detached a microphone from a unit inside. "Mission, this is Cherub. Over." He looked at Royce as he waited for a reply, and observed, "Looks like she's in shock. Mission, this is Cherub. Over," he repeated.

Dragging Royce to the warmth of the stove, Paul tried to put his arms around her, but she twisted away. "Royce, it's all right. You're with me now. Tell me what happened. How did you get out here?" he asked. She stared at the flame of the stove.

"Mission to Cherub. Over," a voice crackled over the radio. Royce jumped.

"Mission, we need a weather report from the lodge," Cherub said.

"Stand by, Cherub," the voice instructed.

He lowered the microphone and said, "I don't like this. Something's gone wrong and we weren't notified. Sweetheart, how did you get here? Did someone bring you?"

Royce turned to look for Dusty, but could not see her in the dark. Paul said apprehensively, "Royce, did you come with someone? We must know if someone brought you."

"I came alone," she whispered. "I'm alone."

The voice came over the radio, "Mission to Cherub. Over."

"Cherub here. Go ahead, Mission," he said into the microphone.

"We have a report of rain at the lodge. Repeat: it has been raining at the lodge," the voice said.

Cherub glanced in alarm at Royce and said, "Requesting a raincheck, Mission. We've caught a cold."

"Stand by, Cherub," the radio said.

"I don't like the smell of this at all," he said, replacing the microphone.

"What? What is it?" Paul demanded. The other two men in sleeping bags had awakened by now.

"There's been gunplay at the lodge. Royce got away, but that means someone is on to us. I've requested that this mission be aborted. I've also told them we've got a visitor," Cherub said.

Paul stood with his head bowed. The radio crackled, "Mission to Cherub. Over."

"Cherub here. Go ahead, Mission," he quickly responded.

"Heaven says no raincheck, Cherub. Over."

"Repeat, Mission?" he asked in disbelief.

"Heaven says no raincheck. Over."

"Let me talk to Rick," Paul said angrily.

"Ah, request a direct line to Heaven," Cherub said, reaching for a dial. "Over."

"Stand by, Cherub," the voice confirmed, and he switched channels.

A few moments later Rick's voice said, "This is Heaven. Over."

Paul took the microphone and said, "Rick, we gotta call this thing off. Our cover's been blown. Over."

"Look, Padre, we've been planning this for months, and we're not about to walk away now. It was your asinine idea to bring Royce, so now you're stuck with her. But if you don't follow through with your end, then the deal is off. Over!"

Slack-jawed, Paul dangled the microphone, then brought it up and replied, "Acknowledged. Over and out." He handed the microphone to the other man, who replaced it on the radio in the truck. Royce stared at the butane flame.

"I don't like this," Cherub repeated. "It feels like a setup. We need to know what happened at the lodge," he said, eying Royce.

Paul turned to her. "Royce, you've got to talk to me.... Why are you looking at me like that? You can't believe that I—! For pete's sake, Royce, can't you see the deep doo-doo I'm in?" he exclaimed.

The other man shook his head. "It's no good trying to get her to talk tonight. Put her in the bag; see if she'll rest."

Paul took her arm but she declared, "I'm not sleeping here with you!"

"You want me to drive back to the lodge? Come on, Royce; come lie down. There now," he coaxed her calmly. He maneuvered her to the bag, where she slowly lay down. She placed her head on his rolled-up jacket. The other men returned to their sleeping bags; Paul took up the gun to resume his watch. He stood by the stove, one hand on his hip, and stared at the figure scrunched up in his sleeping bag.

Royce sank into sleep. But it was a murky, troubled sleep. Images flashed through her mind—of Billy and Dusty, Margaret asking questions in line, and a man stealing across the grounds. A man shattering the window with his gun—Royce sat up screaming, "Paul! Paul!"

Right away he was holding her. "I'm here. I'm here, Royce."

She clutched his shirt. "I was sleeping, and I woke up with this—this awful fear. I knew I had to get out of that room. I got dressed and I ran—I ran to the stables to watch, and a man came—someone came and stood at the window and fired into my room. He fired through the window and ran off. And I saddled Dusty—I rode Dusty to Panther Pass, but I didn't know where you were. . . ." She shivered uncontrollably against his chest.

"It's all right, Royce," he whispered. He gripped her as if to contain her trembling by force.

"How did you know you were in danger?" Cherub asked, crouching nearby.

"I don't know," she gasped. "I woke up and my heart was pounding and I knew I had to get out. I thought you were in trouble. I thought you were praying for me. But then I got here—I found you, and you weren't in trouble at all," she said to Paul.

"Oh no, I'm in plenty of trouble; I just didn't realize how much. And I've been praying continually for your safety, Royce," he said. Gradually, she stopped shivering. "Lie down. It's only a few hours till morning." He tucked her back into the sleeping bag.

"Don't leave me!" She grabbed at his arm.

One of the other men said, "You stay with her and keep her quiet. It's my turn to watch, anyway." Paul borrowed the other man's bedroll, placing it beside Royce. As he crawled in, she scrunched up to him and went right to sleep.

15

---◈---

Sometime in the morning Royce woke from leaden slumber. Paul was standing beside the truck, talking with two of the men. The aroma of coffee wafted by. She struggled up to a sitting position.

Paul came over and knelt beside her. "Good morning. Did we rest well?" he asked. The dark circles under his eyes gave the question an ironic twist he had not intended.

Royce eyed him blearily, brushing errant strands of hair from her face. "If you cared anything for me, you'd pour me some of that coffee," she mumbled.

"Hey, there's nothing I wouldn't do for you," he said, getting up. He used a hot pad to take the coffeepot off the stove and pour brew into a metal cup. This he handed to her wrapped in the pad. "It's hot."

She blew on it with closed eyes. Then she said dully, "I screwed up everything by making you take me. I didn't realize what I was getting into. I am so sorry, Paul."

He sighed and shook his head. "I'm to blame; I brought you.

And now I'm paying my dues for playing Robin Hood. But we're not going to worry about that. We're here; we've got work to do, and we're going to do all that's required."

"What do you want me to do?" she asked tremulously.

"Oh, have some breakfast." He opened a package of sweet rolls and sat down beside her. As Royce pulled out a roll and bit into it, Paul doodled in the dirt at his feet and said, "The latest information we have indicates the drugs will be changing hands tonight. When we get the code describing the exact location, we're going to try to intercept them. We're almost sure there is a wild card in the deck somewhere, but we don't know who that is. So we're just going to try to finesse around it."

"How?" she asked.

"Well, we'll figure that out as we go," he hedged.

As she watched him trace patterns in the dirt, she said, "You're not scared?"

"Not anymore," he replied. "I was, when there was still a chance of backing out. But now that we're here—you, too—and we have to go through with it, I'm ready for whatever's going to happen to go ahead and happen. Does that make sense?"

Royce opened her mouth, then frowned and said, "Not really. If you think you might be walking into a setup, why go through with it?"

"Because Rick said—" Paul began, then his face changed. "Rick *said* . . ." he repeated, slower.

"Yes?" she prodded.

"Rick didn't know you were with me on the helicopter. These agents said nothing about you to him. *I* didn't tell him it was you—" He scrambled to his feet and Royce jumped up after him.

"Charlie, get on the box to Mission," Paul requested urgently.

The man Royce had been introduced to as Cherub backed out of the truck's cab and opened the shell at the rear. He called up his contacts on the radio: "Cherub to Mission. Come in, Mission."

"This is Mission, Cherub. Over."

Paul took the microphone and said, "Mission, this is Padre. I need to know exactly what information was relayed to Heaven about the rain last night. Over."

"Stand by, Padre."

Paul held the microphone, waiting, while Charlie stood by and the other two agents packed up the camp. Royce ate her sweet roll. "What's the problem, Padre?" Charlie asked.

"Did *anybody* tell Rick that Royce was with me?" he asked.

"Not that I know of. Your transport team told me he'd sent her," Charlie said. He had sandy red hair, a few freckles, and an honest, open face that reminded Royce of—yes, a cherub. A two-hundred-and-fifty-pound cherub.

"Well, he didn't," Paul replied. "And he should not have known she was even here, unless—"

"Mission to Padre; over."

"Padre here; go ahead, Mission."

"Following is the text of our transmission to Heaven at 0120 hours: 'Rain at Chisos Basin Lodge at 2430 hours, concentrated on John P. George's room. No flooding. Rainmaker not found.' Over."

"Was there any mention of a third party? Over," Paul asked.

"Negative, Padre. Over."

"Over and out, then." Paul put up the microphone and asked Charlie, "What does 'no flooding' mean?"

"That no one was injured," Charlie replied. "Are you thinking that Rick is our snake?"

"There's no other way I can see that he would have known Royce was with me," Paul asserted. "The same party that sent the 'rainmaker' must have told him."

"I dunno, man. Rick's been with the agency a long time. Still, if he's the one, then we're as good as dead," Charlie muttered, scratching his scalp through his thick reddish hair.

Paul stroked his bristly face, thinking. Then he said, "Can you contact Sheriff Potts of Brewster County on this box?"

"Should be able to," Charlie allowed.

"Do that. Tell him I may need him down here, but not to intervene yet. He'll be our safety net," Paul said. Then he took Royce's arm. "You come help me get the horses ready. But we've only got two. You'll have to ride with me again."

"Dusty!" Royce suddenly remembered. "I forgot about her!" She wheeled to look out in the desert.

"Is this a horse from the stables?" Paul asked.

"Yes, she's the one I rode out here," Royce said anxiously.

"Don't worry, then. She'll have found her way back to the stable long ago," Paul said.

"Are you sure?" Royce asked.

"Oh, yes. They know where their oats are." Paul hauled out tack from the trailer and the other two agents helped him saddle and load the horses. Charlie got off the radio and shut the back of the truck, but then it crackled to announce an incoming message and he had to open it again. Royce stood sensibly out of the way, tying her hair back with a broken leather shoelace she'd found on the ground.

The agents finished their loading as Charlie got off the radio. Paul took a buff-colored hat from the front seat of the truck, combed his hair back with his fingers, and placed the hat on his head. "That's not your hat!" Royce exclaimed.

He gave her a funny look. "Yes, it is. You made sure I brought it."

"But I found your hat in the middle of the trail last night! That's one of the things that led me to you!" she insisted.

"I don't know whose hat you found, but it wasn't mine," Paul said.

"If we've got our wardrobes all coordinated, then I have a message to share from Heaven," said Charlie. "The transfer appears to be going down this afternoon."

"In broad daylight? That's interesting," Paul muttered.

Charlie nodded, handing him a walkie-talkie which Paul placed on his belt. He stood beside a beautiful chestnut horse. Charlie took another unit with him to an elephantine bay. He stroked the horse's nose, cooing, "Howsa Baby this morning?"

Paul climbed up in the chestnut's saddle and pulled Royce up behind him. He paused. "Could I talk you into going with the guys to Castolon?"

"No," she said, hugging his waist gently, remembering his wound.

"Just a thought," he said hopelessly.

Charlie had a few last-minute words with the agents before they climbed in the truck and left, towing the empty trailer. Then, grunting, he hoisted his frame onto Baby's saddle. "Did you raise Sheriff Potts?" Paul asked.

"Yeah, and he was surprised to hear you're back. Said he'd gotten no word from Heaven. He's sending down a unit to be on standby," Charlie told him. Paul said nothing, only reseated his hat. Charlie inquired, "Okay, Padre, where to?"

Paul squinted, thinking. "If the first message you got is still valid, then the area we're looking for is below the South Rim, but not as far down as *Punta de la Sierra*, nor as far west as Ross Maxwell. Better play it close to the chest." He began heading south on a narrow path into the stark Chisos Mountains.

There was no reason to go any faster than a walk as they followed switchbacks up the rugged slopes. Royce leaned comfortably against Paul and watched the clumps of bristly grass pass by underneath. The colored glow of the early sunlight and the remnant of the evening's breeze made last night's events seem surreal. All that mattered to Royce right now was being able to lean her head on Paul's back. Her own sweet, inscrutable Padre. At that point something occurred to her. "You don't talk anything like a preacher," she observed suddenly.

He twisted around to look at her. "That was a lifetime ago. I lost the mannerisms when I lost the job. I can still do it, though." He cleared his throat and began in a stilted, artificial cadence: "Here at First Baptist, we have a special way of recognizing our visitors. If you're a visitor, we'd like for you to remain seated while our members stand in your honor and greet you. Please take a visitor's card and fill it out so we will have all kinds of personal information about you. Then every time you visit us again, we will continue to make you conspicuously welcome until you feel compelled to join."

Royce laughed. Charlie looked over, chuckling. "I don't believe you ever sounded like that!" she declared.

"Sure, I did. I was a good soldier. A good preacher boy. A good Pharisee, until I got the wind knocked out of me," Paul said. Royce squeezed his ribs so hard he gasped, "Like that."

"I guess," he went on, "I had to learn that the externals don't matter much with God—how you look, how you dress, how you pronounce your words . . . where you live, how much money you make, how often you go to church or how many committees you're on—those things count for nothing. All that matters is how much you listen to Him. George MacDonald said, 'If you've been trying to serve Christ for thirty or forty years, it has been a kind of service that He does not care much about, and it is no wonder you can't go on. Perhaps you have been very careful about reading your Bible and going to church, and doing this thing or that thing that you think belongs to religion, but have you been doing the thing Christ told you? If you do that, I do not care whatever else you do; you cannot be wrong then.' I used to think that was heresy. Now I believe it's the simple truth."

He glanced back when she said nothing. "Oops. I see that the ghost of the preacher hasn't been completely exorcised. Sorry," he said.

"I found an old picture in your drawer, of a man in black on a horse, with a Bible. Who was he?" she asked.

"Good heavens, Royce, did you check out my medicine cabinet, too?" he laughed.

"Of course. Who was he?" she pressed.

"That was my great-grandfather on my mother's side. He

was a circuit rider—an itinerant preacher who rode from town to town holding services. When he was thirty-five, he was shot to death by a man angry that his wife was attending services. He left a widow with four children, one of them my grandmother Ruth. But at his funeral, the man who had shot him was converted. My great-grandmother asked leniency for him, but he was hanged anyway," Paul said.

"What was your great-grandfather's name?" Royce asked.

"Paul Raphael Alvarado," he answered.

Royce felt a strange, unpleasant tingle, like a premonition of evil. "How old are you, Paul?"

"I'm thirty-five. Need my social security number?" he asked flippantly. Disturbed, Royce did not answer. Paul looked back and said, "Stop thinking what you're thinking, Royce. My life is not predetermined by anything that happened to him."

"What was his wife's name?" she asked.

"Roseanne. And I'm not answering any more questions," he said. "Subject closed."

They reached the top of the mountain and Royce looked over the exhilarating spread of terrain stretched out around them—the intricate vastness that boggled the mind. Now Royce understood why people kept coming to this inhospitable place: to experience this sensation of being willingly engulfed in something so much greater than themselves.

Charlie and Paul dismounted, and Charlie unpacked a map which he spread out on the ground. "Now show me *exactly* where we are," he told Paul.

"Here," Paul said, pointing.

"Okay," Charlie muttered, unhitching his walkie-talkie. "Cherub to Missionary. Come in, Missionary."

"Missionary here, Cherub. Over," came the reply.

"We're standing at the patio door. Awaiting welcome. Over," Charlie said.

"Stand by for welcome, Cherub," the radio replied.

Charlie nodded at Paul, who turned to lift Royce down from

the horse. "What's going on?" she whispered.

"Charlie's in contact with the guys who just left. They're on their way to Castolon. In a few minutes they'll receive the code words that describe the exact location of the dropoff, which I should be able to identify. We'll check it out, and as soon as we observe the transaction, we'll signal the guys in Castolon to send up the chopper, and they'll make the arrests. At least, that's how it's supposed to work in theory," Paul admitted.

"What are you going to do if Rick double-crosses you?" Royce asked warily.

Paul looked askance at Charlie, who was bending over the map. "I've thought about that, and I just can't see it happening, sweetheart. Not Rick," Charlie said amiably. That did not satisfy Royce at all.

"Okay, Padre," Charlie said, tapping the map. "You've brought us right up to the patio. This area's the foyer, this is the bedroom, the study, the dining room, the kitchen, the hall, the basement, and so on." All these areas were marked out on the map. "When you pinpoint the spot, we'll relay it by room and direction. *High* is north, *low* is south, *door* is west and *window* is east. For instance, a high door in the bedroom would be the northwest corner of this quadrant." He planted a thick forefinger on the map.

"I understand," Paul nodded.

A few minutes brought no message, so they sat in the shade of an overhang. The sun was beginning to warm up the rock around them. Paul offered Royce the canteen; she took a small drink. Then she leaned into his side and played with his fingers—brown, agile fingers that were willingly manipulated by her own. The white stripe on his ring finger had almost disappeared. "What are you going to do when this is over?" she asked reflectively.

"I'm going to marry you," he said.

She looked up into his smiling brown eyes and tossed her ponytail over her shoulder. "You have to ask me properly."

"Ask you properly! After you slept in my underwear?" he exclaimed.

"This I gotta hear," said Charlie.

Royce recalled something, and ignoring Charlie's comment, asked Paul, "Is that a guitar in your room?" His smile faded and he nodded. "Is it yours? Do you play?" she asked eagerly.

"No," he said, looking away. "Well, I used to, but . . . I haven't picked it up in years. I'm sure I don't remember how."

Royce was disappointed at this nonresponse until she remembered Kris mentioning it in her letter. Then she could have bitten her tongue for asking about it. To forestall further questions, Paul got up and stood over the map with Charlie. *You're still doing it,* she thought dejectedly. *You propose and then pull back.* Whatever the cause for his vacillation, she determined not to push him with too many questions. So she sat quietly under the rock, and he soon turned back to her.

At that moment Charlie's radio crackled, "Missionary to Cherub. Over."

Charlie grabbed his unit. "Cherub here. Over."

"Here's your welcome, Cherub: 'Emory's blue elephant dominates over the mule.' Over."

"Acknowledged, Missionary. Over and out," Charlie confirmed. He and Paul bent over the map. Royce leaned over Paul's shoulder to watch.

"'Emory's blue elephant dominates over the mule,'" Paul slowly repeated. He took out a pencil and began drawing on the map, connecting dots. "That refers to Emory Peak, Blue Creek Ranch, Mule Ears Overlook, to Dominguez Mountain, to Elephant Tusk." His drawing produced something of a triangle on the map. Then he bisected the triangle with a line from Blue Creek Ranch to Elephant Tusk. He drew another line through the triangle from Emory Peak to Dominguez Mountain. Paul tapped the point at which those two lines intersected and said, "Here. At the foyer door. That's in the remuda just west of this range."

"Right," Charlie said. While he relayed this information to his contacts, Paul scratched his beard and reseated his hat. "That was easy. It's usually not that obvious," he noted. Royce eyed him apprehensively.

They got back on the horses and picked a path over the rough mountain slopes. Paul led in a careful, steadily westward direction, evaluating the stability of the rocks above and below. They worked their way through some dense brush, then broke out suddenly on the edge of a steep cliff. Royce gulped and closed her eyes, clinging to Paul. But he knew what he was doing, and the horses were sure-footed. He led along the edge of the cliff until they reached a balcony of sorts—a ledge of rock that extended out beyond the rest of the cliff face.

Paul surveyed the area and dismounted. "We can see most of the remuda from here. It's pretty narrow. If I'm anywhere near right, we should be able to see them."

By this time Royce had a physical necessity, so she went off by herself while Charlie and Paul unpacked enough gear to make themselves comfortable for an extended watch. When she returned, Charlie was stretched out on a sleeping bag and Paul was crouching near the edge of the balcony with binoculars. Royce sat beside him. He adjusted his hat and smiled at her.

Royce looked out over the rugged, dry valley. "What's a *remuda?*" she asked.

"Grazing land," he answered, scanning with the binoculars.

"*That's* grazing land?" she wondered, nodding at the sparse clumps.

"Such as it is," he admitted. "Folks have always been trying to figure out how to make a living off this land."

Royce leaned down on his rolled-up sleeping bag. "If you could do anything you wanted for a living, what would that be?" she asked.

He lowered the binoculars. "I'd be a ranchhand," he said. "I'd drive cattle and sleep under the stars and never look back." He paused to scan something that caught his eye, then added,

"I hate the city. I hate the traffic, and the smog, and the noise, the crime, the filth. . . . I'd be content never to see it again. Just give me a bedroll and a good horse."

Royce, city born and bred, listened in dismay. She thought, *But I hate nature. I hate bugs. I hate places without running water or restaurants. I could never live on a ranch.*

Paul looked at her and said, "I bet that doesn't sound very appealing to you." She shrugged indifferently. "Not very appealing at all," he murmured knowingly.

Royce lay with her head on the bag and watched Paul watch for the drug runners. *He's not bad-looking,* she thought sleepily. *He's not a heartthrob like John, but there's something special about him . . . just under the surface. . . .*

She closed her eyes and the picture came to mind of Paul's face on the billboard as the Marlboro Man. But instead of advertising cigarettes, he was advertising a different kind of life—something as alien to her as Big Bend. Looking up at the billboard, she felt the same trepidation that she had first felt about coming here. But his half-smile and steady gaze were irresistible, and she found herself cashing in her IRAs to buy a one-way plane ticket south.

There was a rustling nearby, and Royce opened her eyes. The sun had traveled enough to indicate the passage of several hours. Charlie was lying flat on his belly on the other side of Paul, and they both had binoculars trained on the remuda below. The growling which Royce had thought was her stomach was that of a helicopter landing far below.

"That's them," Paul murmured. "Three guys in the Range Rover. They've got the money. The helicopter will have brought the coke."

Charlie pulled out his walkie-talkie. "Cherub to Missionary. Come in, Missionary." He waited a few seconds, but there was no answer. "Cherub to Missionary. Dinner is served, Missionary. Do you copy?" He waited again, then shook his head. "I'm not raising them."

"They're making the exchange," Paul said, watching through his binoculars.

"It's the mountain above us. I'm going to have to go up on top to transmit," Charlie said, getting up.

"Better hurry," Paul muttered, watching. Charlie jumped on Baby, dug in his heels, and disappeared up the slope into the brush. Royce moved to lie flat beside Paul, holding her breath. Unaided, she could see the helicopter and Range Rover below. Paul was right on the money, as usual. So when would this snake show up?

As Paul monitored the activity below, his brow wrinkled in puzzlement. "What're they doing?" he muttered under his breath.

Royce squinted, but could not see what was amiss. However—"I hear a helicopter," she said. Paul dropped the glasses to listen over his shoulder. His eyes darted to hers in alarm. Then he yanked her up and lunged toward a steep embankment beside the balcony.

16

❖

Grabbing Royce's wrist, Paul jumped off the edge of the balcony onto the rocky slopes. Following, Royce yelped when strands of her long ponytail caught in the brambles. She yanked free as Paul dragged her down the mountainside.

He slid down to a rocky outcropping and pushed her back against the slope. Covering her with his body, he gripped an exposed root to hang on. The roar of the helicopter neared, and in the next moment the balcony was hit by strafing. The barrage of bullets ricocheted off the rocks into every bush and crevice. Royce heard Paul's horse scream. Bits of rock and dust came flying out, showering down on them twenty feet below. Then the helicopter departed, leaving the echo of gunfire bouncing around the mountains.

Paul slowly looked up, shaking fragments of rock from his hat. "Are you all right?" he whispered.

"Y-yes," she said through chattering teeth. "I w-wish people would stop sh-shooting at me." Paul sneezed into his sleeve as the dust settled. "How did you know something was wrong?" she asked.

"It just didn't feel right," he muttered, shifting his weight tentatively on the loose rock. "They were taking their sweet time down there, and the helicopter came from the wrong direction. Castolon is west of us—that one came from due south." He twisted cautiously to peer down into the valley. "I can't see them now."

He moved to the side and kicked a toehold in the crumbling rock. "We're going to have to climb back up. You get in front of me, now," he instructed. Royce edged over and began climbing, Paul hovering beneath. She grasped prickly, unfriendly branches for support as she worked her way up, spitting out dirt. Paul followed, bracing her leg whenever her foot slipped.

Finally, she pulled herself up over the edge of the balcony and looked around. It was splintered and pitted everywhere. There was no sign of the horse.

Paul swung a leg up and rolled onto the rock ledge. Wiping his hands, he looked around the area. Royce turned to him and uttered, "Oh!" at the nasty scratch which bled down his face. He bent to pick up his canteen, miraculously intact. The bedroll Royce had been napping on was riddled with bullet holes.

They heard a sound in the brush and Royce darted behind Paul. Charlie, on horseback, appeared, whistling in surprise. "How on earth did you survive that?"

Paul studied him. "How did you?"

"Me and Baby took cover right away when that whirly-bird came up. That wasn't one of ours!" Charlie said emphatically. "Did you lose Prosperity?" he added.

"He ran," Paul muttered. He splashed a little water from the canteen onto his face, then wiped it off with his sleeve. Directing a cautionary glance at Royce, he picked up the dropped binoculars and scanned the valley. "They're gone. Did you ever reach our contacts?"

"Finally, yeah," Charlie said. "Maybe we can get your horse

back." He started whistling loudly.

The distant sound of helicopter rotors silenced him. The three of them watched tensely as the flying speck advanced from the southwest. The walkie-talkie still on Paul's belt crackled, "Flying Nun to Padre. Come in, Padre."

Paul yanked the unit off his belt. Watching the approaching chopper, he said, "You blew it, guys. They've come and gone, and sent a small arsenal to dismantle the rock we're on. Over."

"Roger, Padre. We have intercepted bird number two. Need a description of vehicle carrying dinner. Over."

"It's a late-model, tan Range Rover. Over," Paul said.

"Roger. Over and out." The chopper veered off in a northerly direction.

Paul picked up his bedroll; Charlie began whistling again. Soon the chestnut horse appeared from the brush, whinnying. Royce was unspeakably relieved to see it alive. Charlie grabbed the reins and Paul ran a comforting hand over the animal, looking for injuries. "Is he hurt?" Royce asked fearfully.

"I don't think so," Paul said tightly. He took off his walkie-talkie and thrust it at Charlie. "I'm done. I've kept my end of the deal. You clowns can take it from here." He started to strap the bedroll onto the saddle, then muttered, "What am I doing? It's ruined." He tossed it to the ground and took to the saddle. Royce grasped his hand to climb up behind him on the skittish horse.

"You might want to keep this—in case we need to advise you," Charlie said, holding out the walkie-talkie.

Paul gathered the reins and leaned forward. "No, thanks." He turned Prosperity's head to find a gradual route down the mountain.

Royce had fancied herself well on the way to becoming an accomplished horsewoman, but this descent jarred her back to reality. Paul urged the horse down any passable route, seemingly regardless of how steep or rocky. Royce leaned far back on the horse's haunches while it slipped and lumbered down, setting off small rockslides below. At one point Prosperity almost sat down, and Royce's feet touched the ground on both sides. Meanwhile, she stared past drop-offs of twenty to fifty feet.

When they finally reached the foot of the mountain, Royce had time to let out her breath before Paul kicked Prosperity to a full gallop. She swallowed hard and held on tight. Soon, she discovered that she had developed no tolerance at all for rocking horses gone berserk: "Paul—please stop," she gasped.

Right away, he slowed to a gentle stop. "Please don't get sick on me, Royce."

"I'm . . . I'm going to be fine . . . just give me a minute," she said, drawing deep breaths. When she felt her insides settling back into proper position, she asked, "Why are we running like this?"

"It stinks. This whole thing smells, and we're getting as far away from it as possible," he said edgily.

"You don't trust Charlie?" she asked.

"I don't trust anybody but you," he stated.

"Well then, I've got to have something to eat. I'm about to die," she moaned.

"There are a couple of packages in the bag on your right," he said, nodding. Royce unstrapped the saddlebag and brought out dried apple rings. As she began eating, Paul started Prosperity walking.

"Where will we go?" Royce asked.

"To the lodge. I have to return this horse, then I'll call Sheriff Potts."

"Do you think Charlie really contacted him?" she wondered.

"We'll find out," Paul said.

They heard the familiar whirring of a helicopter as it topped the mountains behind them. Paul quickly looked around for cover, but there was not so much as a tall cactus in sight. So he held the horse still and watched. The helicopter approached, then passed directly over them without slowing. As it went on north, Paul mused, "Looks like they're keeping an eye on us."

"'They' who?" Royce asked.

"I don't know," he admitted with a sour laugh.

She reached around to feed him an apple ring. He took it in his mouth and she apologized, "My hands are dirty."

"The inside of my mouth is coated with dust. So?" he said. She promptly handed the canteen up to him.

When Royce had finished her snack, Paul prompted the horse to a lope. In the scant hour it took to reach the lodge facilities, they saw no other suspicious vehicles—just campers and trailers. Paul rode straight up to the stable, where he dismounted and helped Royce down. Billy came out to meet them and Royce smiled at him.

Not seeing that, Paul told him, "This is Prosperity. His owner will be coming for him soon. Clean him up for me, please." He handed the reins to Billy and took Royce by the arm. As they walked to the lodge office, Royce discreetly pointed out the boarded-up window of their room. Paul nodded.

They entered the office and Paul told the clerk, "I'm John P. George. My wife and I were on our way back from an overnight camping trip when some folks told us our room had been ransacked or something."

In a gravelly smoker's voice, the woman began, "Oh, Mr. George! We've been looking for you. I am so sorry! The rangers are investigating, but—we've got your things in the back room here, and you're welcome to stay as long as you want—in another room, of course, at no charge—"

Paul held up his hand to interrupt her apologies and said, "If you'd just get our bags and show us to a new room, that would be fine. We have to leave today, anyway."

The clerk brought out their duffel bags and gave them the key to another first-floor room. "It's the last one on the west end. Enjoy your stay," she added reflexively.

"Thanks." Paul took the bags, mustering a smile, and hustled Royce out of the office. It was late afternoon, sporting a last hurrah of golden sunshine before the sun retreated behind the mountains. Paul opened up their room and glanced around it, then shut and locked the door. He dropped his hat onto the table and wiped his face with his sleeve. Royce unzipped her duffel bag and found her new hat—riddled with bullet holes. She gazed at it despondently.

"Well," he said, and she raised her face, "you can shower first while I see if I can find a soft-drink machine."

"Great," she laughed weakly. "I'll try not to use all the hot water. Oh—" She dug in her pocket and found the rest of the money, which she handed over to him.

He left, taking the key. Royce took a long-sleeved, long-tailed shirt with her to the bathroom and gratefully washed off a pound and a half of dirt. In a supreme gesture of consideration, she used only fifteen minutes of water and one towel for both her hair and body.

She emerged from the bathroom dressed in the shirt, her hair wrapped in the towel, and carrying her dirty clothes. Paul looked up from the table, where he had deposited two canned drinks and various snacks. "We might not have a chance to eat dinner till later," he explained. Royce assented, dropping her dirty clothes on the floor and shaking her hair from the towel while Paul watched. Then, clearing his throat, he said, "Guess I'll get cleaned up." He took fresh underwear and his shaving kit with him to the bathroom, and shut the door.

As she listened to the shower run, Royce sat on the bed, working tangles out of her long, damp hair. She ignored the food on the table, having a higher priority in mind. "Got you now, Mr. Arrendondo," she murmured, smiling. She began humming Mozart's *Eine Kleine Nachtmusik*.

A while later the door to the bathroom opened and Royce looked up. Paul, freshly shaven, came out in his t-shirt and boxer shorts. He dropped his dirty clothes on Royce's, and tossed his shaving kit in his duffel bag. "We need to. . . ." He swallowed as Royce stretched out on the bed. "We need to get dressed . . . and . . . get going," he said, weakening by the second.

Royce smiled, having no intention of going anywhere just

yet. "Right now?" she pleaded softly.

Paul came to stand beside the bed. "Yes. Absolutely. Right now," he insisted.

Royce reached up to him and he sank to his knees to kiss her. She lay back and he crawled on to the bed without leaving her lips. Droplets from his wet hair fell on her face. Royce combed his hair back with her fingers so she could kiss all over his face, even the scratch on his cheek. Then she shifted her hips underneath him.

"Oh, no, Royce—I can't," he moaned, trying to raise up.

She pulled him back down, reaching under his t-shirt. "Seems to me you can," she whispered.

"No—I mean—" he had difficulty talking around her lips. "It's not—fair to you. We're not in the clear yet, and we're not— we're not—"

"Married?" she said coolly, pulling back. "Is that the Baptist preacher talking again?"

The cut went deep. She saw it in his eyes, and immediately regretted it. "Some things I didn't leave behind, Royce. Some things are still wrong, regardless of what I want." She realized it was not a Pharisee talking. It was a loving, principled human being.

Paul got up from the bed and put on his jeans. She sat up. "What are you doing?" she asked in alarm.

He jammed his feet into his boots and said, "I'm just going to walk around outside to cool off. When I come back, I want you dressed." He smiled tightly and left, slamming the door. He neglected to lock it or take the key.

Tearfully, Royce fished out a clean pair of jeans. She pulled them on and plopped down on the bed with her socks, but was crying so hard she could not see to put them on.

The door opened. She dried her eyes and looked up expectantly. But instead of Paul, there were two men in suits standing in the doorway. Royce stiffened.

One held up an ID and said, "DEA, Ms. Lindel. Please come

with us." She could not say whether they were the same two from Del Rio or not.

"Where's Paul?" she asked in a low voice.

"He's with us," he stated.

"He said he was coming back," she argued.

"He's with us, and you need to come too," he said with an authoritative tone that enraged her.

"Well," Royce said, outwardly calm, "since you came in without bothering to knock, you can see that I'm not dressed yet. So you can just wait outside until I finish getting my clothes on." With a glance at each other, the two agents withdrew and shut the door.

Royce crossed the room and quietly locked the door, then ran to the window on the other side of the room and opened it. The rear of this unit backed up to the very foot of the mountains. Barefoot, Royce climbed out the window and gingerly picked her way on tender feet toward the treacherous mountains.

She heard a door slam nearby and jumped. Then she recognized Margaret with her Pasadena Baptist group, loading up a travel trailer. And Royce got a better idea. Casting wary glances, she approached the group. "Margaret," she said quietly, and the woman turned.

"Why, hello, dear. How are you?" Margaret was a cute, chubby forty-five-year-old who like chunky jewelry and big blouses. She was a habitual smiler, even when worried.

Royce took her arm and drew her behind the trailer as she saw the two agents come running around the end of the motel. "Margaret, I'm in real trouble. Will you help me?"

"Why, of course. What is it?" Margaret asked, smiling in reassurance.

"My husband has disappeared. He was doing some undercover work for the DEA, but he suspected one of them was a plant, and the only person he trusted was the sheriff in Alpine. Will you please take me—quietly—to Sheriff Potts?" Royce pleaded.

"We certainly will," Margaret said firmly. "Get in." She opened the trailer door and Royce slipped inside. Gratefully, she curled up on a seat of the plush motor home.

A few minutes later the door opened and Royce sat up. A fiftyish fellow in comfortable vacation clothes and bifocals came in. He extended his hand to Royce. "I'm Margaret's husband Bob," he said, "and we're taking you to Alpine."

"I'm Royce Lindel, and I can't thank you enough," she said, squeezing his hand.

"You ought to know that we're in a caravan. We've got a group of six RVs here. Everybody had to know why we changed travel plans, but they're all sworn to secrecy. As far as anybody else knows, we're just Good Sams traveling the highways," Bob said.

"Fine," Royce smiled, for some reason recalling Marla's rendition of "Born to Be Wild."

Margaret came in and gave her a thumbs-up signal. Then Bob sat in the driver's seat with Margaret in the captain's chair beside him, and he turned the key in the ignition. The caravan started off.

"Wild Bob rides again!" he cackled. "Ladies, you just sit back and enjoy the ride with Bob at the wheel," he said, glad of a new audience. He led off the impromptu performance with his best material: an imitation of a television evangelist named Brother Bob Tiltin'.

Taking one hand off the wheel, he pushed his hair up in front to resemble a pompadour and took up an invisible microphone. Screwing up his face, he began, "Brothers and sisters I say unto *thee*, send me thy money and thou shalt be blessed! Or at least, *I* shall be blessed! I bind those demons of doubt that prevent you from sending every last dime you have to keep me on the air so I can continue to ask, nay, *plead* with you for money! So you send me money and your prayers still go unanswered? Let me encourage you with these words: It's your fault! You don't have enough faith! You haven't sent enough money!

And you know what? You'll *never* be able to send enough because I can't get enough! That's the good news I'm here to preach to you today! AMEN!"

Margaret laughed until the tears ran down her face, which unleashed renditions of Elmer Fudd, George Burns, and an unexpectedly straightforward Elvis. As he sang "Love Me Tender" in a smooth baritone, Royce stopped laughing and listened. He sounded really good!

Margaret listened also, with a look of rapture. Royce looked from one to the other. They were not young, beautiful, cool, or rich. But they were as much in love as she and Paul. Margaret once had been twenty-five. Someday Royce would be her age. Would she and Paul still be together, still in love?

Suddenly Royce saw that this possibility was what Paul had been trying to protect, in tearing himself from the bed. Marriage was when two people who loved each other swore to prove it through the toughest tests—through disasters, misunderstandings, changing feelings, and time. Once you had laid that foundation of trust, then you were free to explore all the rooms of love.

Royce put her head down. She could see the fitness of that. Look what happened to Marla, who threw herself at every interested man until her body was nothing more than a commodity. It had made her a bitter, manipulative person bankrupt in self-respect, regardless of her job title.

Paul was divorced, though he had not wanted to be. He had taken both barrels of the pain and betrayal, losing his vocation as well as his wife. He had been through the worst that marriage had to offer and still considered it a prerequisite. Was he that naïve? Or that wise?

"Are you all right?" Margaret asked, looking back at her.

"Her name is Royce, sweetheart," Bob advised her.

"Yes." Royce lifted her head. "I was just worried about Paul." She stared out the window as they rolled up Highway 118. What was happening to him right now?

"Well, we've got everybody in the caravan saying a prayer for your husband," Bob said, looking into the rear-view mirror.

"Thank you," Royce blushed. Would God hear their prayers anyway?

"Poor thing, you ran out without even your shoes," tsked Margaret. "Are you hungry?"

"I'm famished," Royce admitted.

"Well!" Margaret got up and opened the freezer unit of the refrigerator. "I've got a little casserole in here, if you're interested."

"That sounds heavenly," Royce agreed. Margaret took out a ceramic dish and put it in the microwave. "These motor homes have everything, don't they?" Royce marveled.

"It's our little home away from home," Margaret said happily. The microwave timer dinged and she pulled out the steaming bowl, which she set on the table in front of Royce, with a napkin and fork. "What would you like to drink?"

"Water. Anything. Whatever you have," Royce said gratefully, placing the napkin on her lap and taking up the fork. Margaret filled a plastic cup with ice water and Royce thanked her again.

She inhaled the casserole, made of hamburger, cheese and macaroni. Back home she would have turned up her nose in disdain at such a dish, but here she honestly admitted, "That was great," as she put her dishes in the little sink.

"We usually like to eat out when we travel, but it comes in handy to have a little something made up," Margaret said in gratification.

At the mention of travel, Royce thought of Paul's great-grandfather—the preacher named Paul who traveled from town to town, who was shot to death at thirty-five. . . . Royce sat weakly at the table.

Studying her, Margaret began to wonder, "My, that must be dangerous, doing undercover work, and in Big Bend of all places! Who would have thought? How in the world did you get mixed up in that?"

"Now, Meg, don't ask questions. She can't talk about that. Why don't you show her pictures of Jodie and the boys?" Bob interrupted.

"Oh, goodness; I guess I am too curious. Yes, Jodie." Margaret picked up her fat purse and took out wallet photos which she passed to Royce. They showed a smiling young woman with two small boys. "That's our daughter Jodie with her sons Michael and Kevin. Michael is six, and Kevin is four. Larry, our son-in-law, was killed in a car accident last year."

With the question of Paul's fate shrouding her thoughts, Royce burst into tears. Bob exclaimed, "Meg!" in exasperation.

"Oh, dear! Don't cry—they're not alone. Jodie is engaged to a wonderful man and the boys adore him," Margaret hastened to add.

"Don't mind me. I'm just stressed out," Royce muttered, chagrined. She took the tissue Margaret offered.

"Alpine coming up," Bob noted.

Royce looked out the window. "Already?" It was growing dark.

"How do we get to the county courthouse? Isn't that where the sheriff's office is?" Bob asked.

"Yes," Royce said, leaning over his chair. "You just go up this highway and turn—here." She pointed. Bob turned the corner and pulled up before the white stone edifice. "Thank you so much. I can't thank you enough," she said, pumping his hand.

"Wait." Bob reached into his back pocket and Margaret her purse. "You might need a spot." He held out a twenty-dollar bill.

"No. You are too kind," she said, holding up her hands. "All I needed was to get here. No." She adamantly refused the money he offered.

"Wait," Margaret said, writing, as Royce opened the door. Then Margaret handed her a postcard, stamped, with her and Bob's names and address on it. "We want to know that your husband is all right. When you find him, please jot us a note that he's all right and drop this in a mailbox."

"Yes. I'll do that. I promise," Royce said, taking the post-card. Margaret leaned forward and Royce embraced her. "Goodbye," Royce whispered, and backed out of the motor home.

She paused in the night before the jailhouse door to wave. Bob and Margaret pulled away, and the other RVs in the caravan followed, flashing their headlights to Royce as they passed.

She turned and ran into the building. The one deputy on duty looked up from his desk. "I'm Royce Lindel. I need to see Sheriff Potts right away!" she said urgently.

"He was called away on an emergency. What's your problem?" the deputy asked.

"Look, he should have gotten a message from a DEA agent in Big Bend named Cherub. He and Paul Arrendondo were supposed to intercept this drug shipment, but the DEA botched it, and Paul suspected there was a snake in the agency, but they took him and he disappeared and I need the sheriff's help!" she said breathlessly.

"Okay, miss, calm down." He was a deputy Royce had not seen before, and he looked plainly skeptical. "Go on home and I'll raise the sheriff in the morning."

"I can't go home! I don't have a home! I even left without my shoes and socks! They tried to take me, too!" she exclaimed wildly.

"Okay, okay." He came around the desk and took her arm. "You can stay here tonight so 'they' won't get you." He led her to the same cell she had occupied before.

"You'll call the sheriff right away, won't you?" she pleaded as he opened the door and nudged her inside.

"Sure, sure." He shut the door and locked it.

"Don't talk to the DEA. Just the sheriff," she reminded him.

"Sure," he said, settling behind the desk.

Royce gripped the bars. *He doesn't believe me.* "Paul could die if he doesn't get the sheriff's help right away!" she cried.

"The sheriff was called down to Big Bend. He's already

down there, so just chill out," he told her.

Surprised and grateful, Royce sank down onto the bunk. She looked at the postcard she clutched, which pictured a view of the Chisos Mountains. Staring at the photo, she lay down on the thin mattress and sank into sleep.

17

❖

"Well, well. Look who we have here." Hearing the voice, Royce opened her eyes. She saw hazy streams of sunlight splashed on the concrete floor of the cell. Then she turned her head and lifted up to look straight into the iron-gray eyes of Rick. She sprang up, hitting her head on the upper bunk. "You led us on quite a chase," he added, motioning to the deputy to unlock the cell door. Royce backed up against the cell wall, rubbing her head. She saw no way to escape this time.

The outer jailhouse door opened. In rushed Paul, wearing the same t-shirt and jeans he had on when Royce had last seen him. He looked exhausted and slightly wild-eyed. When he saw Royce, he dropped to his knees and uttered, "Thank You, God." Silently, but sincerely, Royce echoed it. Then he jumped up and she met him at the bars. He held her face and kissed her through the bars while the smiling deputy opened the door nearby. Sheriff Potts came in from outside.

Then Paul stood back and demanded, "What happened to

you? I searched that blasted mountain all night long! I railed at God all night that I couldn't find you! How did you get here?"

Bewildered, Royce stayed in the cell and looked from Paul to Rick and back again. "They . . . told me they had you. They came for me too," she murmured.

"She was acting on your suspicions," Rick said with a slightly superior air to Paul.

Now Paul looked sheepish. "Ah, Royce, there was no snake. A half-dozen contacts told Rick you were with me. And they intercepted the Range Rover with the coke, the chopper that had delivered it, and the chopper that fired on us. They arrested a dozen people, including the drug boss's son, who ran the operation. It was a good bust," he said, glancing humbly at Rick.

"But . . . why did they come for us?" she asked, venturing out of the cell.

"To take us home!" Paul shrugged with a little laugh. He gathered her up and rocked her, then shook her. "I could spank you for giving me all that grief!"

"Fun and games later. Ms. Lindel, I am very interested to know how you made it here," Rick said.

"Some friends brought me in their mobile home," she said, looking down at the postcard she still held. She pulled away from Paul and picked up a pen from the deputy's desk. She wrote on the postcard, "Paul found safe. We are going home today. Love, Royce." Then she walked over to the mailbox in the lobby and dropped the card inside. The men exchanged glances. Royce resumed her position in Paul's arms and he kissed her head.

"I suppose you'll be demanding breakfast before we fly you home," Rick said grumpily.

"They won't let me in without shoes," she said, pointing to her bare feet. "Have you got my things?"

Royce's duffel bag was brought in. While she put on her shoes and socks and brushed her hair, Rick radioed the searchers at Big Bend that she had been found. When he got off the radio, he told her, "The park rangers have a request of you."

"'Don't come back'?" she asked sardonically.

"Tell them not to worry. Next time we come back, I won't be walking out," Paul said, eyes steadily on Royce. Rick scratched his eyebrow.

He and Sheriff Potts accompanied Paul and Royce to a roadside restaurant, where Rick told her how they had found Paul outside the motel room, then sent two agents in for her. When she locked the door and disappeared, they assumed she had run up into the mountains. Alerting Paul and the rangers, they had searched for her on horseback and with helicopters, calling down Sheriff Potts to assist.

"When we did not find you we were afraid that a member of the cartel had escaped our net and reached you first. By morning, we had to assume you were dead. Then Sheriff Potts' deputy called him about a crazy female in his jail. There you were, having rolled into town in an RV!" Rick said.

"The agents didn't say anything about taking us home," Royce said defensively. "They just said, 'Come with us.' When I asked where Paul was, they said, 'He's with us.' I thought they were going to kill us. Why didn't you come back?" she asked Paul.

He looked away from her wounded eyes. "I was sore. But it was brought to my attention that I had no right to punish you for a situation I helped create. I had all night to think about it."

Rick added, "Actually, you were an asset, Ms. Lindel. We were having trouble pinpointing the front man at the lodge, mainly because we were looking for a man. But when you and Paul checked into the second room, she got right on the phone to the cartel. We were listening."

"The front man—!" Paul exclaimed, striking his forehead.

"—Was a woman? The reservations clerk?" asked Royce.

"That's right," said Rick.

Paul put his head in both hands. "I forgot. I forgot all about the front man at the lodge. If I had remembered about him—

her—I never would have brought Royce. I'm sure the clerk recognized her the first time we checked in. They just waited until the dead of night to send someone to our room to blow us away." Shaking his head, he took solace in another cup of coffee.

Rick told Paul, "There's a nice little finder's fee coming for your part in the bust. You should get a check in about six weeks. Ought to be enough to buy yourself that ranch you always talk about."

Up until then Royce had been devouring some warm, gooey blueberry pancakes. At once her appetite vanished. Paul drained his coffee cup and said, "Nah, I don't think so. I've been offered a position in Dallas, and I think I'll take it. Can you get used to living there?" he asked Royce.

She thought of the airport, the hotel, the beautiful new symphony center, and her heart skipped a beat. "Yes! But—what about your dream—and how much you hate the city—?"

"Aw, that's just talk. I can go help Buddy's dad whenever I want to play rancher. That's always good for a reality check. I was burned out at the center, sure, but I can live anywhere. Even—New York City," he gulped.

Royce hugged him joyfully. "I'm tired of New York. I like the sunshine in Dallas," she said.

"Well, now, don't that just make your heart swell," the sheriff said sincerely.

Paul and Royce gazed at each other and Rick said, "Time to put you two on a plane and get you out of my hair—what I've got left of it," he muttered, tentatively feeling his head.

So Paul and Royce flew straight from the airstrip in Alpine to Dallas on a cushy Piper Navaho the DEA had confiscated from drug runners. The flight took less than two hours, and Paul slept soundly the whole time.

When they arrived at Dallas/Fort Worth International, Royce had some difficulty waking him. She did not like shaking him, but when she tried kissing him, he just responded in his sleep. Finally she pulled him up by an arm. That woke him.

Bemused at her roughhousing, he reached up automatically for their bags. It took him a moment to realize that there was no compartment where he was reaching.

Upon leaving the terminal, he had to think for a while about where he had parked the car. They found it, though, and as he loaded the bags into the trunk he groaned, "Can you drive us back to the apartment, Royce?"

She felt a momentary panic. "I—don't have a driver's license, Paul. I never drove in New York."

"Oh?" He squinted at her and shook his head vigorously to wake up. "Okay. You'll get one. Soon." He unlocked her door and then went around to the driver's side.

As they drove out to the freeway, she turned on the radio to help him stay awake. Automatically, she turned to the classical music station. He winced. "Spare me," he grumbled, changing to a country station.

"You might like it, if you tried listening to it. Have you ever heard Aaron Copland's *Rodeo*?" she asked brightly.

"You Yankees!" he muttered in exasperation, watching traffic. "It's ROdeo, Royce; not roDAYoh. You say it like that in these parts and you'll get laughed out of town! Shee!" He grinned sleepily at her and she laughed, hugging his arm.

Paul got them safely to his apartment complex and paused to check his mail. Royce made a concerted effort not to look over his shoulder until he said, "Look at this." He dropped their bags to open an envelope.

Royce leaned on his arm. "What is it?"

"A wedding invitation from Buddy and Renetta!" he laughed. "They're getting married at his dad's ranch in less than two weeks." He looked at the envelope again. "It's addressed to both of us."

"I *knew* I hadn't heard the last from her!" Royce exclaimed. "But—how did she know I'd be with you?"

"I asked her for your phone number, remember?" Paul said slyly. "She's sharp; she knew you'd come."

"'On Saturday, June 4, at the Grayson Homestead,'" Royce read from the invitation. "Will I get to see Buster, too?" she asked.

"You'll get to ride Buster, if you want to," Paul replied, kissing her forehead.

"Maybe I'll just say hello to him," she reconsidered. Paul shook his head wryly as he picked up their bags. Vague apprehensions came over Royce, and she asked, "Paul, does the Ferrings' ranch have . . . indoor plumbing?"

"Indoor plumbing?" he hooted. "Royce, have you ever seen Southfork Ranch on *Dallas*?"

"Yes," she said.

"Well, that's a shack compared to the Grayson Homestead. It's been featured in one of those glossy East Coast magazines— I forget which one," he said.

"No kidding?" she exclaimed.

"No kidding. Wait till you see the Rose Room. . . . But I'd have to produce a marriage license before Walt Ferring would let me show you *that* room," he considered, dragging their bags up the steps.

As he unlocked the door, he added, "I bet we beat them." Royce looked around the apartment and tensed. Something was different. Her purse was on the bar in the kitchen. She knew she had left it in the bedroom.

"I hope you don't want a big church wedding," Paul said apprehensively.

"No. Oh, no," she conceded, looking around. "But we should be married by a Baptist preacher."

"No way, Royce," he laughed bitterly, tossing the bags down. "There is no Southern Baptist preacher in the country who will perform a ceremony for a divorced ex-pastor!"

"I know of one," she said smugly, going to the bar and opening her purse. She took out a business card and handed it to him. "Dr. Forrest Oldham. He's in Arlington."

Paul took the card, his jaw dropping. "Forrest Oldham? *The* Forrest Oldham?"

"We're like this," she said, twining her fingers. She glanced into the bedroom. The guitar case was leaning up against the unmade bed. Her suitcases had been rifled and her dirty clothes were hanging half out of the hamper.

"I guess I'll call him," Paul said dazedly, moving toward the telephone.

"Paul," she said suddenly, and he looked up. "Do you think you'll ever—return to the ministry?" she asked.

He studied the wall beyond her for about twenty seconds, then he said, "No. That door is shut and I can't go back. I have to go forward . . . 'forgetting what is past. . . .'" He lowered his eyes. "What on earth—?" he said, picking up a piece of paper from the bar. He read silently for a moment, then threw back his head and laughed.

He was laughing so hard that he could not answer her eager query of "What?" so he just handed her the paper. Royce read:

Thurs. a.m.
Paul,

When I didn't hear from you yesterday I came by your apartment. The manager let me in when I told him I was your wife. I see that you have not been alone, and while I am glad that you found someone to spend time with, I am a little disappointed in that you used to preach so much about self-discipline and self-denial. I am sorry you are no longer the person you were, or perhaps you did not believe what you were saying at the time. However, I am grateful for the few special years we had together. I will love you always.

Kris

Speechless, Royce looked up and Paul wiped tears from his eyes. He took the note from her fingers and crumpled it. "Forgetting what is past," he repeated vehemently as he picked up the tele-

phone and dialed the number on the card. "Hello. Ah, this is—
Paul Arrendondo, calling for Dr. Oldham. Is he . . . ? Yes, I'll
hold."

Royce pensively went to the bedroom to stand over her
rifled suitcases. From there she heard Paul saying, "Dr. Oldham,
my name is Paul Arrendondo. We've never met, but somehow
you know my fiancée, Royce Lindel. . . . Yes, that's her. That's
right. Well—"

Listening as he talked, Royce turned and opened his dresser
drawer. She pulled out the old photograph of the handsome man
on horseback with the Bible under his arm, and set it out on the
dresser. Looking at it stirred up deep, tender feelings that she
knew must also have belonged to Roseanne. "Padre, you passed
down some good genes," she whispered.

She could have sworn he smiled.

PART THREE

18

---❖---

Paul and Royce drove silently on I-30 out of Arlington, coming back from their first premarital counseling session with Dr. Oldham. Today was Wednesday, June 1—six days after their return from Big Bend and three days before Buddy and Renetta's wedding. Paul drove a little less patiently than usual; Royce stared at her pink pumps.

At length she remarked, "Dr. Oldham thinks we should wait."

"Dr. Oldham doesn't have to sleep on the couch with you in the next room," Paul replied vehemently.

"I wish you hadn't gotten short with him," she said.

"I didn't like what he was getting at," Paul answered, applying the brakes as a car changed lanes in front of them without warning.

"I didn't understand what he meant about being 'unequally yoked,'" she confessed.

"Look, Royce, Dr. Oldham is a sincere, dedicated man, but—he's got the same blueprint for every situation, and it just doesn't work that way in real life. I know God gave you to me—He used you to bring me to my knees for the first time since I left the pastorate. He wouldn't have bothered to send you all the way from New York just to leave you hanging. There are any number of ways He could bring you into the fold."

"Of course," she agreed. "There's Buddhism, and Hinduism, and—"

"No, Royce," Paul interrupted. "That's not what I mean. There's only one Person who could reconcile you to God, and only one Person who was resurrected to prove it."

"I'm willing to convert to your religion, Paul. Why wouldn't you let Dr. Oldham tell me what I needed to do?" she asked.

"Because it's not a matter of following a set of rules; it's meeting Someone. And you don't always do that through four Basic Steps," he said, agitated.

"I don't understand you," she said unhappily.

"I know." He reached over to take her hand. "Don't worry about it for now. Listen, why do we have to wait for Dr. Oldham to work us into his schedule to get married? We've got all the paperwork, and it's only good for ten days. Let's just go to a justice of the peace—please, Royce?"

"I don't want you to repudiate your religion to marry me," she said, blinking rapidly.

"I'm not repudiating anything! I'm just trying to save my sanity!" His voice rose and Royce began dropping tears. "Oh, for pete's sake. I'm sorry. Don't cry, Royce. We'll talk about it later," he sighed. She nodded, digging in her purse for a tissue.

They were silent a few minutes as Royce searched for something positive to talk about. "It was nice of Rick to lend you this car." It was a Mercedes 560 SL which had been confiscated from a drug dealer now in prison.

"Yeah. Since I quit at the center, I couldn't use the Nissan anymore. . . . It was for the best. That way they can hire a new director who can bring in his own assistant," Paul reflected.

"And you'll be starting in Dallas on the twentieth!" Royce

said, holding his arm. She looked in approval at his new haircut, which allowed his hair to hang naturally without getting in his eyes. "Thank you for trying a new stylist. Your hair looks great," she added.

He glanced in the rear-view mirror. "I don't like barbers patting me," he muttered.

"Stylists," she corrected.

"Whatever," he said. After a moment he mused, "It's in downtown Dallas."

"What?" she asked.

"Ville Du Havre Hospital. I'll be driving to downtown Dallas every day," he grumbled.

"That narcotics detective said the traffic's not so bad when you learn the ropes—he said never drive the speed limit, signal, or stop at yellow lights and you'll do fine. It was nice of him to show us around. He loves the work," she noted, smiling.

"Uh-huh. He just arrests 'em—he doesn't have to help them piece their lives back together," Paul mused.

Moving right along, she enthused, "I can't wait to set up housekeeping! And I'm sure to find a job right away."

"A deposit, and first and last month's rent . . . you'll need a car . . . *I'll* need a car. . . ." He shook his head. "I hope Rick gets that check to us soon."

Royce snuggled against his arm. "I'm so excited. I can't wait to see Buddy and Renetta again."

Paul stopped at a red light and turned to kiss her on the mouth. "Why don't we tell them how much fun it is being married? There's a JP down this street. All we have to do is walk in. Please, Royce?" He kissed her again. "There's a bed at the Ferrings' that's big enough to swim in." He tilted her head back to kiss her again and the driver behind them honked as the light changed.

Royce glanced back and capitulated, "All right."

"Yes!" he exclaimed, turning down the street.

"Do you have the license?" she asked.

He slapped his coat pocket and moaned. "Oh, no. It's back at the apartment. But if we hurry—" He glanced at his watch.

Royce sat back and smiled. "We're supposed to go to San Angelo tomorrow," she reminded him.

"I know, I know," he said, focused on weaving in and out of slow-moving traffic.

"It was *so nice* of the Ferrings to invite my parents down from New York to meet you!" she sighed. "My dad will love you, and—"

Paul suddenly uttered an expletive. Royce looked back at the flashing red and blue lights of the patrol car behind them. Exhaling in frustration, Paul turned down a side street and pulled over. He rolled down his window and stroked his forehead.

The patrol car pulled up behind them and stopped. Paul stared glumly down at his watch as the seconds ticked by into minutes. Royce asked, "What's taking him so long?"

"He's running a check on the plates—" Paul began, then looked at the rear-view mirror in alarm. The officers had jumped out of their car with guns drawn.

"Come out with your hands up!" one policeman shouted.

Paul closed his eyes briefly. "Do what he says, and move slowly, Royce," he said as he opened the door. They emerged from either side of the car. Paul automatically turned and put his hands on the hood.

One officer frisked Paul and took out his wallet. "Call Rick Canzoneri of the DEA. His number's in my wallet. He'll tell you about the car," Paul said.

As the other officer turned Royce toward the car, her heel caught in a crack in the pavement and she fell against him. "Take it easy on the lady, man!" Paul said angrily. The officer behind him shoved him against the car and handcuffed his hands behind his back. "Will you just call Rick?" Paul insisted. He was placed in the back seat of the patrol car. Royce was cuffed and led limping to sit beside him.

While the officers searched the Mercedes and radioed in, Paul stared out the side window. Royce nudged him with her shoulder. When he turned around, he saw her smiling. "We won't make it before they close today," he informed her.

"So we'll stop at the first JP we find when we get back from San Angelo," she whispered. She leaned over and kissed him softly.

"Oh, Royce, you'll have to lock the door to keep me out tonight," he moaned.

"No, I won't. I understand why you want our honeymoon to be special. Since both of us want it to be that way, it will be," she promised.

"I love you so," he murmured. He moved to kiss her, but stopped as one officer opened Royce's door.

The policeman took off her cuffs and gave her a hand out of the car. "Sorry about that," he apologized.

"No harm done," Royce replied in spite of Paul's glowering.

The officer who released Paul was not so conciliatory. "You can go. But you had better slow down," he warned.

"There's no rush, now," Paul said civilly, taking his wallet back. As the patrol car departed, Paul asked Royce, "Well, since we can't go get married, where would you like to go eat?"

"Oh, let's see. Know any good Chinese restaurants?" she asked.

"Sure." He opened her door for her. "How's your foot?"

"It's okay. I just turned the ankle a little," she said, rubbing it. He looked down at her legs before closing the door.

As he sat and started the engine, she resumed, "Like I was saying, I'm so excited that you'll get to meet my parents."

"Yeah," he said unenthusiastically.

"You haven't told me anything about your parents. Where do they live?" she asked.

After a few seconds Paul replied, "In Fort Worth."

"Here?" she exclaimed, and he nodded. "Your parents live here and you haven't taken me to meet them yet?"

"After we're married, I'll take you," he said stonily.

"Paul," Royce protested, hurt, "why? Why not sooner? Are you ashamed of me?"

"Hardly." He glanced at her with a dry laugh.

"Then why won't you take me to see them?" she asked.

He pulled up to a stop sign. "Because . . . oh, Royce, don't give me those wounded eyes. I hate that."

"Well then, just tell me why I can't meet them!" Royce exclaimed.

"Because . . . because. . . " he hedged. Royce waited, bewildered. "All right; I'll take you," he groaned. He turned the car down the street in the other direction.

"Good. Now?" she asked, and he nodded. "Shouldn't we call first?"

"They don't have a telephone," he answered.

Royce did not ask any more questions, but sat patiently as Paul first stopped at a drive-through teller machine, then turned past a shopping center into an old part of town.

Royce watched as they passed dilapidated storefronts and broken-down cars. Then he turned onto a narrow, gutted street lined with large old trees and sagging shotgun houses. He pulled up into the front yard of one of these houses, where the grass refused to grow. He got out and helped her from the car.

Looking across the street, he called to a young boy: "¡Vamos, Luis!"

The boy came running. "¿Qué pasa, Paul?"

Gesturing to the car, Paul told him, "Vigile el caro. Arita regreso. Voy a llevar la señorita a dentro." He reached into his wallet and handed Luis a five-dollar bill.

The newly enriched boy answered, "Si, Paul. No es ningún problema."

Paul took Royce's hand and led her up crumbling front steps to a torn, rusted screen door. Opening the door, he called, "Mama! Mama, it's Paul." Royce looked around the dark, shabbily furnished front room with the stained and torn wallpaper. A large cloth hanging depicting the Last Supper hung tiredly over the couch.

"Paul?" A woman came from the rear of the house. "Paul!" She threw open her arms and hugged him around the neck. She was a plump, lovely woman with sad eyes, wearing an old print dress and apron. Her dark brown, gray-streaked hair was pulled up in a bun on the top of her head. She had to reach up to hold her son's neck.

"Mama," Paul said, putting an arm around Royce, "I want you to meet someone. This is Royce. We're getting married."

The woman turned her large, dark eyes on Royce. "Oh, Paul! She's beautiful! What is her name?"

"Royce," Paul repeated loudly, close to her ear. "We're getting married."

"Married?" his mother exclaimed, taking Royce by both hands. "We must have a dinner for you—"

"No, Mama," Paul shook his head firmly. "We're going to do it simple. No dinner." As he reached into his back pocket, he asked, "How's Papa?"

"Papa?" she asked, and Paul nodded. "Oh, not too good. He's not been himself lately, Paul. Don't mind what he says to you," she warned. Paul gave a slight nod, taking fifty dollars from his wallet and pressing it into her hand. Then he put his finger to his lips and she nodded, sealing her lips with a finger as she put the cash in her apron pocket.

"Come inside," she urged them, pushing Paul and Royce past the front room to a small, dingy kitchen where they sat at an old Formica table. Royce looked at the curling, pitted vinyl on the floor.

"Papa!" His mother called into the one back room. "Papa! Paul is here." She then withdrew to the tiny gas range.

A man came shuffling out of the back room and Paul stood. Royce stood as well. The man paused at the doorway to peer up at Paul. At first Royce thought his father to be very elderly because of the way he walked, and how shriveled he appeared.

But his hair was still dark and his eye steady as he gazed at his son, who was looking at the floor. Paul wholly resembled his mother; he looked nothing like his father.

"You got a church yet, boy?" The hostility in his tone made Royce cringe.

Still looking down, Paul replied, "No, sir. I'm not in the ministry anymore, Papa. I—"

"All I ever wanted was for you to be a preacher. That's all I ever worked for and prayed for," his father stated.

"I tried, Papa. I gave it my best shot. It just wasn't meant to be," Paul said.

The father shook his head and waved away the excuses. Then his eye landed on Royce. She tried to smile but her face felt paralyzed. "Who is that?" he rasped.

"This is Royce, Papa." Paul took her hand protectively. "We're going to be married."

"You're *what?*" the man uttered. "You can't marry her! You're already married. Where's your wife?"

"Kris left me to marry another man, Papa; you know that," Paul said. "I've been divorced for five years."

"Not in God's eyes!" the father declared, pointing in Paul's face. "You're committing adultery to marry another woman!"

"That's not true!" Paul objected, his voice stronger.

"Don't you raise your voice at me, boy! And don't you bring any tramps to this house!" He turned his back, then swung to point at Paul's mother. "You didn't take any money from him, did you?" he asked loudly.

"Papa!" she said in an injured tone.

"Don't you take any money from him. We don't want anything from you, boy!" He shuffled back into the other room.

Paul stood looking at the floor, then gripped Royce's hand, which already ached from being squeezed, and headed for the front door. His mother followed them to the door. "You come back when he's feeling better, and talk to him again. He'll be feeling better later," she said encouragingly.

"Yes, Mama," Paul said, bending to kiss her cheek. "Later."

Paul took Royce outside, where the boy was fending off a group of interested young men from the car. As soon as Paul appeared, they dispersed. "*Gracias*, Luis," he said.

The boy replied, "*De nada*." Then he looked at Royce, waved his hand back and forth, and remarked, "*¡Caliente!*"

Paul rebuked him, "*¡A callar!*" Luis laughed and ran off.

Paul and Royce got in the car and drove off in silence. After a few moments Royce said, "Stop the car, Paul." He pulled over and looked at her attentively. It was the same look she had encountered that first day at the lodge, when he thought he would never see her again.

Royce swallowed back tears and said, "You're the most wonderful man I've ever met. I'm so glad I fell in love with you."

Paul put his head down on the steering wheel. "Give me just a minute," he whispered.

Shortly, he straightened. "Chinese food, huh? There's a great place off of Camp Bowie. They have a Hunan Beef that'll make your ears ring."

"Sounds great," she smiled with watery eyes as he turned back onto the street.

They drove to the restaurant, were seated and given menus before either spoke another word. After the waiter had taken their order and departed, Paul said, "I'm waiting."

"Waiting?" Royce repeated blankly.

"For the barrage of questions about my family," he said.

"Tell me what you want," she said softly.

"I guess there's not much to add," he said, gazing absently around the dining room. "I hope you won't object to taking my mother in some day."

"Not at all," she told him.

"I'm the oldest. I guess that's why I've taken the brunt of Papa's ambitions. My brother Ed has done much better for himself, though. He's a lawyer, living in Westover Hills. You should see his house—it's more like a mansion. The outside of it, anyway. I've never seen the inside." He paused as the waiter brought their water and hot tea.

Royce poured her tea and squeezed in some lemon. As Paul poured his tea, he said, "I have three sisters, but none of them lives in Fort Worth. I hear from them every now and then. My sister Christine works in the governor's office in Austin. Rita is an artist and Vicki runs a day-care center. I'm probably the least successful of the lot."

"That's not true. That's a good position in Dallas," she firmly contradicted him. He shrugged.

The waiter brought their orders. Royce zealously attacked her steaming chicken cashew, but Paul picked at his chow mein. At length he gave up on the chopsticks and picked up a fork. "I always thought that God blesses obedience," he murmured. "And I guess He does—just not in the ways you'd prefer. I always tried so hard to do the right thing, and got knocked flat on my back for it. Ed, now—he does whatever he wants, and he makes more money in a year than I'll see in my lifetime." Paul shook his head at the irony of it.

Royce wiped her mouth on her napkin. "I don't know Ed, but most of the people I know are like him. From the first moment I saw you I knew you were different, only I didn't know what it was. I know now. You carry your wealth around on the inside instead of the outside. Isn't that better, in the long run?"

Paul smiled faintly as he wound the noodles around his fork. "Maybe I can find a JP who has night hours," he considered.

19

❖

Early the following morning, Paul and Royce loaded their suitcases into the Mercedes to drive to the Grayson Homestead south of San Angelo. "It's an easy drive," Paul assured her, "only about four hours. We just take I-20 to Abilene, and 277 south from there to San Angelo. That way you can see more of the state."

"I'd like that," Royce agreed. Unfortunately, once they got out of Fort Worth, there was not much to be seen from the interstate. They passed through whole towns before Royce even knew they were there.

"There's a good antique shop," Paul said, nodding to the right.

"Where?" Royce asked, looking.

"Ah, we passed it. We'll hit it on the way back," he said.

Before long, the monotony of the landscape induced Royce to put her head back and close her eyes. Paul smiled and held her hand.

She woke up at the junction of I-20 and 277 in Abilene.

From there, it was only an hour and a half to the Ferrings'. Royce stared out the window as they passed acres and acres of farmland. "What crop is that?" she asked.

"That's sorghum," he replied.

"Sorghum? What's that used for?"

"Feed, mostly. Walt grows some for his cattle," Paul said.

"Does he have enough land for both crops and cattle?" she asked.

"With twenty thousand acres, I guess he does," Paul grinned.

"Wow," she breathed.

They passed through San Angelo, which struck Royce as a quaint, pretty town, then they continued down the highway another few miles until Paul turned off at a white wrought-iron entrance which spelled out "Grayson" at the top. They went down a long driveway and pulled up in a circular drive before a gray stone mansion.

Royce gaped at the huge house, the front fountain, the side gardens, the lush lawn—and that was just what she could see. Paul watched her as he got out their suitcases. She turned on him. "When you said 'homestead' I thought, like, a log cabin!" she exclaimed. He grinned.

The massive double front doors opened and Buddy and Renetta came running down the steps. "Renetta!" Royce cried, embracing her. "I could have killed you for leaving without saying goodbye! You look terrific!" she added, holding Renetta at arm's length. Wearing makeup, with her hair falling softly around her face, Renetta did look lovely.

She murmured, "Thank you," and shyly held out her left hand to show Royce her engagement ring. Buddy and Paul shook hands warmly, and Buddy threw an arm around him.

"Oh, Renetta!" Royce breathed in awe, examining her ring. It was a large, brilliant marquis-cut diamond. Royce felt a stab of envy. "I am so happy for you!" she exclaimed, hugging her again.

"Can I get one of those?" Buddy said to Royce, and she obliged by throwing her arms around his neck.

Paul leaned down to kiss Renetta on the cheek. She held him a moment and whispered something. Paul laughed, "But it makes such a good story—how my best friend's fiancée shot me." Renetta colored.

"So when are you two tying the knot?" Buddy asked.

"As soon as we get back to Fort Worth," Royce replied. "It would have been yesterday, but we got stopped for speeding."

"And they ran a check on the plates of the car—it's a loaner from the DEA," Paul said, patting the Mercedes. "For a while there, I had visions of spending the night in jail."

Buddy asked eagerly, "Yeah, now what happened when you went back out to the Bend? You told me something about that over the phone."

Standing beside the car, Paul told them how Royce had come to Fort Worth at his request and then accompanied him out to Big Bend—"via blackmail," he noted. It was Royce's turn to blush.

He described how she had escaped the motel room before it was shot up and had found his camp; how they had intercepted the code and deciphered the location of the drop-off; how Charlie had trouble raising their contacts and they had been fired on by the helicopter.

"By the time we got back up to the ledge the party was over and everybody had left. I thought they'd bungled it, but they managed to pull off a good bust. Remember the front man at the lodge, who we heard over the radio?" Paul asked, and Buddy nodded. "It wasn't a man—it was a woman! The reservations clerk!"

"The reservations clerk . . ." Buddy mused. "The lady who always had the cigarette stuck to her lip?"

"That's the one. They arrested her and about eleven others, including the drug boss's son," Paul related. Royce was relieved that he omitted certain parts of the narrative, such as their close encounter in the second room and her mistaken flight.

"For my part in it, the area supervisor promised a finder's fee. Hope it comes through soon." Paul paused to turn and whisper inconspicuously to Royce, "When it does, I'm buying you a bigger diamond than Renetta's." She winced that he had noticed her reaction.

"Perry was down here the other day, wanting to borrow horses for another trip to the Bend," Buddy mentioned.

"Perry?" Renetta asked.

"'John,'" Buddy clarified. "I told him no way—we were through with that business. Besides, it was getting to where I didn't trust him anymore."

"No kidding," Paul muttered. "What did you tell your folks about how you met Renetta?"

"You know, I thought and thought about that. I couldn't see any way around it but to tell them the whole truth," Buddy confessed.

Paul nodded. "I'm glad. And they're still going to let me in the house?"

"You can do no wrong in their eyes, Padre," Buddy assured him. "So what are you doing standing out here? Come on in!" Buddy bounded up the front steps and yanked open the stained-glass doors. "Mom! Dad! They're here!" he shouted. Paul carried their suitcases and Renetta held Royce's hand as they went up the steps.

They entered a large marble foyer which opened to rooms on either side. A double staircase rose grandly from the far end of the foyer. "Paul! So good to see you!" Royce turned at the woman's voice to see her hostess warmly embrace Paul. A man beside her grabbed Paul's hand and pumped it up and down, then forsook that gesture for a bear hug.

"Walt—Jeannine—I want you to meet someone," Paul said. His face was radiant as he reached for Royce. "This is my fiancée, Royce Lindel. Royce, these are Buddy's parents, Walt and Jeannine Ferring."

"I'm so pleased to meet you," Royce said, shaking the hands of two people she instantly liked. They were both about fifty—Jeannine had frosted blond hair in a bob, expressive blue eyes, and a comfortable, thoughtful manner. Walt was the tanned, easygoing cowboy with Buddy's curly hair and angular features. Royce could not decide whom Buddy resembled more.

"And we are thrilled to have you here," Jeannine said sincerely, holding Royce's hand in both of hers. "We love Paul so, we call him our oldest son."

"You're too young to be my mother," Paul objected, smiling.

Jeannine hugged him with one arm while still holding Royce's hand. "Come into the drawing room, you two, and have some lunch. Jesse," she turned to a young ranch hand standing nearby, "please take Paul's suitcase to his room, and put Royce in the Rose Room."

As they walked into a room off the foyer, Walt poked Paul and said, "I've got a bone to pick with you, young man."

"Yes sir, I imagine you do," Paul acknowledged. Royce dropped her jaw at the heavily laden buffet table set up in front of floor-to-ceiling windows dressed in pink silk.

"That business of taking on the drug runners in Big Bend was mighty risky. Wherever did you come up with that hare-brained scheme?" Walt asked roughly, but his eyes twinkled.

"We just kind of fell into it, sir. But we're all done. No more robberies," Paul vowed, taking up a plate behind Royce at the buffet table. A maid standing nearby smiled at him in a welcoming way.

"That's good, 'cause I hear you almost got killed," Walt added, as if approaching a punch line. Renetta cringed.

"Nah. We just staged that, so I could see if Royce cared anything about me," Paul said artfully, then pointed to cocktail wieners simmering in a brown sauce. "Try the smokies. They're one of Jeannine's specialties," he told Royce. She obligingly loaded her plate.

As they sat around the room, Royce admired the padded

wallcovering with pink piping. "Your home is gorgeous," she said.

"Thank you, dear. I hope you'll see much more of it. Buddy tells us you certainly proved yourself under some difficult circumstances," Jeannine responded.

Buddy looked at Royce meaningfully from the buffet table and she lowered her head. "They saved our lives," Royce murmured. "And I never will forget how Buddy loaded up Paul on his horse and rode like crazy to the hospital. I'd never seen real people show such courage and loyalty. As a matter of fact, until I met them, I never knew that men like Buddy and Paul even existed." She looked from one to the other, both of whom were listening intently.

"That's our boys," Walt said proudly.

"You don't know the half of it, Dad. The DEA caught up with Paul in Fort Worth and talked him into guiding them on a bust at the Bend. He and Royce almost got killed, but they pulled it off," Buddy told him.

Jeannine looked startled. "Are you with the DEA?" she asked Royce.

"No; I just foolishly insisted on going with Paul. I'm a writer," Royce said.

"Who's also proficient at blackmail," Paul added.

"Really?" Jeannine responded to Royce. "What kind of writing do you do?"

"Mostly magazine articles. At my last job I was a copywriter for The Chocolate Conglomerate in New York City, where Renetta worked," Royce said, nodding toward Renetta, who was comfortably perched on a hearth cushion with her plate.

"That's interesting," Jeannine remarked.

"Yeah, Mom, didn't you have to produce a series of articles for that magazine—what was it?" Buddy asked.

"We were discussing it, but I just didn't have time to pursue it," Jeannine replied.

Royce, who had begun staring dreamily out the window, sat up. "You do have cattle! Right out there!"

Buddy smothered a laugh and Walt said, "Yep, we're a work-ing ranch, though I'm down to 'bout two hundred head. It's dang near impossible to get good help nowadays. Sure wish I had Paul out here all the time."

Paul practically jumped up. "Show me what you need done."

"Now, son, sit down," Walt said. "You didn't come here to work."

"Sure I did. Let me go get my jeans on—" Paul started out the door.

Jeannine interrupted, "No, Paul; not now. Sit down." She gave Walt a purposeful look.

Paul reluctantly sat back down and Walt said, "That's right. We wanted to give you your wedding gift." He took a check from his shirt pocket and handed it to Paul. Buddy grinned broadly.

Paul glanced at it, then did a double take. He looked up at Walt in shock. "I can't take this."

"Yes, you can," Walt said easily. "It'll clear."

"No," Paul protested to Jeannine. "It's about three zeroes too much." She only smiled.

"Son, if I paid you minimum wage for every hour you've worked for me, that check still wouldn't cover it," Walt said affectionately.

"No," Paul repeated. "Everything I did, I did it because I wanted to, not so I'd get paid. I can't take this." He tore the check up and put the pieces in Jeannine's hand. "I'm going to change. You come show me what needs to be done," he told Walt. Then he turned and walked out. Walt raised his brows at Jeannine as he followed Paul out.

Jeannine sighed, sifting the pieces of paper. "You can see why we love him," she said to Royce.

"That's the Paul I know," Royce agreed. "He's telling you the truth. His fondest dream is to work on a ranch the rest of his life."

Jeannine looked up quickly, then covered her reaction with a smile. "Buddy brought him here for the first time right after his divorce. I never saw such a broken man. He didn't know a thing about ranching—had never been on a horse—but threw himself into helping Walt. He stayed for about a month, working twelve-, fourteen-hour days. I fussed at Walt for working the poor man so hard, but he said, 'It's good for him.' I guess it was. We would have been happy for him to stay forever, but I suppose he felt he was imposing on us. Still, he comes back many weekends just to work his fingers to the bone." Royce listened, taking in Jeannine's soft pink complexion, watching her play with the remains of the check.

"Walt's getting older, and can't do all that he used to, but this ranch is his life. I just don't know. . . ." Jeannine trailed off.

Renetta said, "Royce, come up to my room. I want you to see my dress."

"You bet!" Royce agreed. "Excuse us, Mrs. Ferring."

"Jeannine," she smiled.

"Jeannine," Royce repeated fondly. She paused, as it appeared that Jeannine wanted to say something more. But Renetta tugged on her arm, so she followed her up one of the broad staircases to an airy guest bedroom with French doors that opened onto a balcony.

As Renetta shut the door behind them, Royce confessed, "I envy you, Renetta. I've never seen such a beautiful home. And the Ferrings are so nice!"

"Yes, but there's more you should know," Renetta said. "They are very nice, and very wealthy, and Buddy is their only child. He's been struggling for years to gain some independence from them. They've always assumed he would take over the ranch from his dad, but Buddy just doesn't want to. Well, last night he told them that we're going to New York after the wedding so that Buddy can continue his education—oh, they were not happy campers," Renetta said. She went to the closet and pulled out a white tea-length dress with stacked ruffles, lace and pearls.

"I'm sorry to hear that," Royce murmured. "Renetta, this

dress is—incredible." Touching the intricate lace, Royce felt the pangs of envy again. She would be lucky to get her white linen suit back from the cleaners to be married in.

"Royce, I know the Ferrings are hoping that Paul will stay on at the ranch when we leave. Do you suppose he would? Oh, it will make it so much easier for us if he would!" Renetta said, pleading with her large gray eyes.

"I'm sure he'd love to, but—he's supposed to start his new job on the twentieth. . . ." Royce mused. *And where would I fit in here?*

"Could you talk to him—ask him to consider it?" Renetta asked again, holding her arm. "Buddy needs so much to leave the nest!"

"I'll talk to him," Royce said blankly.

"Thank you," Renetta leaned on her with a sigh. "You're such a good friend."

Renetta then began talking about the preparations for the wedding the day after tomorrow, but Royce hardly heard her. It was only too apparent that Paul would jump at the invitation to take over the ranch from Walt. True, the place was a mansion, but what would she do out here? The closest town was just that—a small town. She looked out the window at the endless stretch of pasture, and suddenly ached for the city.

There was a knock on the door and Renetta opened it. Jeannine stood outside. "Royce, our man is about to go to the airport to meet your parents' charter, and I thought you would like to go with him," she said.

"Oh, yes! Thank you!" exclaimed Royce. "Renetta—I'll talk with you later." She turned, giving her an excited hug. "Where's Paul? I want him to go too," Royce said to Jeannine.

"Oh, dear. There's no way to find him before you have to leave. He and Walt get out there and they can be gone for days, literally," Jeannine said regretfully.

"Oh. Well. I'll—go without him, then," Royce said, feeling strange.

She freshened up in a downstairs bath and then climbed into the Ferrings' Jeep Cherokee with Jesse, the hired man. He touched his cowboy hat and they headed out to the airport. He did not say two words along the way. As Royce watched the monotonous scenery zip by, she grew unaccountably uneasy.

They arrived at the airport in plenty of time to meet the three o'clock flight—especially as it was delayed. This facility was newer and nicer than the one in Alpine, but it did not have regularly scheduled air service, either—only charters and private planes. Royce sat in the waiting area and watched the minutes tick past 3:30. Jesse leaned back in his chair, put his hat over his face, and went to sleep. Royce went to the reservations desk to ask the lone clerk the cause of the delay for the chartered flight, but she did not know.

Other flights came and went; Royce idly watched people board and disembark. She got a candy bar from a machine and bought a *Texas Wildlife* magazine, which she read from cover to cover. By 4:15 she was wandering around the small terminal, counting planes through the wall-sized windows.

A few minutes later she approached the reservations clerk to ask again about the delay. "Apparently it's weather related," the woman answered from under her headset. "They've been having heavy thunderstorms and hail around D/FW."

"Hail? Here? In early June?" Royce marveled.

"Not here—in Dallas. Spring hailstorms can be a real problem for light aircraft," the woman noted.

"That's just wonderful," Royce muttered. A delay like that would not put her mother in a good frame of mind, and Royce wanted her to be in the best possible mood to meet Paul—not that she had any doubts about the impression he would make; Paul looked especially good with his new haircut. But her mother could be blunt, and Paul did not wear polite veneers easily.

Royce settled back in the hard plastic chair to think about her parents. Her father Lowell had done well enough as a garment wholesaler to buy a home three years ago in Forest Hills

Gardens, where he and her mother Sue Anne lived. Royce still got most of her clothes through him. In another era Lowell would have been called henpecked—he allowed his outspoken, strong-willed wife to dominate their relationship without much argument. Royce's older brother Lowell Jr. still lived in Queens as well, although he had not spoken to his mother for years.

Royce watched the second hand on the clock glide past 5:05. Jesse started snoring; she nudged him and he shifted, quieting down. Mother liked Mack. Royce never quite understood why, since he was so domineering himself. But he always acquiesced in Sue Anne's presence. He did treat her royally—much better than he treated Royce, actually. Maybe that was why Royce was a little uneasy about her mother's first meeting with Paul: he was just not cunning enough to play up to her need to be in control. He would be himself, regardless. But as honest, selfless, intelligent, and loving as he was, Royce was certain that not even her mother could find fault with him.

At 5:25 the clerk waved to Royce. "They're here," she said, pointing out the window. Royce jumped up and ran to the glass wall to look. There was the charter, pulling up on the runway! She grabbed her purse and ran out to the fence.

Shortly, her parents disembarked. "Mother! Daddy!" Royce shouted and waved. She met them at the fence with hugs.

Her dad, tan and handsome, smiled. His silver-gray hair was as full as it had been thirty years ago. "You look great, Royce."

"Thanks, Daddy. It's because I've met a man who really loves me," she said, holding him.

"Just so you're happy, Royce," he said. "I just want you to be happy."

"Where is this man?" asked Sue Anne, looking around. Her auburn hair was perfectly coiffed, her face without a wrinkle, her designer suit elegant.

"Oh, Mother, I can't wait for you to meet him! He's an angel! But he was out helping Mr. Ferring, and we couldn't find him before we had to go—they have twenty thousand acres, you know. Anyway, you'll meet him at dinner," Royce said excitedly, taking her mother's hand. Her dad carried three suitcases off the plane. "How long can you stay?" Royce asked.

"Just overnight, pookie. I have an arts league meeting tomorrow," her mother replied. "Now what is his name?"

"Paul Arrendondo," Royce said. They entered the terminal and she shook Jesse by the shoulder. He sat up, snorting, then took the bags from Lowell and carried them to the Cherokee.

"What does he do?" Sue Anne asked in faint disapproval. She gingerly sat in the back of the Jeep beside Royce as Lowell sat up front with Jesse.

Royce's stomach tightened. "He was director of a substance abuse clinic until just recently, when he was offered the position of drug counselor at Ville Du Havre Hospital in Dallas. He'll start there on the twentieth."

"How much will he make?" Sue Anne asked, looking out appraisingly as the Cherokee bounded down the highway toward the Ferrings' ranch.

"About $45,000," Royce answered.

"A year?" her mother asked in dismay.

"Mother, that's a good salary here. The cost of living isn't as high as it is in New York," Royce said anxiously. "Anyway, that's not important. He's such a gem, Mother. He's—he's—" Mrs. Lindel was no longer listening, as they had pulled up to the front of the Grayson Homestead.

"This is the ranch?" Sue Anne asked with arched brow.

"Yes. Walt and Jeannine Ferring's ranch. Their son Buddy is marrying my friend Renetta on Saturday," Royce explained again.

Sue Anne looked at her daughter in hapless bemusement. "Why couldn't you have 'fallen in love' with Buddy?"

Royce did not have an answer. As Jesse unloaded suitcases, the front door opened and Jeannine came out. Mrs. Lindel instantly put on a gracious demeanor.

"We were beginning to worry about you! I hope your flight

was uneventful. I am Jeannine Ferring," she said before Royce could speak.

"I am Sue Anne Lindel and this is my husband Lowell. Actually, we had to wait several hours at the Dallas airport, which was terribly uncomfortable, but—we're here now! It was so kind of you to invite us." She deliberately looked past Jeannine to the house.

"Jesse, please take their bags to the Colonel's Room. Walt and Paul just came in a few minutes ago from fence-mending. They're getting cleaned up, and will meet us in the parlor for hors d'oeuvres," Jeannine said. She turned to give Royce a hug and warm smile. "We have a lot to talk about," she whispered, and Royce wondered what had transpired while she was gone.

They entered the front parlor—a room with comfortable, overstuffed furniture in pastel Southwestern colors. It was a less formal room than the drawing room opposite it. The young maid brought in a tray of appetizers, and Jeannine said, "Shana, please go tell Paul and Walt that the Lindels are here."

As the maid left, Jeannine passed the tray herself. "I'm sorry that we don't have any alcohol, but I can offer you anything else under the sun you'd care to drink."

"Mineral water, please," said Sue Anne. Lowell shook his head.

"Let me get it, Jeannine," Royce said, heading for the beverage table. She was anxious to accommodate her mother's idiosyncrasies right now.

"You have an—interesting home," Sue Anne observed regally.

"It's formally known as the Grayson Homestead. Walt's grandparents had it built back in the 1920s. I will be happy to show you around later," Jeannine offered in true graciousness. "It can be big and lonely sometimes. It wants special guests." She dropped a glowing smile on Royce again.

Walt came to the door then, and right behind him was Paul.

20

❖

Taking a cue from his host, Paul wore clean jeans, boots, and a fresh cotton shirt. His hair hung damp on his forehead, and when his gaze landed on Royce, he smiled with full contentment.

Royce handed her mother the glass of water with a sliver of lemon and went to Paul. He put an arm around her and kissed her head. "Mother, Daddy," said Royce, "this is the man who saved my life. Paul, these are my parents, Lowell and Sue Anne Lindel."

Royce's father stood and Paul shook his hand. "Mr. Lindel."

"Call me Lowell," he offered, and Paul nodded.

Paul bent to shake Sue Anne's hand: "How do you do, Mrs. Lindel." She smiled coolly.

Jeannine introduced Walt to the Lindels and then said, "What took you men so long out there today?"

"About a hundred yards of broken fencing and a pasture full of locoweed," Paul said happily, scooping up a handful of appetizers.

"The cattle were everywhere," added Walt, easing down in

a chair. "They'd be halfway to Matamoras by now, if I hadn't had Paul out there."

"He has been so helpful to us, we call him our oldest son," Jeannine confided to Sue Anne.

"You're Mexican, aren't you?" Sue Anne asked. A stillness fell around the room.

"I am Hispanic, yes," Paul said slowly.

"You speak English well," Sue Anne noted, "for a Mexican. Do you have citizenship papers?"

Royce felt the blood draining from her face, but Paul calmly replied, "I was born in Texas. We grew up speaking English; my father insisted on it."

"I see. And what does your father do?" Sue Anne asked.

"He was groundskeeper and janitor at a small Baptist church for many years before he retired," Paul said.

"Well. I'm sorry your parents were not able to fly down to meet us," Sue Anne said gravely.

"My father has not been well lately. But Royce has met them," Paul said.

Royce started to confirm that but Sue Anne asked, "And you've known Royce for—how long?"

Paul looked at Royce's pale face. "Oh, I guess almost—three weeks now."

"Three weeks?" gasped Sue Anne.

"Royce hasn't known Paul that long, but she's an excellent judge of character. We've known him for years. He's solid gold," Jeannine affirmed warmly.

"And you met her—where? In Big Bend?" Sue Anne asked, with widening eyes.

"Yes, I told you all about that on the phone, Mother," Royce said nervously. "He and his friends rescued me, Marla, and Renetta after our guide dumped us."

"How convenient," Sue Anne observed. Paul studied her. "Tell me about this job you'll be starting in Dallas," she added.

Paul turned to Royce, taking her hands. "We have to talk

about that. With Buddy leaving, Walt has asked me—us—to stay here. He needs my help running the ranch."

Royce opened her mouth but her mother interjected, "You're going to be a ranch hand?" Paul turned to her with an explanation but she said, "Excuse me. What kind of education do you have?"

"I . . . have a master's degree in divinity," Paul answered.

"Divinity? What, like a cleric?" Sue Anne asked.

"I was a Southern Baptist pastor for several years," Paul said.

"Why aren't you now?" asked Mrs. Lindel.

Several silent seconds ticked by before Paul answered, "I left the ministry after my divorce."

"You're . . . divorced," Sue Anne said levelly.

Royce gazed desperately at her father. *Rein her in, Daddy!* she silently pleaded. "Mother, Paul has told me all about that, and it's not relevant. He—"

"I understand," Sue Anne said, sipping her sparkling water. "You must be—ten or twelve years older than Royce."

"I'm thirty-five," Paul admitted.

"And a ranch hand," she muttered into her glass. "Well. You had an interesting vacation at Big Bend. Do you normally go there to meet women?"

Paul looked down at Royce and she said, "Mother, we met by accident, just like I told you. He and Buddy had been vacationing out there for years. We stumbled on to their camp. They took us to the lodge, but had to come back for us when the—" Royce suddenly stopped. She had recited this story so many times that she momentarily forgot her parents knew nothing of the drug runners.

"When what?" asked her mother. Paul was gazing down at Royce.

"When it became apparent that we were in danger," Royce answered weakly.

"Danger? What kind of danger?" Sue Anne asked in exaggerated alarm.

"We . . . we had come across . . . some money that . . . didn't belong to us. . . ." Royce stammered pathetically.

Paul dropped his head and laughed silently. "Buddy and I were out there robbing drug runners," he said, helping himself to a soft drink from the beverage table. "We gave the girls some of the money, and they were a little too free about spending it."

"You—you were *robbing drug runners*—!" Mrs. Lindel put a hand to her chest.

"That's right," Paul said drily.

"Don't they—arrest people for that?" Sue Anne asked in an offended voice.

"Oh, we got it all straightened out with the DEA," Paul assured her.

"I'm so glad," she breathed in a tone that was anything but. Then she seemed to remember something. "Oh, Royce—Mack has been frantically trying to get hold of you. He was so upset that you left without any explanation."

"I'll bet," Royce muttered.

Sue Anne reached into her purse. "He asked me to give you this letter."

"Mother!" Royce exclaimed. "I am not interested in anything Mack has to say!"

"But, pookie, for as long as your relationship lasted, I think you at least owe him the courtesy of saying goodbye." She held out the letter.

"I don't owe Mack anything, and I can't believe you brought that with you!" Royce said angrily. Paul was coolly examining the hors d'oeuvre tray.

"At least give me your Fort Worth address, so I can give it to him," Sue Anne said, taking out a gold pen. Paul smiled.

Royce slowly opened her mouth. "No."

"Well, will you give *me* your address?" her mother asked in exasperation.

"We're not going to be there—" Royce began, then caught herself.

"I see." Mrs. Lindel put up her pen. "You're living with Paul."

"We haven't slept together!" Royce cried. "Paul just let me stay at his apartment! He's been sleeping on the couch!"

"And where did you sleep in Big Bend?" Sue Anne asked.

Royce sagged helplessly. Paul looked up. "Tell her, Royce," he urged. As far as he was concerned, the truth could not hurt a situation this far gone. But she numbly shook her head. "She slept in my sleeping bag, Mrs. Lindel," Paul said helpfully.

Walt covered a sudden laugh by pretending to blow his nose in his handkerchief. Royce wanted the floor to swallow her up; Paul met Sue Anne's glare with unflinching, unapologetic steadiness.

"Well." Sue Anne stood; her husband did likewise. "You're a grown woman, Royce Anne; I can't tell you what to do with your life. But I certainly will not stand by and watch while you ruin it. Don't expect that we're going to pay a penny toward this wedding or any future needs. Mrs. Ferring, please have our suitcases brought down. I see no reason to stay longer."

"I'm sorry you feel that way," Jeannine murmured, turning to get Jesse. Her eyes, full of sympathy, lit not on sturdy Paul but on battered Royce.

The Lindels' bags were brought down and loaded into the Cherokee. Royce followed her parents out to the car. "Mother," she pleaded, "if you'd just give him a chance—get to know him—he's such a good man."

"You're welcome to come home at any time without him," Sue Anne said. She took Mack's letter from her purse and handed it to Royce, who started to rip it up. Sue Anne advised, "I wouldn't do that. There's money in it for plane fare back to New York. Goodbye, pookie." She puckered her lips beside Royce's cheek and looked back up to where the Ferrings stood silently on the grand front porch. Then Sue Anne climbed in the back seat beside her husband. Jesse started the engine and drove off.

Royce watched the Jeep go, then looked down at the letter. She opened it and removed the cash—over five hundred dollars.

Then she dropped the letter unread to the ground. With heavy steps she turned back to where the Ferrings stood.

Jeannine opened her arms to Royce, who laid her head on Jeannine's shoulder and cried. "I'm so sorry," Jeannine whispered, stroking Royce's hair.

The maid came out to announce that dinner was ready. Royce wiped her eyes, pocketed the cash from Mack, and held Jeannine's hand as they went in. Walt came in a few moments later.

The long dining room table was beautifully set with crystal and china for eight. Buddy and Renetta entered. "Did your parents make it in, Royce?" asked Buddy. Then he looked at her face and said, "Uh oh. Does that have anything to do with why Padre's standing out on the back veranda?"

"Buddy, we've asked you repeatedly not to call him that," his mother said sharply.

"Habit, Mom. He doesn't mind. What's the big deal?" Buddy shrugged.

"Well, here he's Paul. Please remember that," she said.

"Where is the back veranda?" Royce asked faintly.

"Up the staircase, all the way to your right," Buddy pointed.

"Thanks." Royce quickly left the room and found her way up the spacious corridor toward the stone veranda. Through the open door at the end of the hall she saw Paul leaning on the balustrade, looking out.

Royce came up behind him and circled his waist. She laid her head on his shoulder and kissed it. He turned his head. "Your mother doesn't like me much."

"You're not marrying my mother," she whispered.

"Thank goodness," he said drily. "You look a lot like her," he remarked.

"But I'm a lot different," she answered uneasily.

"Maybe. But I see where you get your penchant for asking questions." His tone alarmed her.

"Paul, I love you," she said, pressing close to him.

He drew back. "I love you, Royce; I really do. But I don't

know that I want to—that I want to—"

"Get married," she finished for him, her stomach turning to stone.

He turned back toward the open land. "I don't want to drive to downtown Dallas to work every day. I'm tired of pouring myself out for self-destructive people. I'm not going to apologize for my background or my family. And I'm not going to disappoint the Ferrings." Royce opened her mouth but Paul said, "Listen, Royce; I just have to think things through. Just let me think about it awhile." He walked off the veranda.

Royce stood at the balustrade, looking over the rolling acres dotted with cattle. As twilight fell in heavy purple and night stretched out, she watched the stars come out and glimmer one by one.

Jeannine came up quietly behind her. "Royce, would you like some dinner?"

"No, thank you," Royce whispered. Jeannine stood beside her, looking to the horizon, saying nothing. "Paul doesn't want to marry me now," Royce added, her voice breaking.

Jeannine gathered her in her arms. "Yes, he does, Royce. I know he does. He just feels ambushed. Give him a little time to get over it, and he'll be fine. I promise."

"I've never seen him like this," Royce sobbed.

"Honey, I know he loves you. He must; he's never taken off his wedding band for anyone before—not even the woman who followed him down here last year," Jeannine said.

Royce looked up. "What woman?"

"Well," Jeannine said hesitantly, "there was a woman who became infatuated with him, and followed him down from Fort Worth, though I know Paul did nothing to encourage her. She practically camped on our front porch while he was out on the remuda with Walt. He finally had to go tell her he didn't want any entanglements before she would leave. But—that has nothing to do with you."

"Oh, I think it does," Royce said distantly. "He's still avoiding entanglements." Of course. That's why he would not sleep with her. That might lead to all kinds of unwanted entanglements. Had he learned that from this woman—that freedom was better than sex?

Royce gently pulled away from Jeannine. Certainly she and Walt would defend Paul—look what they were getting out of him. Royce closed her eyes at her rash foolishness in abandoning everything to come join him. But he could truthfully say she did it of her own free will. And he could truthfully say he promised her nothing. She came simply on the strength of her own hopes. "Please show me my room now," Royce said quietly.

It was a lush, feminine room upholstered in dusty rose satin, appointed with antiques. Royce smiled wanly when she remembered Paul's appraisal of this room's possibilities. Apparently his ardor had cooled since then.

Royce bathed in a sumptuous private bath and turned down the covers on the four-poster bed. As she lay down, she began some intense soul-searching. She saw her father sitting mute while her mother ravaged Paul, and she knew why she had always been attracted to men stronger than herself. She wanted somebody to prevent her from becoming a human steamroller like her mother. She needed a solid outside influence to check the excesses of her personality.

But such men were not likely to compromise their own agendas: Mack needed to be in control; Paul needed to be free. Knowing that, why must she have a man at all? Somehow, she was just going to have to learn to live for herself, by herself, without Daddy, without Mack . . . without Paul. Royce draped her hair over the pillow and turned out the light.

✳ ✳ ✳

The next day, Friday, preparations moved into high gear for the Saturday afternoon wedding. Royce did not see Paul at all that day, which was just as well. When she came down to breakfast, she found Jeannine swamped with chores, with precious little help. The kitchen was a disorganized mess, guests were due to begin arriving from out of town, and the wedding consultant Jeannine had hired called to say she had a stomach virus. Shana, the maid, was a willing worker when she was told exactly what to do. Until then, she stood unoccupied.

The cook could not be bothered with such mundane matters as breakfast for Royce when she had two days of wedding festivities to oversee. Her name was Patricia—not Pat, Patty, or Tricia, and woe to anyone who tried to butcher her name. She was efficient and moody, a five-foot powderkeg who respected Mrs. Ferring alone. As soon as Royce set foot in the kitchen, Patricia took the van keys from a hook on the wall and left for the grocery store in San Angelo.

So Royce took over the tumult in the kitchen and Jeannine gratefully abdicated to receive delivery of the folding chairs. Royce fixed herself a light breakfast and loaded both dishwashers. She began answering the telephone and, when questions surfaced and Jeannine could not be found, Royce had Shana fetch Jeannine's wedding folder, which was full of notes and receipts.

"White roses,—no, *white*," Royce said over the telephone to the florist in San Angelo. "Look, Mrs. Ferring placed this order two weeks ago," she noted, holding the carbon copy of the order.

She paused, cupping a hand over the mouthpiece as Shana came up. "Miss Lindel, the Porters are here from Tulsa and I don't know where to put them."

"How many?" Royce asked.

"I'm not sure," Shana frowned.

"Well, find out. What guest rooms are available?" Royce asked.

"I don't know," Shana said.

"Well, *find out*," Royce repeated. She removed her hand from the mouthpiece and said, "Twenty baskets of a dozen each. No, *baskets*. This is a wedding."

"How do I find out?" Shana asked doubtfully.

"Go to each room and look in to see if there's luggage in it," Royce told her. "Bring me a list of all the empty rooms. And find out how many are with the Porters!"

From then on, Royce was fully occupied helping Jeannine handle food, decorations, guest accommodations, the florist, the caterer, the photographer, and a hundred thousand details. Renetta, of course, walked around in a useless daze, and Buddy was a clown.

Around noon Walt sent Jesse in to bring sack lunches for himself and Paul. When he approached the cook about it as she and Royce unloaded sacks of groceries from the van, she nodded impatiently toward Royce. "You can fix lunches, can't you?"

Lovingly, Royce put together two large lunches of sandwiches, fruit, chips, and some pastries she found in the refrigerator. The cook stopped her: "The cream-filled pastries are for the out-of-town guests."

"They're good enough for Paul and Walt," Royce huffed, packing them anyway. Patricia scowled, but began treating Royce with almost the same deference she reserved for Jeannine.

As Royce handed the lunches to Jesse, Shana came up: "Miss Lindel, Mrs. Silberson wants to see the bridesmaids' dresses. She wants to find out if her dress clashes with theirs."

Royce had no idea who Mrs. Silberson was or why she should care if her dress clashed, but she told Shana, "Tell her we'll call her as soon as the seamstress brings them." Shana nodded and then Royce asked, "Has anyone heard from the seamstress recently?"

"I don't know," Shana replied as usual. Royce opened the file to find a phone number for the seamstress.

With all that needed to be done, Royce was on her feet until late evening, eating on the run. She did not know any of the guests who trickled in throughout the day. There were Renetta's family and friends from Texas and New York, Grayson-Ferring people from Texas and Oklahoma, and Jeannine's friends from around the country. Each new arrival added to the cordial chaos at the Grayson Homestead.

Royce saw Paul come in just in time for the rehearsal dinner, newly showered. He was Buddy's best man. Royce was not in the wedding party, so she ate with the cook in the kitchen while she supervised Shana's serving of the dinner.

Afterward, during the rehearsal, Royce washed dishes. Shana was there to help her, but the mountains of china and delicate stemware which could not go in the dishwashers still required hours of careful hand washing and towel drying. Drooping at the sight of yet another batch of dirty dishes being brought in, Royce made herself deaf to the laughter and light conversation coming from the formal living room, where the wedding would take place.

As she lowered the last stack of dessert plates into the sink, Shana came in from the living room with dirty glasses. "Miss Lindel, Mrs. Louden is mad about being put in the Hunters' Room. She says they always stay in the Colonel's Room when they're here."

Royce leaned on the edge of the sink, hanging her dripping hands over the sudsy water. "Get out the guest room list for me," she said tiredly, nodding toward the bulging file folder on the table. Shana found the list and held it under Royce's nose. "Okay," Royce sighed, straightening to look at it. "The Hamptons are in the Colonel's Room. Go ask Mrs. Hampton if she would mind moving to the Hunters' Room."

"Yes, Miss Lindel," Shana said, backing up.

"Shana." Royce suddenly turned. "Tell her *Mrs. Ferring* wondered whether she wouldn't be more comfortable in the Hunters' Room."

"Oh. Right," Shana nodded slowly. Another burst of laughter erupted from the living room. Royce submerged the last glasses in the sink, wondering if it were possible to drown oneself in eight inches of water.

Several hours later, when the kitchen was clean and all the out-of-town guests were situated for the night, Royce crept up to bed without another glimpse of Paul.

21

❖

Saturday morning, Royce was up very early, mediating between the cook and the caterer over infringed territories. The caterer suffered a major disaster when the cake toppled while being transported up the front steps. As Patricia flatly refused to do it, Royce found herself baking layers for a new cake while the caterer fetched her decorating supplies from San Angelo. By meticulously following the recipe's directions and Patricia's suggestions, Royce turned out four fluffy layers. She had about five minutes to admire them before the florist showed up with the wrong flowers. Straightening that out required almost two hours.

Then they discovered that Renetta's sister's dress did not fit. The sister, Susan, was Renetta's maid of honor. "What am I going to do?" she wailed, trying in vain to fasten the buttons. She was a little older and a lot heftier than Renetta.

"Here—all we have to do is move the buttons over a half-inch. I can do that," Royce assured her, eyeing the long row of tiny buttons on blue satin.

As Royce helped her out of the dress, Susan turned to Renetta and said, "Buddy's best man is a hunk. What's his last name?"

"Actually, Paul is engaged to Royce," Renetta said quickly.

"Oh? Nobody told me," Susan said in surprise. Royce began snipping off buttons.

She finished that chore and ate a quick bite, then the photographer asked her to stand in for a light reading. By the time he was finished setting up, she had just long enough to change into her pink suit before the wedding began.

Royce stood in the back behind the white slipcovered chairs and watched the nuptials with moist eyes. It was a dream set in the spacious living room, overflowing with white roses and orchids. Buddy looked debonair; Renetta was a vision in her white ruffled dress; and Paul looked so good in his blue suit—his "interview suit," he called it. As he walked Susan up the aisle before Renetta came out, Royce happened to catch his eye. He looked away.

The music was sung, the vows were said, and the party turned out onto the canopied grounds in back of the house for the reception. The scene was so beautiful, it was heartbreaking. The silky green lawn was hedged by pink rosebushes in full bloom on one side and Indian hawthorn on the other. The glowing afternoon was graced with just enough breeze to ruffle the scalloped edges of the canopies.

In the receiving line, Royce was one of the first to embrace Renetta, whispering, "Write me from back home."

Renetta squeezed her. "Thank you for talking him into staying!" Royce nodded wryly and retreated to a serving table covered in white linen and lace. She picked up a sterling silver ladle and began filling punch cups as the guests filed by. Paul passed through the line and took a cup without even seeing her. Reeling from the slight, Royce concentrated on filling all the little silver circles as quickly as they were demanded. When she chanced to glance up, she saw Paul mingling far across the grounds. She felt a sharp pain in the center of her chest.

Much more of this is going to kill me, she thought. *But what can I do? I rode down here with him. Even if I had transportation, where would I go?* She ladled punch, smiling automatically while she thought out her options. First, she would have to get the rest of her things out of his apartment in Fort Worth. They did not amount to much, but it was all she had. Then where? Back to New York? She recoiled at the idea of crawling back home. And she did not have the money to waste on air fare. That five hundred dollars of Mack's would have to be spent very carefully.

She looked up long enough to see Susan leaning on Paul and laughing. He glanced toward the table where Royce stood and she lowered her head, determinedly smiling and ladling. She could rent a room in Fort Worth, Dallas, or anywhere in between and get a job—anything to put food on the table while she reordered her life.

As she handed a cup to the next person in line she was greeted with, "Hello, Royce."

Looking up, she saw that she had served punch to "John"—Perry, actually. He was dressed in casual clothes, as if coming today were an afterthought.

"Hello. It's Perry, isn't it?" she nodded carefully.

"Tsk, tsk, tsk. They tattled," he smiled. "Nice wedding—if you go for that kind of thing."

There was no one in line behind him, so she poured a cup of punch for herself. "I hear you have," she said.

"My wife and I split some time ago. Marriage is too confining," Perry said with a slight shudder.

"So it would seem," she murmured, glancing toward Paul, who had his back turned to her.

"And I hear you and Paul are making it legal," he added.

"We talked about it, but . . . decided not to," she said. Would that pain ever go away?

"Really?" Perry asked, putting down his cup. "You're free?"

Royce raised an eyebrow. "What's it to you?"

"That's the best news I've heard all week," he grinned. Royce smiled sadly. It was nice to have someone paying attention to her, even if it were Perry. Besides, he was definitely the best-looking man here. "What are you doing hanging around here, then?" he asked. "Let's split."

Royce tried to look bored. "Look, Perry, I'm not interested in any—entanglements right now. All I'd want from you is . . . a ride back to Fort Worth."

"My chariot awaits, lady," he said with a sweeping gesture.

Royce studied him, then put her cup down. "Let me go get my suitcase, and I'll meet you out front." She went inside and ran up the stairs to throw her things together before she could think twice about it. She did check her purse to make sure she had the money and a key to Paul's apartment.

She paused at the door of the Rose Room, knowing she needed to tell her hosts goodbye. She dropped her suitcase and fished stationery from the antique rolltop desk. She wrote, "Dear Jeannine, Thank you so much for your hospitality. I am so glad I got to meet you, and I am so happy for Buddy and Renetta. But it's time for me to leave. Perry is giving me a ride"—here Royce paused. She did not want to leave open the possibility of someone tracking her down—"into town. If I don't see you again, God bless. Royce."

She hesitated over the letter, wondering why she had closed it that way. She had never before invoked the Lord's blessing on anyone. Maybe the pastor's prayer during the wedding had affected her thinking, because it just seemed appropriate. Being in too much of a hurry to rewrite it anyway, she left it out on the desk and trotted down the stairs with her suitcase.

Perry was waiting out front in an idling Ford Explorer. Royce put her suitcase in the back of the truck with a lot of camping gear, then plopped down in the front seat. "Awright," Perry growled, pulling out around the cars of wedding guests. As they left the Grayson Homestead behind, Royce entreated the pain to go away.

Perry turned the radio to a loud heavy metal station; Royce leaned her head back and closed her eyes. Suddenly she ached for Paul so intensely that her hand felt for the door handle. She wanted to throw herself on him and beg him to marry her. After a moment's reflection, she took that urge as proof that she needed to leave, seeing some pathetic, unwanted woman camped on the Ferrings' doorstep. Royce stared out the window, sternly forbidding tears to come. Somehow, she managed to hold them back, and fancied it was because her heart was getting harder.

It was impossible to talk over the loud music, so they rode without a word between them. Perry drove very fast, drumming the steering wheel with his thumbs as he roared down the two-lane highway. Royce looked over at the glowing orange sky on her right and sighed. It reminded her of the sunsets in Big Bend—of riding with Paul, and sleeping beside him—Royce braced for the pain and then realized vaguely that something was wrong. They had not yet passed through San Angelo. And she was looking out her window at the sunset, which meant they were traveling south. But even with her limited knowledge of Texas geography, she knew that Fort Worth was north of San Angelo.

"Where are you going?" Royce shouted at Perry. He did not hear her, so she reached over and turned off the radio. "Where are you going?" she repeated.

"Fort Worth, darlin'," he replied with a half-smile.

"Fort Worth is north, and we're heading south. Where are you going?" she demanded.

"I'll get you to Fort Worth, don't worry. We just have something else to take care of first," he told her.

"What?" she asked suspiciously.

"Well, see, it's like this," Perry began as if he were on to the greatest idea since ice cream. "I've been thinking about it, and I think Paul was a doofus to dump out all the coke. We could've made a hundred times the amount from each trip if we'd held on to it and resold it. So we're going back to the Bend for another job. Only this time, we keep it *all*."

Royce gripped the armrest. "No. Perry, you're crazy. You can't do that. The sheriff and the DEA are on top of all that down there. They just pulled off a major bust—"

"Which would leave the field wide open for another supplier to step in. Piece of cake," Perry smirked.

"You just stop this truck right here and let me out," Royce demanded. "I don't want anything to do with this."

"I don't think you have much choice about it now," Perry observed, traveling at eighty miles per hour.

"Look," Royce said desperately, "I wouldn't be any help to you. I'd just get in the way."

"Oh, no. Not at all," he replied. "Fact is, you're just what I needed. There's no better decoy than a pretty woman."

Royce's hands got clammy. Perry turned onto four-lane Interstate 10 so that they began heading directly into the sunset. He turned the radio back on, and Royce pressed against the door in a vain attempt to get away from the harsh, ugly music. To get away from the terrible predicament she had gotten herself into.

You are stupid beyond words, she lashed herself. What kind of foolish pride drove her out of the Ferrings' house today? Even if Paul were forever set against marrying her, he was certainly gracious enough to see that she got back to Fort Worth, or even New York, safely. And how unutterably blind of her to assume that because Paul and Buddy were trustworthy, Perry was, too—especially after repeatedly demonstrating his lack of scruples in Big Bend.

Royce closed her eyes. There was no way Paul could rescue her out of this mess. There was no point in even wishing it. But in her desperation the inner cry escaped anyway: *Padre. . . .*

The old photograph of Paul's great-grandfather came to mind. *Padre.* But what the lens of her memory focused on was the Bible under his arm, and a prayer learned in childhood came to mind: *Our Father who art in heaven*—Padre!

Royce opened her eyes. The blazing sunset before them almost blinded her, overwhelmed her with rays she could practically touch. Rays of love that found her whether she was lost in the desert or stranded in Fort Worth. Rays that reached into the truck with its unwilling passenger and bathed her in illumination. Padre—her heavenly Father—was really there, and knew of the distress of His naïve, homeless child. And He was no wimp who sat idle when His child asked for help.

Padre ... help me, she pleaded. In response she felt cradled in protective assurance. It was almost like being in Paul's arms when he had found her in the desert. She was bathed in something as delicious and refreshing as the cool water from his canteen. Royce curled up on the seat, letting the love block out the vicious sounds from the radio.

✳ ✳ ✳

She awoke sometime later. It was deep into the evening, and Perry had turned off the radio. Royce sat up, groggily rubbing her stiff neck. "Have a nice nap?" he grinned over at her. Royce looked out the windshield and saw a road sign which indicated they were now traveling south on Highway 385. The mountains crowded up to the two-lane highway.

"So how long before we get to Alpine?" she asked casually.

"Oh, we're not going through Alpine," he replied knowingly. "I've seen all I want of Sheriff Potts and his boys."

Royce tensed, but then that glowing assurance came back, like Paul saying, *I'm here, Royce; I'm here.* She sat quietly and watched.

They passed the entrance to Big Bend; Royce noted that it was a different one than she had seen so often before. *That's okay; when he gets to the lodge I know exactly where to go for help.*

Perry drove on down the road until they came right up to the park headquarters, which was closed. But then he drove past it and left the road, shifting to four-wheel drive. Royce groaned.

Keeping an eye on his odometer, Perry drove past a low range of hills right into the Chisos Mountains, until the grade was so steep and rocky that he could go no farther. He stopped to make camp, pulling supplies from the back of the truck.

Royce got out and walked around a bit to loosen up her stiff legs, as well as she could in high heels on the rough, sloping ground. Looking dismally up at the rugged mountains, indistinct in the darkness, she felt there was no way she could endure being stranded out here again.

Perry set up a radio receiver and turned it on. Then he pulled out a package of wieners and opened it. "Hungry?"

"Yes, I'll take whatever you have," Royce said guardedly. He pulled out three-fourths for himself first, then tossed the remainder of the package to her, which she ate.

"Sorry I don't have any Fig Newtons," he said, popping open a can of beer. "Want one?" He held up the can.

"I'd rather have water," she replied.

He smirked as he handed her a thermos. "Don't want to get drunk?"

"Don't like the taste," she said.

He unrolled his sleeping bag and stretched out. Royce gingerly sat on a crate of supplies, taking a package of crackers from the bag he threw at her. They were salty and stale. "So you and Paul split, huh?" he said with a note of satisfaction. She did not answer. "I didn't think it would last. He doesn't like women," Perry added.

"He's not gay," Royce said.

"I didn't say he was. I said he doesn't like women. His wife jerked him around pretty bad. He told us about coming home to find her in bed with another man," Perry said.

"That would be a shock," she said softly.

"I'd 'a' killed her. But poor ol' dumb Paul tried to get her into 'counseling' with him. His problem is, he's too nice. He lets them push him around until he's had it full up to here." Perry burped contemplatively. "A man's gotta show a woman he's in charge, or she won't respect him. He's gotta take what he wants and not let her give him any lip about it."

"Paul's not such a wimp. He just knows that a man doesn't have to be an ogre to be strong," Royce said defensively.

"Did he ever tell you he was a preacher?" Perry asked with curled lip.

"Yes," Royce said.

"Well, there you are," he said, as if his case were proved.

"I suppose being a wimp enabled him to rob the drug runners," she observed.

"Hey, *I'm* the one who set that up! They couldn't do a thing until they brought me in!" Perry declared. Royce did not respond, but her face indicated what she thought. Perry stewed over it for a while, then blurted, "What did you see in him, anyway?"

"He has character," she said quietly.

"What do you mean, 'character'? That he's safe and predictable? Well, that's true. Safe and steady. No moods, no temper, just the same ol' Paul. That would drive me crazy, living with someone who couldn't get crazy now and then. C'mon now—isn't that why you dumped him?" Perry taunted.

"I didn't dump him. He dumped me," Royce said.

"Yeah. Right," Perry said sarcastically. "You're so noble I could puke."

"It's true. He wasn't sure he wanted to get married after all," Royce said offhandedly.

Perry flailed his arms in exasperation. "You stupid broad! Don't you know how to stroke a man who's got cold feet?"

"You—said you weren't surprised that we broke up," Royce stammered.

"This is different, stupid. A man's *supposed* to get cold feet before his wedding. It's *traditional*. The *woman* has got to convince him that he *needs* to be married. Don't they teach you anything in New York?"

"Not about Texas mating rituals!" she fired back.

Perry threw back his head and laughed. "That's good. That

was a good one. Well, you screwed up big time." Opening his second can of beer, he began to mellow. "Aw, I guess you two deserve each other. You're too much of a princess for me. I like my women with a hard edge."

"You broke Marla's heart," she observed quietly.

"Who?" he said.

"Marla!"

"Oh, her." He snorted mildly. "She gave me the royal kiss-off, didn't she? Don't talk to me about breaking hearts," he said with sudden vehemence. "Marla's in it for Marla. She came down to have herself a fling with a cowboy, then she went on back to New York. Would she have dropped everything like you and Renetta and come down if I had asked her?" he demanded.

Royce thought it over and replied honestly, "No."

"So there!" he said, vindicated. He eyed her as he took a swig of beer. "Well, I owe it to him," he said to himself. "He helped me make a lot of money. I owe it to him to take you back so he can slap you around for walking out on him."

"Thank you," she breathed.

"*After* we take care of business here," he amended.

"Perry, you can't be serious about going through with this," she said urgently.

"Dead serious, darlin'," he confirmed. Unzipping the sleeping bag, he said, "Time for bed." He held the bag open with a lewd smile.

Royce got up. "If you don't mind, I'd rather sleep in the truck," she said, opening the passenger door.

"Aren't you curious as to whether I'm as good as Paul?" he baited.

"I already know the answer to that," she said, closing the door.

"Well, don't get any ideas, 'cause I've got the keys!" he shouted back.

"Oh, to know how to hot wire," she wished as she took off her suit coat and rolled it up to go under her head.

22

❖

Perry woke Royce the next morning by stretching over her and kissing her full on the lips. She brought her knee up sharply and he doubled over in pain. "Whadja do that for?" he shouted.

"Sorry. Reflex," she muttered, sitting up and blinking.

"Well, get out and get yourself something to eat!" he said crossly.

Royce climbed out of the truck and rummaged in his supplies, finally settling for the snack cakes. Perry sat down to listen to the receiver, as apparently he had been doing for some time. Also apparent was that he was not getting the information he wanted. He gave up on one channel and began to scan another.

Royce ate and took care of her business. It was probably no later than eight o'clock, but the air was already heavy and warm. She looked up at a golden eagle riding on the thermals high overhead, and she wished for the gift of rising above the turbulence so effortlessly.

Returning to the truck, she pulled out her suitcase to get a pair of jeans. Perry looked over. "What're you doing?" he asked.

"I'm going to change. This suit isn't exactly desert wear," Royce said.

"You leave on what you got. It'll do just fine," Perry ordered. Royce bit back an argument and shut the suitcase. She wasn't exactly afraid of him, but she did not want to push him, either.

Royce looked past him to the splendid mountains, towering in the fog. They did not fill her with apprehension today. They were Padre's mountains. In their starkness, and harshness, and unyieldingness, they were His. And in her weakness, so was she.

"Okay," Perry muttered meaningfully as he leaned closer to the radio. Royce was too far away to hear what he heard. He quickly pulled out his map. "They're giving coordinates," he mused. "Hmmmm. . . ."

He worked over his map with a compass for some time, plotting distances and degrees and so forth. Royce unobtrusively came up to look over his shoulder. It was a topographical map with many numbers which Royce could not interpret; however, she did see that Highway 385 led north out of Big Bend to Marathon, east of Alpine. She memorized as many major features of the map as she could until Perry folded it up and said, "Got it. We're ready."

He packed the truck while Royce climbed halfheartedly in front. Then he got in, started the engine, and said, "It's going down in the Grapevine Hills. I thought that was pretty far north, but they musta thought the South Rim was getting too hot." *As if I were interested,* Royce thought scathingly.

It took half an hour to reach the area, and that was only because Perry had to circumvent the park headquarters again going north. They crossed a paved road which Royce immediately identified as 385, then Perry intercepted a primitive road up to the hills. They bounced along until they reached a plateau. Perry stopped the truck, looked all around, and consulted his map.

"Okay," he said. "Get out." Royce did, reluctantly. They were high enough so that she could see the ribbon of 385 to the east. Perry hauled out her suitcase and took it to the middle of the dusty plateau. Apprehensively, Royce followed when he beckoned with a finger.

He set her hard-sided suitcase on the ground and patted it. "Have a seat."

"Why?" Royce asked.

"Because," Perry answered, "the drug runners are going to come flying directly over this spot. When they see you stranded here, they're going to land to find out what the deal is. Then I'm going to come out and rob them." Royce's stomach began churning as Perry turned back to his truck. "Oh—" he said, taking a pistol out of the back, "don't try to go anywhere." He aimed and shot a couple of rounds in the dirt at her feet. Royce gasped and jumped back.

Perry started up his truck and moved it out of sight in the brush that surrounded the plateau. Royce could not see him, but to remind her that he was there, he loosed a few more rounds at the ground beside her suitcase. She cringed.

As she sat on her suitcase, Royce looked up pleadingly to the clear blue sky. "Padre," she whispered, and felt a faint tingle, just a reminder of His loving embrace.

She sat in the full glare of the sun, waiting for whatever would happen. Her pink pumps were gray with dust; her toes uncomfortably sweaty. Her hose had a large, brand-new run. Royce thought about Perry's selfish cruelty in using her this way, and she thought about Paul. It was easy to take his gentleness and restraint for granted, and to assume everyone was like that.

He thought himself a failure—oh, how accurately her mother had zeroed in on his weaknesses! But he could not see how successful he really was, in putting a human face on her Padre. When she tried to think of what God must be like, she could think of no better example than Paul, raised to superhuman levels.

Royce wiped sweat from her forehead and sighed. There was no shade from the glare of the sun bouncing off rocks and dirt. "At least you could have left me some water, Perry." She remembered how Paul was driven to prayer to save her life, and at once she knew that it was God hounding him out here, chasing him down until he succumbed, to save his life. Had God chased her out here as well, to save her life? "You have a strange way of doing things," she muttered.

She gathered her heavy hair and held it off of her neck. This long hair, of which she had always been so proud, was a hot, unwelcome burden right now. How stupid to be proud of something that weighed her down so much. She closed her eyes and rested her weary head on her hand. Keeping her eyes closed made it easier to bear the heat and the anxiety.

Then she heard something. It was faint, but her throat constricted at the sound. She lifted her eyes toward the south, where a helicopter rose from the distance.

Pinned in place by Perry's gun, Royce helplessly watched the chopper approach. It got bigger, and louder, and the dead air began to move across her face. The helicopter hovered above her, then descended. As it landed about twenty feet away, Royce covered her eyes from the flying dust.

A man in a straw cowboy hat, jeans, and boots hopped out of the helicopter and ran toward her. Right away Royce knew this was no drug runner. He shouted at her, but she could not hear him over the rotor blades. However, she did see the dirt jump around them from Perry's pistol, and let out a warning cry.

The cowboy grabbed her arm and her suitcase. He ran her to the helicopter, put her on board, and they quickly took off again. Coughing, Royce looked out the window as Perry came helplessly roaring from the brush in his truck.

The pilot glanced back at her in the narrow cockpit as he talked over his radio. The cowboy beside him shouted, "What were you doin' down there?"

Royce opened her mouth and cried, "My—boyfriend

stranded me for a joke! He's drunk!"

"We'll take you to the ranger headquarters," the cowboy offered.

But Royce cried, "No! Please—not there." She was just too embarrassed to face those park rangers again.

"Where do you want to go?" he asked loudly.

"Marathon?" she shouted, and he nodded. She covered her ears from the loud drone.

In a very few minutes the pilot was setting down on the outskirts of Marathon, population 800. The cowboy climbed out and reached over to help her down. He carried her suitcase a ways from the helicopter and told her, "The Gage Hotel is on Highway 90 there, if you need it."

"No, thanks. I can't thank you enough for picking me up," she said repeatedly. He was very brown, with a lined, kind face. "I just need—they have a bus line through here, don't they?"

"A bus? No, miss. Where do you need to go?" he asked, perplexed.

"Oh, dear." She sagged. "Where do I need to go?" The Ferrings' sprang to mind, but Royce refused to consider it. She did not put any credence in what Perry said about men's cold feet. Paul did not play those kinds of games.

"Are you okay, miss?" he asked, squinting at her.

"Yes. Really. Thank you. I'm just trying to decide where to go. I need to get to Fort Worth," she mused.

"I can't take you that far," he shook his head. "I can take you as far as San Angelo; that's about it."

She stared at him. "Why on earth would you do that?"

"I guess I'm just a sucker for gals in trouble," he chuckled, then stuck out a brown hand. "I'm Joe Salinas, owner of the Salinas Ranch."

"The Salinas Ranch. . . ." In a flash Royce recalled this from the map—private ranchland within part of Big Bend, just north of the Grapevine Hills. She shook his hand warmly. "I'm Royce Lindel. Can you take me to . . . the Grayson Homestead south of

San Angelo?"

"Walt Ferring's place? Sure," he said.

"You know the Ferrings?" she asked.

"I know Walt; I see him at auction all the time," Joe replied.

"That's incredible," Royce murmured. "Do you know—Paul Arrendondo?"

"Now him I'm not sure of. But I'll be happy to say hello to that ol' cuss Walt. Hop on board." Joe took her suitcase back to the small chopper and provided her with some earplugs.

Wondering if she were dreaming, Royce huddled in the helicopter as they flew over hills and long stretches of remuda. "Thank you, Padre, for sending an angel to pick me up," she added as she clutched her suitcase up against her knees.

In less than ninety minutes they were setting down in a pasture a hundred feet from the Ferrings' house. It was almost exactly twenty-four hours since Royce had left the reception with Perry. All the other wedding guests had left. With Joe at her side and a queasy stomach, Royce walked to the house, mounted the wide front steps and rang the doorbell.

Shana answered the door. Seeing Royce, her big eyes widened, and without so much as a hello she ran back into the house calling, "Mrs. Ferring! Mrs. Ferring!"

With a weak smile at Joe, Royce brought him into the foyer and set down her suitcase. Jeannine appeared through a doorway and cried, "Royce!" She ran forward to embrace the shame-faced refugee.

Walt came up behind her. "Joe? Joe Salinas!"

"How do, Walt. This little girl belong to you?" He reached out to take Walt's extended hand.

"She sure does, Joe. Did you bring her?" Walt asked.

"Yep. I need to refuel my chopper," Joe said.

"Well, come on back and I'll fix you up. My whirly-bird's been on the blink and I can't seem to find the problem," Walt told him.

"Let me get my pilot to have a look at it—Sam's a pret' fair mechanic. Then we can talk about that ornery old Angus you were itchin' to get rid of," replied Joe.

"You sly devil!" Walt slapped him on the back and they headed out.

Royce turned with penitent eyes to Jeannine, who said, "I'm so relieved to see you safe. You gave us quite a turn!"

"I'm sorry. It was rude of me to leave like that, but I felt that ... since Paul ... " she gulped. "Is he around? Or out in the pasture?"

Jeannine shook her head. "He took off, Royce. Oh, what a scene." She put a hand to her forehead.

"What happened?" Royce asked in alarm.

"Yesterday, when the photographer was taking pictures at the reception, Paul asked if we could get a picture of you and him together—he said it was probably as close to wedding pictures as you'd get."

"This was—at the reception?" Royce asked weakly.

"Yes. Well, we looked around and couldn't find you—first place I looked was in the kitchen—oh, Royce, I wouldn't have made it through that wedding without your help. Anyway, Paul went up to your room looking for you, and found your note. He came tearing down the stairs—he was just livid. I've never seen him so angry. He seemed to know where Perry was taking you, and it wasn't into town, was it?" Jeannine asked. Royce shook her head. "Well, Paul took one of Walt's trucks, and a gun—"

"A gun?" gasped Royce.

"Yes, he took a gun and left. That was the last we've heard. Oh, Royce, I'm so relieved to see you. I could hardly get through my morning prayers. Come up—"

"He's coming after me with a gun," Royce whispered. Safe, steady Paul, livid, with a gun.

Jeannine urged, "Come up to your room—"

"I've got to get out of here," Royce declared, picking up her suitcase.

"Royce, Paul won't hurt you! He loves you! You've got to

wait here until he gets back," Jeannine insisted.

"No!" Royce cried with a pounding heart. She could not imagine facing an angry Paul with a gun. "Jeannine, I can't. I've got to get my stuff out of his apartment, and—"

"Royce, I'm begging you to calm down and wait for him. I was right the first time, wasn't I?" Jeannine implored with tender blue eyes.

"Where are the keys to the Mercedes, Jeannine?" Royce asked tremulously.

Jeannine gazed at her and quietly replied, "In the kitchen." Royce turned and ran to the kitchen, where a row of hooks on the wall held keys to several vehicles. She seized the keys to the Mercedes and ran back to the foyer.

As Royce bent over her suitcase, Jeannine said, "I won't make you stay, even though you should. But I want you to know that any time you want to come back, we'll welcome you with open arms."

Royce's eyes blurred and she hugged Jeannine tightly. "I'm afraid of Paul," she whispered.

"If you knew him better, you wouldn't be," Jeannine replied softly.

Royce stepped back and picked up her suitcase. She threw it in the back seat of the Mercedes, still parked out front. Trembling, she sat in the car and started it. Then she paused to regain control of herself. Okay, she still had no driver's license, but getting to Fort Worth from here was easy: up 277 to Abilene, then east on I-20 clear to Fort Worth. All she had to do was remember not to speed. She pulled out of the driveway, glancing back at Jeannine on the front steps of the magnificent house.

The trip took five nerve-racking hours. She gripped the wheel tensely and drove no faster than the speed limit with almost paranoid watchfulness. Every car that appeared in the distance she took to be a patrol car, and every truck behind her had to be Paul. She peered at unfamiliar highway signs and jumped when faster cars roared around her.

A warning light on the dashboard came on. Royce stared at it in dread: she was low on fuel. At the first open gas station she spotted, she pulled in beside a row of pumps and got out to stare at them in perplexity. Unleaded? High octane? What? An attendant took pity on her and came out to assist her in filling the tank. Royce paid him with some of Mack's cash (including a tip), then pulled back on to the highway.

Getting on I-20 in Abilene, she almost caused an accident when she found herself at the last minute in the wrong lane to exit to the interstate. Irate drivers notwithstanding, she made it over and then almost relaxed. "I can't go wrong now," she squeaked.

The traffic thinned out in the long, monotonous stretch to the Metroplex, and she had to fight to stay alert. However, as soon as she reached the western suburbs of Fort Worth, the cars multiplied exponentially. The congestion was as bad as anything she had seen in New York City, and today was Sunday, yet. Worse, she got lost trying to get on the loop, and found herself wandering up and down one-way streets in downtown Fort Worth for a while. Then it began to get dark.

Royce was on the verge of hysteria when she chanced upon Phoenix Street, and remembered how to get to Paul's apartment from there. Since she had not eaten anything since morning, she stopped at a fast-food restaurant on the way. Getting out of the car and sitting down in the dining room to eat helped her regain some composure. But when she looked out and saw how dark it had grown, she quickly returned to the Mercedes.

Shortly after nine o'clock that evening, Royce let herself into Paul's apartment and practically collapsed. "In the morning, I'll get a bus out of town to . . . to. . . ." Leaving all such unhappy decisions for later, she shed her wrinkled, soiled pink suit and crawled into bed.

23

❖

Royce opened heavy eyelids and saw sunshine peeking from behind the bedroom drapes. Another morning. She groaned, covering her head. Another day of fear and uncertainty. "Where are you when I need you, Padre?" she mumbled.

There was a movement in the room. Royce sprang upright in bed. And there was Paul, standing by the bedroom door. The first thing she noticed was that he was unarmed. The second thing she saw was his cool, speculative gaze.

"Get dressed," he said, and turned out of the room.

Royce, shaking, pulled out a wrinkled cotton shirt and jeans from her suitcase. She did not even want to look in the mirror at her stringy, greasy hair. She quickly threw her meager possessions, including her dirty clothes, into her two suitcases and duffel bag. *I still have the money,* she reassured herself, checking her purse. *That will help.* But she took out Paul's key and laid it on the dresser beside the photo, which she could not bring herself to even glance at one last time.

She carried her belongings out to the living room. Paul hung up the telephone and appraised her clothing. He himself was fresh and clean, wearing a coat and tie. Without a word he picked up her suitcases and carried them down to Walt's dusty pickup, parked behind the Mercedes.

He threw her bags in the back of the truck and Royce climbed meekly into the passenger seat. Then he got in and drove right out into Monday morning rush-hour traffic. They averaged twenty miles an hour on a four-lane thoroughfare, and the silent minutes crawled by with maddening indifference. Royce stole a furtive glance or two at Paul. He did not look angry, just contemplative. But he did not say a word. It was agony sitting next to him as Royce realized all over again how much she loved him.

Finally, he turned onto a downtown street and pulled up to a large building. The first thing Royce saw was the sign for the Greyhound Bus Terminal. Her eyes began to water. *Who am I kidding?* she thought. *It sounds so noble, so tragic—"all by myself." But I could never endure being truly alone. The first thing I would do is look for friends. I couldn't make it through this miserable life without knowing that somebody loved me . . . like you.*

Paul opened her door. She almost stumbled getting out, but caught herself before he had to reach out a hand. With an eye on the Greyhound sign, she hauled a suitcase out of the bed of the truck. Paul took it from her and locked it with the other two in the cab.

Then he led her by the arm up the side steps of a building near the terminal—the county courthouse. They walked down an echoing hallway until Paul stopped at a wood and frosted glass door and pushed it open. A clerk looked up.

"My name is Paul Arrendondo. I called this morning," he said, drawing papers from his breast pocket.

The clerk took his papers, perused them, then scrutinized Royce through her no-nonsense glasses. "Are you Royce Lindle?"

Royce nodded, but Paul corrected her, "LinDELL."

"Come this way." The clerk got up and knocked at an inner door. Entrance was granted. The clerk opened the door and stood just inside.

A woman in bifocals and a lovely beige suit stood up behind a cluttered desk. "I hope you don't mind if we cut this to the bare bones. I'm just swamped today. Do you have the ring?"

"Not yet," Paul said.

"It's not essential." She adjusted her glasses and glanced at Royce's jeans. "All right. Paul Arrendondo, do you take this woman Royce to be your wife, et cetera and et cetera?" asked the justice of the peace.

"Yes," Paul replied.

"And do you, uh, Royce Anne Lindle—"

"LinDELL," Paul interrupted.

"—Royce Anne LinDELL, take this man Paul, et cetera and et cetera?"

Royce looked away. "Well, I don't know," she prevaricated. Paul turned menacingly toward her and she quickly added, "I guess I don't have anything better to do today."

"Then by the authority vested in me, I now pronounce you husband and wife," the JP finished on a skeptical note. She signed the marriage certificate and the clerk signed as witness. "You may pay the twenty-five-dollar fee on your way out," the JP added, handing Paul the certificate as she sat back down.

Turning to the outer office, Paul slowly took out his wallet. "The fee. . . ."

"Do I have to do everything?" Royce pouted, opening her purse.

She produced the required fee and the clerk gave her the receipt. "Congratulations," she said almost sardonically.

Paul took Royce back down to the truck and opened her door, replacing the suitcases in the truck bed while she sat. As he started the engine, she said, "I'm hungry."

Without a word Paul went through a drive-through for an egg biscuit and coffee. When the order-taker announced,

"That'll be two ninety-five," Royce held out a five-dollar bill toward Paul but he ignored it, paying out of his pocket. Then he handed the order across to her without looking up. Royce had breakfast on their way back to the apartment, where he parked behind the Mercedes.

He turned off the ignition and they sat in the truck without looking at each other or speaking. Royce gathered her trash in the white paper sack, wadded it up, and placed it on the floorboard. The truck was a stick shift, she noted. Probably ten years old. The dashboard was discolored from sitting out in the sun, and some of the air vents were cracked. There was some gunk imbedded in the carpeting, and—

"Nice wedding outfit," Paul deliberately turned to comment.

"I thought you were coming to kill me!" she exclaimed.

"That's asinine! Why did you leave with Perry?" he asked hotly.

"Because you didn't want to marry me!" she cried.

"I have, haven't I?" he shouted.

Without further discussion they embraced in a flare of passion. Royce tried to explain herself but he would not free up her lips. Then he pulled her from the truck and bounded up the stairs to his apartment with her in tow. "My suitcases," she fretted, looking back down to the pickup.

Paul threw up his hands but ran back to the truck and reloaded her bags in the cab. Then he sprang up the steps and unlocked the door. He scooped her up, carrying her back to the bedroom and laying her across the bed. Smiling, he took off his jacket and began loosening his tie. "This," he said, "is what I've been waiting for."

The telephone in the kitchen rang. "Telephone," she said.

"Ignore it." He took off his tie. The phone continued to ring.

"It might be important," she said, sitting up.

Expelling a frustrated breath, he went to the telephone and answered it: "Hello. Yes, Jeannine." He glanced up as Royce came in from the bedroom. "Yes, everything's all right. Royce is here. We just got married." Royce could hear Jeannine's reaction from where she stood. Paul listened a few seconds, then told Royce, "She wants to have a reception for us."

"Oh, no. There's no way I'm going to put her through that again so soon," Royce avowed.

"She says—" Paul began, then handed the phone to Royce. "She wants to talk to you."

Royce took the receiver. "Hello, Jeannine," she said sheepishly.

"Royce, I never had a chance to talk to you about this, but I want you to think about something. I'm involved in so many things—arranging the Distinguished Lecturer series at Angelo State, chairperson of the symphony fund-raiser committee, sponsor of the Concho River Walk—I desperately need an assistant. You were so extraordinarily helpful at Buddy's wedding—you seemed to read my mind. If you and Paul come back here, I wish you would consider helping me in a professional capacity. I promise not to run you ragged."

"Jeannine—that would be wonderful," Royce said earnestly. Paul leaned forward.

"Great, then. We'll discuss details when you get here. Oh—did Paul ever find Perry and kill him?" Jeannine asked.

"I don't know. You'd better ask him." Royce handed the phone to Paul. "She wants to know if you killed Perry."

Paul put the receiver tosear. "I would have, if I had gotten to him first. But he wasn't at any of our usual spots at the Bend. The rangers picked him up when a helicopter reported sniper fire from the Grapevine Hills. By the time I got to the office, they had him in custody and I couldn't get close. I'm sorry I didn't tell you all this when I got in last night, but you know how anxious I was to find Royce. . . . Yeah, she was here. . . . Yeah, she slept here last night. Okay, we'll be there by six o'clock, at the latest. Okay. 'Bye."

As he hung up, Royce asked, "Where did you sleep last night?"

"On the couch, as usual," he said. "I showered and dressed before you stirred. You were really zonked. Why did that idiot take you with him to the Bend?"

"He was trying to use me as a decoy to lure down the drug runners in their helicopter. But Joe Salinas flew over instead. He's the one who brought me back to the Ferrings'," she told him.

"And you turned around and left again!" Paul muttered in disbelief. "After leading me to believe you couldn't drive."

"Hey, when Jeannine told me that she had never seen you that angry, and you had one of Walt's guns, I just freaked out," she said.

"I was going after Perry. But I wasn't really going to kill him—just shoot off selected body parts. Shee, Royce, you should've known I wouldn't hurt you. And you should have known I wouldn't back out of marrying you." He sounded hurt.

"You were so cold at the wedding!" she chided him.

"I was nervous for Buddy. Did you see Renetta's family?" he shuddered.

Royce laughed, then demanded, "Why didn't you tell me we were going to a justice of the peace this morning?"

He looked at her wistfully. "After all that happened, I was afraid you'd say no. Figured I'd better try an ambush." Then he leaned over the bar to kiss her. "Now, where were we?" he murmured.

The telephone between them rang and Paul jumped, grabbing the receiver. "Hello!" He listened a moment, then a smile spread across his face. A crafty, wicked smile. "Why, hi, Mack! Good to hear from you! Yes, this is Paul. Why yes, Royce is right here." He held out the receiver. "Royce, it's Mack, calling all the way from New York!"

She shook her head in refusal. Paul replaced the phone at his ear. "Gee, I'm sorry, Mack; she doesn't want to talk to you. But I want to tell you how much I enjoyed your letter to Royce—especially the part about her 'sensual green eyes and warm lips.' I just couldn't agree with you more."

He briefly held the phone away from his ear and Royce winced at the stream of obscenities she heard. "Wait—okay, calm down, Mack. Royce and I agreed that we could read each other's mail now that we're married. That's right—this morning. You'll be sure to tell Mrs. Lindel for us, won't you? Thanks, guy." He hung up and Royce burst out laughing.

Then he reached down and unplugged the telephone. "There's nobody else I need to hear from right now."

In the bedroom, Paul stretched her out on the soft sheets. Her hand, dangling over the edge of the bed, brushed the guitar case. Royce looked back to see what it was. "I'll take it with us to San Angelo, if you want," he murmured into her neck.

She smiled, closing her eyes to experience his warmth and tenderness. "Thank you, Padre," she whispered in bliss.

"My name is Paul," he growled in her ear.

"I know," she breathed.

Trusting in his sense of humor,
I affectionately dedicate this book
to William Walter Melton (1879–1967),
who was a cowboy before he was a preacher